THE BESSIE BLUE KILLER

A film studio sets out to create a documentary about the Tuskegee Airmen, a unit of African-Americans who flew combat missions in World War Two — but filming has barely begun when a corpse is found on the set. Hobart Lindsey, insurance investigator turned detective, enters the scene, aided by Marvia Plum, his policewoman girlfriend. Soon he uncovers a mystery stretching half a century into the past — and suddenly and unexpectedly is flying through a hazardous murder investigation by the seat of his pants!

RICHARD A. LUPOFF

◆

THE BESSIE BLUE KILLER

Complete and Unabridged

LINFORD
Leicester

First published in Great Britain

First Linford Edition
published 2016

A catalogue record for this book is available
from the British Library.

ISBN 978–1–4448–2844–3

Published by
F. A. Thorpe (Publishing)
Anstey, Leicestershire

Set by Words & Graphics Ltd.
Anstey, Leicestershire
Printed and bound in Great Britain by
T. J. International Ltd., Padstow, Cornwall

This book is printed on acid-free paper

1

International Surety had done it right for once. Hobart Lindsey had spent a career working for the company, starting out as a trainee just weeks after he got his degree from Hayward State.

He sat up in bed. Cletus Berry was pounding him on the bottom of one foot.

Lindsey rubbed his eyes. Back in the room to dress for dinner, he'd put his head on the pillow and fallen sound asleep. Taking an afternoon nap at his age.

He sat on the edge of the bed and reflected on his years of service with International Surety. He'd got his BA in '75, and here it was 17 years later. And he was sitting on the edge of a bed in the Brown Palace, the oldest and most prestigious hotel in Denver, Colorado, pulling on his socks and getting ready to attend a graduation dinner at the Broker, one of the finest and most expensive restaurants in the city.

He blinked at Cletus Berry. Berry was

black and Lindsey was white. International Surety was not going to run afoul of civil rights legislation.

Lindsey hadn't done so badly for a small-town boy — if you could call Walnut Creek, California a small town. It had been a small town when he was growing up there, caring for his widowed mother, learning in painful increments the true story of his father's death. He had been killed in a MiG attack on the destroyer *Lewiston* off the coast of Korea early in 1953. It was just weeks before the end of the war, and just weeks before Hobart Lindsey was born. He had never known his father; never seen him except in a few snapshots that Mother treated as holy relics. The ship's anti-aircraft batteries had picked off the two incoming MiGs. One of them plunged into the Sea of Japan, but the other crashed onto the *Lewiston*'s deck, sending a wave of flaming jet fuel roaring into the battery.

'Better get a move on,' said Cletus.

Lindsey snapped out of his reverie.

'Don't want to keep the Duck waiting, Bart. You know what a stickler he is.'

'Right.' Lindsey pulled up his socks, pushed himself upright and looked for his shoes. He'd sent them out to be shined, and he wore his best suit for the occasion. You didn't graduate from a course like this every day. And in fact, a third of the people who'd started it were back at their former jobs — or out of the company — already.

International Surety had splurged, putting up its employees at the Brown Palace during the seminar, but it had also put them two to a room. Class was all very nice, as the corporate brass were forever reminding their underlings; but International Surety had to protect its resources, and one person didn't need a room all to himself. Not when he was attending workshops all day and struggling with study assignments and papers every night.

Lindsey and Cletus walked the five blocks to the Broker. A couple of their classmates had been mugged on Seventeenth Street the week before, but they had decided not to let themselves be intimidated, and that was final. They kept their International Surety name badges in their pockets until they reached the restaurant, then pinned them on when they entered the marble lobby.

Happy hour was subdued. Lindsey and Cletus drifted apart as soon as they arrived. You had to mix at this kind of corporate function: you never knew who was going to be your boss someday, in a position to do you good or harm.

And Lindsey had already crossed his boss, Harden at Regional, more than once. He'd done a lot of good for International Surety; saved the company plenty of bucks in earlier cases that he'd handled. A claims adjuster didn't just shuffle papers and authorize checks. It was his job to get the facts; to track down the truth when a claim had a peculiar odor to it. Especially if it was a big claim.

Trouble was, when Lindsey had saved the company six-figure amounts on stolen collectibles, he'd outshone Harden. Ms. Johansen at National was aware of Lindsey's work, and of the fact that he'd done it despite Harden's obstructionism.

Harden had managed to squeeze

Lindsey out of the district office and had replaced him with the odious Elmer Mueller. Now Lindsey was completing the training seminar for International Surety's corporate troubleshooting team. They gave it a fancy name — Special Projects Unit/Detached Status — and a funny logo, a russet potato with SPUDS lettered across it. Everybody in SPUDS got to wear a little cloisonné potato on his lapel. Still, Lindsey knew that the team had been the graveyard of careers.

He found himself standing next to a thin, pale woman from Grant's Pass, Oregon. She'd hardly spoken during the course; had sat far from Lindsey. He let his eyes flash to her badge. Aurora Delano, right. Beneath her name, her home town. Practically a neighbor. Behind her, a white-jacketed bartender was doing slow business.

'So, Hobart, you had enough of this? Eager to get home to California?'

Lindsey grunted. 'I'm a little worried about Mother. She — '

The bartender caught Lindsey's attention. Aurora Delano was holding an empty glass, Lindsey noticed.

5

'Aurora, would you like a — '

She turned toward the bartender and held up her glass. 'Refill, sure.'

The bartender said, 'And you, sir?'

Lindsey said, 'I'll have the same as the lady.' He paid for the drinks. International Surety ran a no-host bar.

Aurora said, 'We never got to talk during the course. I don't mind Denver, but I'll be happy to get out of here.'

'And go back to Oregon. How do you feel about working in SPUDS?'

'No way am I going back to Oregon. I only went there because my ex's work was there. I'm a southern girl.'

Lindsey was surprised. 'I would have guessed New York.'

Aurora smiled. Her long, thin face was surrounded by a wash of auburn hair. Definitely the Katherine Hepburn type. 'A lot of people think that. I was born and raised in New Orleans. That's why I took the SPUDS job. Get out of Grant's Pass. Get out of range of my ex. I talked Ducky into sending me back to Louisiana.'

'And your ex is going to stay in Oregon?'

'I hope to hell he does! Besides,

6

SPUDS will be a change. It gets pretty dull, paying body shops to pound out dented fenders and replace broken windows. Not to mention comforting grieving widows and greedy offspring with checks.'

Lindsey smiled. He raised his glass. Aurora did the same and they touched rims.

There was music coming over concealed speakers, something totally unidentifiable and equally undistinguished. Lindsey's musical tastes had been growing in recent months, largely due to the influence of a Berkeley police officer he'd worked with on a couple of his more interesting cases.

Now the music was interrupted by a polite chiming. It was the signal to proceed to the dining room.

Inside the private dining room Lindsey found his assigned seat. Happily, Aurora Delano was to be his dinner partner. He spotted Cletus at another table, and recognized the others in the room from the classes and work groups of the past weeks. The music had resumed.

Aurora Delano was an interesting conversationalist, going on about her ex-husband and how they had climbed the Himalayas, rafted down the Snoqualmie, explored the Great Barrier Reef. It took her a while to get around to the reason for their split.

'Well, he was a great guy, my ex.' Aurora sipped her wine. 'He designed nuclear triggers for a living, and he was good at it. Made a nice living, too. Then the bottom fell out of the market for nuclear triggers. Blooey. No more Evil Empire. No more money. All of a sudden, instead of the headhunters sniffing after him, he had to start sending out résumés. He was hot stuff as long as the money kept rolling in. Those guys make a lot of money, you know. Nuclear trigger designers: making the world safe for our children and our grandchildren; holding the forces of tyranny and oppression at bay. Those Stepford husbands with their sports cars and their big houses and their pert little wives with the big station wagons.'

'You drive a station wagon?'

'The Red Octopus dies and Uncle Sam doesn't need all those weapons factories anymore, so they have to start looking for an honest job.'

Lindsey didn't pursue the station wagon.

Aurora put down her glass, picked up her fork, speared a piece of lamb chop, and chomped down on it. 'All of a sudden, nobody wants nuclear trigger designers. And there's not much positive transfer of skills.'

'What happened?'

'He had a couple of offers from universities, for about a quarter what he was making.'

'What did he do?'

'He called some of his old buddies. You know, they network, those nuclear trigger designers. I don't know what went wrong. Maybe they didn't like him. Maybe there's just no work out there.'

'So what did he do?'

'He took it as long as he could. Then he couldn't take it anymore.'

She picked up her glass again and looked at Lindsey. The roll baskets were empty. The waiters were clearing away the dinner plates. At the head table a major corporate bigshot, Ms. Johansen from National, was looking around. Clearly, she was getting ready to make a speech.

Desmond 'Ducky' Richelieu, the director of International Surety's Special Projects Unit/Detached Status, was on his feet, waiting for the room to quiet so he could introduce their distinguished guest, Ms. Johansen from National. The murmured conversation dropped to a dead silence.

Aurora Delano whispered, 'He came home from a job interview. I knew it had gone badly; and the poor lamb was so upset, he had to do something. So he broke my arm.'

* * *

The International Surety suite was upstairs in a glittering office tower just off Speer Boulevard. The receptionist had a sign on her desk: 'Mrs. Blomquist.' She wore her hair on top of her head like a Gibson Girl. Lindsey could not remember ever seeing a woman with skin that looked so pale and powdery.

The thin air made for a snappy morning even in May, but Lindsey had packed his topcoat and taken a cab wearing a medium-weight gray suit. He usually dressed a little more casually than this, but he was on his way to visit his new boss.

Mrs. Blomquist made Lindsey wait while she buzzed Mr. Richelieu, then made him wait some more. Finally he got the nod.

Richelieu stood up when Lindsey walked in. The sign on the inner door said simply, 'Desmond Richelieu.' Nobody called him 'Ducky' to his face. He wore a neatly trimmed moustache and rimless bifocals that glinted in the sunlight pouring through his office window. He looked like a steel engraving of the French cardinal whom Lindsey had once seen in a high school library edition of *The Three Musketeers*.

'I always like to have a chat with each of our graduates before they head out on their first assignment. I imagine you'd heard that,' Richelieu said, gesturing for Lindsey to take a seat.

Lindsey nodded. He'd carried his attaché case with him and he placed it carefully on the carpet beside his chair.

'The way the Chief used to do it when I worked for the Bureau,' Richelieu added, making a barely perceptible motion with his head.

Lindsey followed Richelieu's gesture with his eyes. A tastefully framed diploma-like document stood out against the elegant paneling. Beside it hung a blown-up glossy of a boyish Richelieu shaking hands with a dumpy, bulldog-faced man in a double-breasted pinstriped suit. The picture was cropped so you couldn't see either man's feet.

'It's a funny thing,' Richelieu said. 'The FBI is like the Mafia. Once you're in it, you're never really out.' He shook his head sadly. 'But once John Edgar was gone, the Bureau was never the same. Mixed up in Watergate; White House interference. They never got away with that when the Chief was alive. He took on everybody — the Kennedys, everybody. But once he was gone, why, it was never the same.'

Lindsey had heard that J. Edgar Hoover had been sensitive about his height; had stood on a box for photo ops with his underlings. Bureau photogs knew that they had to keep the focus up and not show the box. Agents knew that they had to keep their eyes up and not see it, either. Failure to comply could cost a man his career. He might not get tossed out of the Bureau, but he'd reach age 65 counting pencils in the Fargo, North Dakota branch office.

Richelieu leaned his forearms on the polished glass top of his desk. 'When Harden at Regional recommended you for SPUDS, he said you were reluctant to take the job, Hobart. Is that right?'

'Yes, sir.'

'That's all right; a lot of my people join up reluctantly. What happened to your job in Walnut Creek?'

Richelieu didn't have Lindsey's personnel folder on his desk. He must have studied it before Lindsey was admitted to the inner sanctum. Lindsey said, 'I was hospitalized.'

'Yes. Shot in the shoulder, wasn't it?'

'Mr. Harden brought someone else in to run the office. I thought Ms. Wilbur could handle it until I got back, but Mr. Harden brought in Elmer Mueller instead. When I reported back, Mueller had my job and I wound up in SPUDS.'

Richelieu leaned back. 'You've doubtless heard that we have a high rate of attrition in SPUDS.'

Lindsey nodded.

'You'll get tough cases. Some people think SPUDS is International Surety's own little Gestapo, its own little gulag. Neither of those is true, Hobart. We're not police. We don't torture anybody. We're very law-abiding. We are a little bit like detectives, but then I understand that you like to play Sherlock. Is that true?'

'No, sir. I just try to do my job. I'm a claims adjuster, that's all. Somebody's store is burgled, we pay for the loss. Somebody's car gets stolen, we pay fair value.'

'Yes, yes. But if you can recover the stolen goods you can save International Surety a lot of money. You've done that, haven't you?'

Lindsey nodded. The man w[...] cat and mouse with him. He ha[...] that Lindsey had saved the c[...] fortune in rare 1940s comic bo[...] even bigger fortune on a stolen 1928 Duesenberg. Each case had involved a murder as well, but the company paid him to save money, not to catch killers. He did that on his own time, and Harden had used it against him more than once.

'I'm not going to spend a lot of time reviewing material that you learned in your seminars,' Richelieu said. 'If you do a good job for me, you can make a good thing out of SPUDS. You'll have lots of freedom. I understand you have a penchant for breaking rules, Hobart. You should be happy working for me.'

'I think I'm ready for my first assignment,' Lindsey said.

Richelieu's eyes behind his rimless bifocals flashed. Clearly, he did not like having anyone else take the lead in a conversation. Last night at the Broker he'd deferred to Ms. Johansen, but as Lindsey knew, she represented the corporate structure. Richelieu had saluted not man — or woman — but the rank. nd Richelieu outranked Lindsey, and expected Lindsey to acknowledge that relationship.

Once upon a time Lindsey would have quivered and apologized for his faux pas. Now he stood up and said, 'I have to catch a flight for Oakland. If there's nothing else . . . '

A transient smile flashed across Richelieu's lips. 'Sit down, Lindsey. Mrs. Blomquist can phone Stapleton and take care of that. Harden is still running Regional, and Mueller is running Walnut Creek, but you're working for me now. For me. You get that?'

Lindsey hesitated for a moment before slipping back into his chair.

Richelieu smiled. 'This is your first assignment for SPUDS, and I'm going to make it a nice easy one for you. Just to help you get your feet wet. You understand?'

Lindsey nodded. If he answered verbally, even grunted, Richelieu could turn away and still continue the conversation. But if Lindsey spoke only in body language, Richelieu would have to stay focused on him. It was a subtle tug-of-war. Maybe it was something in the Rocky Mountain air that was changing Lindsey. Maybe it was his encounter the night before with Aurora Delano. What kind of man would break his wife's arm because he'd lost a job? What kind of man was Hobart Lindsey? What kind of man had he been since Hayward State, and what kind of man was he becoming?

'Make it a good one,' he said.

The ghost-smile flickered across Richelieu's lips again. He reached under the edge of his desk. Lindsey assumed he was pushing a button to summon Mrs. Blomquist.

The door opened behind Lindsey and he swung around to see Mrs. Blomquist carry in a folder and lay it on his desk, then retreat back to the outer office.

'This is practically in your backyard,' Richelieu said. He hadn't opened the folder, just left it lying on his desk. 'Elmer Mueller has written a special policy for a film company that's going to shoot some footage at the Oakland airport. You can stop and check this out on your way home today, Lindsey.'

'How much is involved?'

'Ah, this is a big policy. Cost of the aircraft, indemnity to the Port of Oakland, personal liability, life coverage of people involved in the film.'

'Why didn't the movie company set up their own coverage?'

Richelieu tapped the folder with one fingertip. 'It's an odd situation. Not a commercial studio. Somebody got a line on a bucket of foundation money and put together an ad hoc organization to make a film.'

'I don't understand. Is there a claim on the policy?'

Richelieu shook his head. 'If there were it would be Mueller's problem, not mine. This is a risky operation. We're getting a nice premium out of it; but if we have to pay off, we'll be in a deep hole. We're covering their aircraft, the flight crews, ground crews, passengers, the film crews, bystanders, physical plant — the works.' He pulled his rimless glasses down his nose and peered at Lindsey over their tops. 'What if a plane crashes and takes out a schoolyard full of kids? Or an office building? You had a lightplane crack up in a shopping mall out there, didn't you?'

'I remember it,' Lindsey said.

'Well, what if — say, what if one of these people pancakes into the ballpark out there during a baseball game? Can you imagine the claims? It could cost us millions. It could put us out of business!'

'And you want me to go out there and babysit these people? Make sure they run a nice safe operation? Is that it?'

'That's it,' Richelieu said.

'I'll need to study the file.'

'Take it.' He shoved the folder across his desk. Lindsey peered at him questioningly. Richelieu said, 'It's all photocopies.'

Lindsey locked the folder in his attaché case and stood up. This time Richelieu didn't try to stop him.

Mrs. Blomquist hadn't changed his reservations, but he caught a United 737 as he'd planned, and he was in Oakland in time to face the afternoon rush hour on his way home to Walnut Creek.

Marvia Plum had offered to pick him up at the terminal if she could clear her schedule with the Berkeley Police Department, but Lindsey had promised Mother that she could come out to the airport. She'd been staying in the present most of the time — a slow, steady improvement over her condition in recent years — and he wanted to reward her for staying connected.

As he'd grown up, Mother had got more and more disconnected from the calendar. Her point of reference was always that dreadful day in 1953, the day she had received word of her husband's death in the China Sea. Sometimes she knew what year it was and what day, and connected with people around her perfectly. Other times she thought Jack Kennedy was in the White House, or Harry Truman, or most often Ike. But as Lindsey had grown away from her, as his relationship with Marvia Plum had ripened from a partnership to a friendship to a troubled and intermittent romance, Mother had somehow regained her grasp on the reality of time. She was still young enough to build a life for herself, and Lindsey wanted to do all that he could to help her.

Now he made his way down the faux terrazzo corridor, carrying his attaché case and flight bag. He spotted Mother: a thinner, older, female version of himself. But not really very much older. She'd been a young bride, just a teenager, when her husband had died and her son was born. With her was Joanie Schorr, their neighbor. Joanie had babysat with Mother when Lindsey had to go out at night. Mrs. Hernandez came during the day. Lindsey stayed with Mother most nights and weekends. But Joanie had been the real lifesaver. Even today, she had driven the Hyundai from Walnut Creek. With a start, Lindsey realized that little Joanie was as old as Mother had been when she'd given birth to him.

Both women waved. Lindsey couldn't wave back, but he hoped they could see his smile. He wanted to get in the Hyundai and get home.

2

The telephone's burbling woke Lindsey from a strange sleep. It was wonderful being in his own home, in his own bed. Mother was asleep in her room, and he'd spoken with Marvia the night before and made a dinner date with her.

The voice on the phone was female, and Lindsey hadn't identified it as that of Mrs. Blomquist before she said, 'Stand by for a call from Mr. Richelieu.'

Lindsey blinked at the clock. It was an hour later in Denver, but still, he couldn't expect Richelieu and Mrs. Blomquist to be at work this early. What —

'Lindsey, get yourself together and start earning your paycheck. They beat you to the punch.'

'Mr. Richelieu? I've just — '

'Never mind what you've just. I should have sent you back there early, or put someone else on this thing.'

'You mean — '

'*Bessie Blue.*'

Lindsey said, 'Who?'

'Haven't you read the case folder yet? That's the name of the star airplane. And of the movie. *Bessie Blue.* They've already got their film crew in Oakland and they're at work at the airport. Look for North Field. Find out what's going on. Elmer Mueller's already there — talk to him and take charge of the case. But don't step on Elmer's toes, Lindsey.'

'Yes, sir. But what happened?'

'Somebody got himself killed on the set. You just came through that airport; you must barely have missed the party. It's still going on. Get your tail out there and see what's happening. You're off to some great start in SPUDS, Lindsey. Well, what are you waiting for?'

'You're talking to me, Mr. Richelieu.'

'I don't care. You should be on your way to Oakland by now. Try to get there before everybody else leaves. What do you think — '

Lindsey took him at his word, cradled the handset and headed for a quick shower. Minutes later he was en route to

Oakland. The *Bessie Blue* folder, still unread, lay in his attaché case on the seat beside him. It was still dark out, the first rays of dawn raising a mist off the hills beside the freeway.

The Hyundai's dashboard clock said it was four-thirty a.m. Lindsey had turned on an all-news radio station, and heard a piece about the aircraft carrier *Abraham Lincoln* sailing from Alameda with its battle group for maneuvers in the Pacific. Made sense. America had to be defended against aggressive Easter Islanders, or maybe swarms of penguins attacking from the south pole.

He switched to a jazz station. That was one thing Marvia Plum had done for him.

It was easy to find the *Bessie Blue* set. There were half a dozen police cars with their roof-lights flashing red and blue. Lindsey parked the Hyundai behind them. A TV news van was pulling out of the lot as Lindsey pulled in. There was another vehicle there, a coroner's wagon. The body might still be in place. Lindsey had never seen a fresh murder victim.

He felt an adrenalin rush. He'd been

involved with murders twice before, and there was nothing like the excitement they produced. He was getting addicted.

He'd parked the Hyundai in a square clearing behind an aircraft hangar. At first the surface looked like blacktop, but then Lindsey realized that it was an old-type dirt and gravel lot where they sprayed a layer of oil every now and then to keep down the dust.

The police cars were pulled up near the hangar. At the end of the line was a decade-old Cadillac. Area lights illuminated the parking area. They were bright enough for Lindsey to read the vanity plate on the Caddy: SURETY-1. That had to be Elmer Mueller's car.

The hangar's huge rolling doors were closed, and only a smaller metal door stood open. A uniformed Oakland policeman stood outside the door. He stopped Lindsey. 'Can't go in, sir. Crime scene.'

Lindsey tried to talk his way past the cop. He flashed his International Surety ID. Insurance credentials usually got him past cops. This one chose to be difficult.

Twenty feet away a figure in a brown

tweed jacket and slacks was pacing back and forth. His face was directed down as if he was studying the hangar floor. His hair was thick, dark, curly, unkempt.

Lindsey kept trying to talk his way past the cop. The rumpled man turned, startled. He recognized Lindsey at the same time that Lindsey recognized him. He headed for the doorway, put his hand on the officer's arm, and said, 'Let him in, Walter. This is Mr. Lindsey. He helps us out sometimes.' Walter touched one finger to the bill of his uniform cap and let Lindsey pass.

'How are you, Lindsey?' High said. 'You don't mind if I call you that? I feel as if we're friends, after that Duesenberg case. I remember we put you through a lot on that one. But it all came out in the end, didn't it? It usually does. You're here because of Mr. McKinney?'

'I don't know. I — It's nice to see you again, Lieutenant High. Is Mr. McKinney the, uh, victim?'

'Looks like it. Name on his coveralls, ID tag with a photo and his name: Leroy McKinney, resident of Richmond. Come on — you want a look, you'd better look now. Coroner's here, crime scene technicians are almost finished, and Mr. McKinney will be leaving in a few minutes.'

He took Lindsey by the elbow and steered him across the oil-stained cement surface. The hangar was cavernous and had the feeling of age. North Field was the older part of Oakland International, dating from the daredevil era when Earhart and Hegenberger flew out of Oakland to make their Pacific hops, back in the days when airplanes were exotic machines and aviators were celebrities.

The body lay face up, presumably where it had fallen. The forehead was caved in and brains and blood had filled the unnatural cavity, forming a horrifying triangle with the staring eyes. The brains and blood looked like scrambled eggs in dark ketchup. Lindsey's stomach lurched and he turned away.

'You all right, Lindsey?'

Lindsey pulled a folded handkerchief from his trousers and mopped his brow. 'I'm okay. It was just . . . '

'Understand. You'll start taking it in your stride after you've seen your first few hundred.'

Lindsey turned back and looked at the body. The technicians had marked its position with white tape. The man was black and elderly. His short hair was mostly gray. His head was tilted slightly, and one hand rested against his cheek. There was a startled expression on his face. His other arm lay outstretched, the elbow bent so the hand lay palm up, even with the face. The fingers were horribly deformed; clawlike.

Lindsey felt cold; an old-fashioned woodstove in the hangar did little to dispel the cold and damp of the previous night. North Field was built on marshy flatlands, and men had died in the cold that crept in from the Oakland Estuary and San Francisco Bay.

'You have to pay a claim on this fellow?' High cocked his eyebrow at Lindsey.

'I don't know. That, uh, that would go through Walnut Creek. I don't know if we carry a policy on him.'

High said, 'I meant to ask you about that. Thought you ran your company's office out there. What's this fellow Mueller doing in your job?' He jerked a thumb toward an overdressed individual who had seated himself at a makeshift desk near one wall. A mug of something steamed invitingly in front of him. He was filling out papers attached to a clipboard.

Behind Mueller a metal door led to another, smaller room. It was an old-style office complete with filing cabinets, girlie calendars and a hotplate. A black man in civilian clothes and a gray-haired woman were hunched over a metal desk with a uniformed sergeant. Lindsey could see only the woman's back. The male civilian was talking and the sergeant was writing, nodding, looking up from time to time — obviously to ask a question, then bending once more to write when the man answered.

Lindsey said, 'I guess I should talk to Elmer. He's got my old job, Lieutenant. I've been sort of kicked upstairs. Working out of Denver now.'

'Just like Perry Mason!'

Lindsey smiled. He handed High one of his new business cards.

'Special Projects Unit,' High read. He looked up at Lindsey. 'Very impressive. Congratulations.'

Elmer Mueller looked up from his clipboard. He didn't seem surprised to see Lindsey at the murder scene. Their eyes caught and held briefly. Lindsey nodded. Mueller returned to his papers.

High steered Lindsey away from Leroy McKinney's cadaver. 'Can't say I like your Mr. Mueller too much, Lindsey. He used to run an insurance agency in Oakland.'

'I know.'

'Never quite got in trouble with the law. But a lot of the gang at Broadway and Sixth know him. Too many times over the years, we'd get involved in something messy and shake hands with Elmer.'

Lindsey grunted. He didn't like Mueller either, but he didn't want to run down another International Surety man.

'Well, before we get back to the case at hand,' High said, 'If Elmer is your company's man on the spot, what can I do for you, Lindsey? You're not here just out of curiosity, are you?'

'Hardly. As a matter of fact, I just started this new job, and I'm afraid I'm in trouble already. I was supposed to prevent losses on this project. *Bessie Blue*. You know about that?'

'Just a little. I expect I'm going to learn a lot more about it.'

'International Surety wrote an umbrella policy for *Bessie Blue*. Anything goes wrong on the project — mechanical failure, equipment loss, public liability — we have to pay.'

'Just like Lloyds of London, eh? I guess you're in trouble, then, with Mr. McKinney.'

'I don't know. I'll have to study the case folder, then get together with Mueller. What happened to — the victim? And what's the matter with his hand?'

'What happened, almost certainly, was a monkey wrench. Come on over here.'

The wrench lay a few yards from the body. It had been marked off with white tape, too. The wrench was made of some dark metal, and its head was discolored with the same red goo that had seeped into the cavity in the middle of Leroy McKinney's forehead.

'It'll be bagged and taken away and tested,' High said. 'If we're lucky we might get some useful fingerprints off it. And we'll compare the blood from the wrench and from the victim, then run a genetic scan just to make sure. But I'd give big odds that we'll get a match.'

'Who found the body?'

High nodded toward the office where the uniformed sergeant and the civilians were still huddled over the metal desk. 'Mr. Crump and Mrs. Chandler.'

Lindsey studied the trio as best he could. The male civilian was wearing a leather jacket like a World War Two aviator. Lindsey saw that he was gray-haired, like the murder victim. He was nodding and gesturing in response to the police sergeant's questions.

Lindsey said, 'Did they do it?'

'I don't know who did it. My guess is, somebody who was known to the victim. Look at that — hit him right between the eyes, no sign of a struggle. How could somebody get that close, with a heavy wrench in his hand, and the victim not try to fight back, not try to escape, not even put up his hands to ward off the blow?'

Lindsey forced himself to look at the corpse again, then waited for High to resume.

'The body was already cold, and rigor had set in when our kids got here. So McKinney had to be dead several hours when Chandler and Crump found him, unless they killed him and stood around for five or six hours before they phoned it in. I think we're probably looking at a third party.'

Lindsey peered through the glass at Chandler and Crump and the police officer. He said, 'Still, who are they?'

'He's our movie star, Lawton Crump. One of the original Tuskegee Airmen — the World War Two outfit.'

'He's still got his jacket.'

High grinned. 'Hardly any Negro combat troops at the start of the war. Mostly they used them for service troops. Cooks, laundry, mechanics. You know. There was a lot of agitation to let

Negroes fight. We had a whole Nisei brigade, and the Japs were the enemy. The blacks had been here for hundreds of years — why couldn't they fight for their country?'

Lindsey shook his head. 'You tell me.'

'Somebody even got the cockeyed idea that Negroes could learn to fly airplanes and go into combat. So they set up this segregated training base in Alabama, and pumped out whole units of black fliers. Called them Tuskegee Airmen. Now they want to make a movie about them. Times change.'

'And Mr. Crump was one of the Tuskegee Airmen?'

'Pleasant, soft-spoken elderly gentleman.' High nodded toward the office again. Through the windows it appeared that Crump and the uniformed police sergeant were concluding their business. 'Flew everything we had, or so I'm told. It was before my time, Lindsey.'

'And the woman?' Lindsey asked.

'Mrs. Chandler? She's from Double Bee Enterprises. They're the outfit making the movie.'

'I don't see any cameras. Or any airplanes, for that matter.'

'They haven't arrived yet. You'll have to get the details from Mrs. Chandler or Mr. Crump. She's the producer, he's their technical advisor. In fact, I think the movie's pretty much about him. But they're merely the advance party. McKinney was a janitor here. We have to find out what he was doing in this hangar. The maintenance boss vouches for him — that he's legitimate. But he wasn't scheduled to be working in this building. The signs are that he was killed here, not just brought here and dumped. So — what's the story?'

Lindsey grinned. 'You tell me.'

High shrugged. 'Mrs. Chandler and Mr. Crump found him. They arrived at the building together. Crump spotted the body first and got a good look at it, then he called us. He's really upset.'

Inside the office the sergeant and the two civilians rose and headed toward the door, back into the hangar. Simultaneously, a coroner's squad lifted the remains of Leroy McKinney onto a folding gurney and headed out of the hangar.

★　★　★

Mother sounded nervous and Lindsey apologized for leaving the house without telling her, but all in all she handled it pretty well. Lindsey explained that he'd been called out of Walnut Creek by a work emergency and he'd be home in a few hours.

Mother had dressed and breakfasted and was waiting for Mrs. Hernandez to come and take her shopping. She was so happy that her son was home from Colorado, she wanted to make a big dinner just for him. Lindsey told her that he'd promised to have dinner with Marvia Plum in Berkeley.

'Oh, that nice colored girl. Well, she can come and eat at our house. She can sit right at the table with us.'

Lindsey pressed his hand to his forehead. He was phoning from the same desk where Lawton Crump had given his statement to Sergeant Finnerty. The evidence squad were packing their gear, preparing to leave the airport. Mr. Crump was gone, Lieutenant High was gone, and Lindsey had passed up the pleasure of breakfasting with Elmer Mueller.

He was entitled to desk space at the Walnut Creek office, and to admin support. Meaning that Ms. Wilbur would handle his mail and keep him posted on company gossip. But he wasn't going in today. There was a chance that Elmer Mueller would show up.

As long as he was in Oakland, Lindsey drove to Lake Merritt and parked near the Kleiner Mansion. The mansion was closed at this hour, so he found a bench on the grassy bank and opened his attaché case. There were joggers and dog-walkers on the footpaths and ducks on the lake.

The *Bessie Blue* folder was in standard International Surety format, with plenty of paperwork. The company had computerized its operations in recent years, but cautious heads still insisted on keeping hard copies of everything, and a series of computer virus scares had left the corporate structure in a state of electronic paranoia.

The umbrella policy was made out to Double Bee Enterprises, as Lindsey had expected after talking to Lieutenant High. The policy covered all equipment, personnel, and operations of Double Bee and all its officers, employees, consultants, agents, and independent contractors engaged in lawful activities on behalf of the company in the course of the development, production, post-production, promotion, distribution, and exhibition of the film tentatively titled *Bessie Blue*.

The coverage included the insured's operation at Oakland International Airport, all grounds and facilities thereof, travel and transportation to and from, and other related movements and activities taking place at any location throughout the entire universe.

Lindsey turned to the policy appendixes. Double Bee Enterprises listed the airplanes it was going to use in *Bessie Blue*: a Stearman PT-17, a North American AT-6, a Lockheed P-38, a Bell P-39, a Curtiss P-40, a Republic P-47, a North American

P-51, a Boeing B-17F, a Messerschmitt 109, a Focke-Wulf 190, and a Mitsubishi A6M2 Zero. There were photos of all the aircraft. Wonderful machines, all of them packed with character. They were like something from another age. But where in the world were they going to get a fleet of 50-year-old warplanes in flying condition?

The folder revealed that the aircraft were to be provided by the National Knights of the Air Historical Association and Aerial Museum of Dallas, Texas. One more question answered.

There were signatures from all sorts of corporate officers at Double Bee and at International Surety. Every item in the policy carried a separate dollar value. The whole policy faced out at $100,000,000.

Lindsey placed the airplane photos, the appendixes and the policy itself back in the folder inside his attaché case and snapped the brass locks closed. He locked the attaché case in the Hyundai and found a restaurant on Grand Lake Boulevard.

When he phoned Oakland police headquarters he was able to reach

Lieutenant High. He had the number of High's private line and was able to avoid the Broadway bureaucracy. High agreed to see him. Lindsey headed across town.

There was even a visitor's badge ready when he hit the front disk. Upstairs, High greeted him. 'You should have come over earlier, Lindsey. You could have attended the autopsy on Mr. McKinney. You're following up on that, of course.'

'Coroner must have been in an awfully big rush.'

'Well, yes. We don't usually get to post-mortems this fast, but Sergeant Finnerty had an interesting theory about the McKinney killing. The evidence squad hasn't brought in its report yet, so we don't know about that, but I thought we should get the PM report on the victim as quickly as we could.'

'What theory was that?' Lindsey asked. 'Sergeant Finnerty's theory.'

'Narcotics.'

'Every story in the paper seems to be about narcotics.'

'Well, we get pretty close to a homicide a day here in Oakland. That's no match

40

for LA or Chicago. Half a dozen cities beat us, but then we're not nearly as big as they are. Most of the homicides are related to narcotics. Not the users. Well, sometimes we'll get somebody so strung out, he'll kill for a fix. But not often. Mostly it's the dealers. It's turf wars, just like Prohibition.'

'Sergeant Finnerty thinks that's what happened at the airport, to Mr. McKinney?'

'We had one woman a few weeks ago — couple of crack dealers were fighting over who got sidewalk rights in front of her house. She went out and tried to chase them away; they killed her. Right there, on the spot, just pulled out their automatic weapons and killed the poor woman.'

'Finnerty's theory?' Lindsey said.

'These old airplanes are coming up from Texas for this movie they're making here in Oakland. Most of the stuff comes up from South America, a lot of it comes via Mexico. Most of the heroin still comes From Asia, but crack is a cocaine derivative. The coca grows mainly in South America, and they bring a lot of cocaine in by air. If they could get it as far as Texas, Sergeant Finnerty thought, they could load it onto those old airplanes. Nobody thinks they'd be carrying cargo. They're museum pieces; they're just for this movie, right? So why not use them to carry the cocaine? Who would suspect?'

'But none of the planes have arrived yet, have they?'

'No. I think they're due in tomorrow. Mrs. Chandler would know that. But Sergeant Finnerty thinks that Mr. McKinney might have been involved. So we were really eager to see the post-mortem, just in case he's a user himself. Most of the dealers at the higher levels aren't users; they're too smart to get hooked on their own wares. But at the lower levels . . . Well, Sergeant Finnerty thought Mr. McKinney might be a user. So we rushed the autopsy.'

'And?'

'He was pretty clean. Coroner found a little cannabis in his bloodstream, and a little alcohol. My guess is that Mr. McKinney was not a happy individual, sweeping up a hangar and swabbing out urinals at the airport. I can understand his wanting to start the day with a little fortification. A little something added to his morning coffee. A joint before he leaves the house. Then down the freeway, it's just a hop, skip and a jump from Richmond to Oakland, and it's another day, another dollar.'

'What about the crack?'

'Nothing to indicate he was involved at all.'

'But those planes are coming in from Texas tomorrow.'

High smiled. 'We've already talked to the Feds. They're all over those airplanes. Even as we speak, Lindsey, even as we speak. You didn't think I'd tell anyone about this now, do you, if we were going to wait until they arrive to check them?' High pushed himself to his feet. 'Did you say you had another appointment, Lindsey?'

'Actually, I have to make a phone call.' High started to say something but Lindsey headed him off. 'No, it's all right, thanks. I'll use the pay phone in the lobby.'

3

Lindsey headed for Walnut Creek and the International Surety office after all. As he crossed the threshold he felt a wave of emotion sweep over him, a feeling of homecoming mixed with a sense of loss.

Ms. Wilbur was at her desk, the same as ever. She looked up and came around her desk and wrapped Lindsey in her arms. She planted a kiss on his cheek. They separated, laughing.

'I thought you were too high and mighty to come and see us again, Bart!'

He shook his head. 'I missed you. I'll still be working out of the office. You'll see me around.' He took her hands. 'How's it been?'

'You mean since Mr. Mueller took over here?' She made the title sound like an epithet. 'He's out of the office this afternoon — on business, he says. I think he's looking after those real estate interests of his in Emeryville.'

44

'Not good, eh?'

'I have almost enough years in for retirement. My husband is still working. My kids are grown up. I'm a grand-mother, Bart. I think I'll just be a housewife and a grandma for a while. I think I'll enjoy that.'

Lindsey plopped into a familiar chair. 'You going to do it?'

'I think so.'

'That bad?'

'You wouldn't believe it.' She changed the subject. 'And what are you doing for International Surety now? Ever since you went off to the mysterious SPUDS, I've been wondering.'

Lindsey told her about *Bessie Blue* and Double Bee Enterprises and about the murder of Leroy McKinney.

'I'll take a look and see if we have life coverage on him.' She called up the alpha file of policy holders. 'No policy. You don't think they're going to try and claim a death benefit under the umbrella policy, do you? He wasn't even working for Double Bee, was he? Wasn't he some kind of mainte-nance man or janitor at the airport?'

'That's right. No, I'm only afraid that the investigation is going to hold up the project and Double Bee will come after us with an indemnity claim. If we could clear up this killing it would be a big help.'

Elmer Mueller strode into the office. He dropped his briefcase on his desk. 'Lindsey, Harden says I have to let you use this hole. I guess he's sucking up to Ducky Richelieu; God knows why. But I want you to you remember who's the boss here now. I am. Get it? You're supercargo.' He turned and pointed a finger at Ms. Wilbur. 'As for you, Mathilde, if you don't have anything better to do than gossip with visitors, maybe we should see about cutting your hours.'

Lindsey settled into a spare desk and began writing up his notes on the day's work. He'd been back in California for a mere matter of hours, and he was already involved in another murder case and in an intracompany mess.

He shot a covert look at Ms. Wilbur. All he could see was the back of her neck. It was flaming red.

He clicked on the computer on his desk and called up KlameNet. Ms. Wilbur had determined that there was no policy in the name of Leroy McKinney, but he knew the umbrella policy issued to Double Bee would appear. He called up the full text of the policy and verified that it contained a moral turpitude clause. If Double Bee suffered a loss through its own illegal or immoral conduct, the coverage was void.

Not that he expected anyone from Double Bee to have killed the janitor. Ina Chandler had arrived with Lawton Crump when Crump discovered the body. Still, it wouldn't hurt to have a talk with Mrs. Chandler. Or even with Mr. Crump. Sergeant Finnerty had already questioned them, but Lindsey would approach the man from another angle. Sometimes that made a big difference.

He phoned Berkeley police headquarters and reached Marvia Plum. Now that she was a sergeant in Homicide, she was spending more time at her desk and less time in the field.

Lindsey would pick Marvia up and

drive her back to Walnut Creek for dinner. That way she couldn't go home afterwards by herself. He'd have to drive her back.

'You're a schemer,' she said, laughing. The sound was like a hot jolt that ran through his body.

When he arrived at Oxford Street, one of Marvia's housemates let him into the restored Victorian house. She was another woman, heavyset and orange-haired. She said, 'Well, if it isn't Mr. Suburb. Back to grace the land of peace and progress with your presence?'

Lindsey managed a polite banality before racing up the stairs two at a time. He reached Marvia's turret apartment gasping for breath.

Marvia had showered after work and was standing before a full-length mirror, drying her hair. Lindsey ran across the carpeted room and put his arms around her. She shut off the dryer and turned to him.

'I missed you,' he said. 'Denver was okay but I really missed you.'

'I love you, Bart,' she replied.

She finished dressing and they drove to Walnut Creek, fighting the thousands of commuters struggling home from San Francisco and Oakland to the bedroom communities of Contra Costa County. In the car Lindsey said, 'Mother's doing well. She's making dinner. But we can't expect too much.'

'Does she still think I'm your football coach's daughter?'

'I don't know what she thinks. I told her you were coming for dinner. She said something like, 'Oh, that nice colored girl.' I don't want you hurt. When you are, I feel it too. I know I can't feel it the way you do, but I can see it and — '

Marvia touched his shoulder. They'd left the classic Mustang that Marvia's brother had restored as a gift for her at Oxford Street. She said, 'I have some vacation time coming up. I've been saving my days. You think we could get away for a little while?'

'I'd love it! What about Jamie? You don't mind leaving him with your parents?'

'We could do that. Or maybe we could

take him with us. I thought we might go down to Monterey. He's interested in fish; he'd like the aquarium.'

'As soon as I wrap up this case.'

Dinner went amazingly well. Mother had stayed with a simple pasta dish. The result was far from gourmet fare, but for a woman who had been almost helpless a few months before, it was an achievement.

Mother served coffee and ice cream and told Lindsey and Marvia that she had seen a wonderful movie on cable while Lindsey was away. She'd enjoyed it so much she'd got Mrs. Hernandez to take her to the video store; she'd bought a copy, and now she watched it every day. It made her think, she said.

Lindsey asked what movie it was.

Mother said, 'It's called *Sunset Boulevard*.'

'I know the picture,' Marvia said. 'Gloria Swanson and William Holden and Erich von Stroheim.'

'Yes.' Mother's eyes were shining. 'Gloria Swanson. And Norma Desmond, don't you see? She was an old-time movie star, but she was Gloria Swanson, but she was really an old-time movie star. An actress playing an actress. A silent star. But she couldn't bear it. Everything changed and she couldn't bear it. She lived in this huge mansion and she had a butler and she just pretended it was the old days. But it wasn't, don't you see? Everything was changed. *Everything was changed*.' She took a paper napkin from the table and wiped her eyes, then buried her face in the napkin in her hands. Lindsey held her by the shoulders. She looked up, looked at him, looked at Marvia, and said, 'Everything was changed.'

After a few minutes she said, 'Well, if everyone is finished with their coffee, I'll clear these cups and saucers away.'

A little later she said, 'Hobart, if you and your friend want to go on, I'll just clean up a little and go to bed. I'm so glad that you're back. I'm a little tired, though.'

Lindsey stood holding her hands, studying her face. 'You're all right, then, Mother. Is Mrs. Hernandez coming in tomorrow?'

She said yes.

'Then I might stay over in Berkeley. I'll phone you in the morning. And Joanie Schorr is right next door, if you need her.'

When they reached Marvia's home and climbed to her apartment, Marvia put on a CD and knelt to light the fire. She had worn a loose shirt and dark jeans for dinner at the Lindsey house. She had not changed her clothing since.

Lindsey sat in an easy chair, watching Marvia and listening to the music. A woman sang to a judge, pleading guilty as charged. The fire flared up with a crackle, sending a huge shadow of Marvia dancing around the circular room. She stood up, fetched a bottle of wine and two glasses, and filled them up. She gave one to Lindsey and raised the other. 'Welcome home,' she said.

'That's a blood-curdling song. That's a murder song. Who's singing it? Is that new?'

Marvia laughed. 'That's Bessie Smith. She's been dead since 1937. That's a great song. 'Send Me to the 'lectric Chair.'

'I caught him with a trifling Jane
'I warned him 'bout befo'
'I had my knife and went insane
'And the rest you ought to know.'
Lindsey said, 'What happened to Bessie Smith? How did she die?'
'She was hit by a cab. They rushed her to the nearest hospital. She might have survived, but they refused to treat her there. It was a white hospital, you see. So they took her to a black hospital, but then it was too late. She was 42 years old.'
Bessie Smith was still singing. She sounded happy. The song was 'Take me for a Buggy Ride.'
Lindsey and Marvia finished their wine and climbed into bed.

★   ★   ★

The Oakland *Tribune* and the San Francisco *Chronicle* both ran stories on the Leroy McKinney murder. The *Chron* gave it a couple of paragraphs on an inside page. To the San Francisco papers, events in Oakland were by definition minor stories. The *Trib* gave it a banner above the logo and a top position on page three.

There were a pair of photos of the crime site. The body had been removed and the photo centered on the taped outline on the hangar floor. The monkey wrench was still in place, and it could still be seen, surrounded by its own outline of tape, in a corner of the picture.

The *Trib* photographer had got a picture of the body, and in fact he must have gone back to the hangar for a second shoot to get the tape after the body was gone. He'd somehow also managed to shoot a close-up of McKinney's ID badge photo, and the *Trib* had blown that up to column width.

The story in the *Trib* gave McKinney's address in Richmond and quoted the usual reactions of family and neighbors. McKinney had been friendly and outgoing, had kept strictly to himself, had been a wonderful man, nobody knew much about him, he was a pillar of the community, everyone loved him, he was a victim of society.

Next of kin seemed to be a young

woman named Latasha Greene. After reading the story, Lindsey wasn't quite sure whether she was McKinney's daughter or granddaughter. She was described as distraught but calm, bearing up courageously. A memorial service was planned.

Marvia was on the day shift and left Oxford Street early for police headquarters. She had her own case-load. Lindsey hadn't burdened her with the Leroy McKinney killing and she hadn't unloaded any of hers onto him.

He read the newspapers over a second cup of coffee and a stack of pancakes in a hole-in-the-wall restaurant on Shattuck Avenue. He phoned Mother and assured her that he was all right; that he would probably be home for dinner. Mother was expecting Mrs. Hernandez.

He borrowed a pair of scissors from a waitress and clipped the *Trib* and *Chron* stories on the hangar killing. The *Trib* ran a jump that butted against an aerial photo of the *Abraham Lincoln* at sea. It didn't look like the *Love Boat*, but Lindsey could think of worse ways to spend a few weeks.

When he finished his breakfast he walked to an instant printing service and made copies of the stories on the killing and extra blowups of the ID photo of Leroy McKinney. The dot-pattern of the newspaper photo didn't enlarge too well, but the pictures were recognizable.

★ ★ ★

Latasha Greene's address was on 23rd Street in downtown Richmond, just off Nevin Avenue. Lindsey found a parking spot between a rusted-out Corolla and an ancient Buick the size of a gymnasium. He'd driven home, checked on Mother and Mrs. Hernandez, showered and changed his clothing. Working for Ducky Richelieu certainly had its compensations.

He'd passed kids skateboarding on the sidewalk; groups gathered around ghetto blasters practicing their rap moves; some derelicts slumped in vacant doorways, paper bags in their laps, their eyes as vacant as the doorways where they made their homes.

Latasha Greene lived in a 1930s frame and stucco bungalow. It might once have been a pleasant little house, but it had not seen a paintbrush or received the attention of a carpenter in decades. The paint had faded to a nondescript tan, the wood was cracked, and there were holes — they looked like bullet holes — in the stucco. Several windows were cracked and patched with cardboard. The lawn was spotty and strewn with litter. On either side of Latasha's house were vacant lots, overgrown with weeds and scattered with old tires and miscellaneous trash.

The kid pointed his weapon as Lindsey turned from the Hyundai and started to slip his keys into his pocket. He said, 'Drop the tachy-case, gringo, and reach.'

He had pale, almost albino features marked with blotchy freckles and crinkly blond hair. He wore a baseball cap with the visor turned sideways. He must have been wearing some kind of clothes, but all Lindsey could focus on was the gun in his hands.

He dropped his attaché case as the kid had ordered.

'Too slow, gringo!'

Time froze. Lindsey could see three or four more kids behind the one with the gun. They couldn't have been more than 12 years old. They all wore baseball caps with the visors over their ears and plastic straps hanging onto their cheeks. They were all grinning, all baring white teeth in black faces. Lindsey's eyes moved back to the kid with the gun.

The kid's finger tightened on the trigger. Lindsey felt his knees buckle. He saw the stream of water coming from the muzzle of the gun. He heard the kids bursting into hysterical laughter. Then they ran away, all except the one with the gun in his hands.

The kid said, 'I was only joking, mister. It's only a water-gun, see?' He held the gun in front of Lindsey and pulled the trigger again. A stream of water squirted from the muzzle and splashed onto the lawn in front of Latasha Greene's house. 'I didn't mean to soak your jacket. I don't got any money. I don't know how to . . . Don't tell my Grandma. She's kill me if you tell her. Don't tell . . . '

'I won't tell,' Lindsey said. 'Do you know Latasha Greene? Is this her house?'

'That's her house all right. You gonna visit her? She's all broken up. Mr. McKinney, he got offed. *Wham*, some sucker got him with a monkey-wrench. I saw it all on TV. *Wham!* Right in the face! Must have been some sucker he knowed. Right in the face!' The kid grinned, turned around, and ran off in the direction his friends had gone.

Lindsey climbed three rickety steps and knocked on the door. After a while he heard the latches opening. There were a lot of them.

The black man who opened the door had hair cropped short around his ears. The dome of his head was hairless and shone as if it had been polished. A pot belly pushed out the front of a vest beneath a dove-gray clergy suit. He said, 'I'm the Reverend Johnson. Did something happen to you?' He was looking at Lindsey's soaked jacket.

'I ran into some kids outside. They didn't mean any harm, but . . . '

'That's too bad,' Reverend Johnson

said. 'But why are you here? This is a house of grief today.'

'I know. I'm very sorry. I hoped I could talk with Miss Greene. I represent International Surety.' He fumbled for a business card, then handed it to Johnson.

Johnson took the card. He studied it for a long time, then slipped it into a pocket. 'An insurance man.'

Johnson seemed to think that Lindsey was here to arrange a payment. Let him think it. People talk to you when they think you're going to give them money. 'It's about Mr. McKinney.' He managed a note of detached sympathy.

Johnson said, 'Come in, young man. I expect that Miss Greene will receive you in the parlor.'

The furnishings were shabby and the air was musty inside, as if the house hadn't been aired thoroughly in years. Johnson disappeared through a dusty, rust-colored curtain. Lindsey heard him speak softly: 'Latasha, dear, there's a man to see you. It's about Grandfather's life insurance.'

Latasha Greene was tall and brown. She wore a T-shirt with a picture of a brown-skinned Bart Simpson brandishing an assault pistol, faded jeans and wooden clogs. She balanced a baby on her hip. She said to Lindsey, 'What happened to your jacket?'

'Some kids outside. It was just an accident.'

'What kids?' She seemed distracted, only partially present, asking her questions in a remote voice.

Lindsey described the kids in their baseball caps and team jackets.

Latasha said, 'Oh, that's just Ahmad. Mrs. Hope's grandson.' She blinked. Then, as if she'd just wakened, she said, 'What about my Grandpa?'

Lindsey extended another business card. She looked at it for a time. Then she sat on the couch. Lindsey slipped the card back into his pocket. The Reverend Johnson sat on a reversed chrome and plastic kitchen chair. Lindsey looked around, found a faded, overstuffed easy chair, and settled uneasily on it.

He said, 'I was very sorry to learn of Mr. McKinney's demise. He was your grandfather, then, Miss Greene?'

Latasha said, 'Grandpa had insurance?'

'We have to find out. Under the circumstances of his death, I don't know whether he was covered or not.'

Reverend Johnson said, 'Now wait a minute, mister! You mean you're trying to weasel out of paying off?'

'Not at all. You see, Mr. McKinney was not directly covered. But there's an umbrella policy, so we may be able to . . . ' He let it go at that. He hated to mislead them. It wasn't his job to pour out International Surety's funds, but to preserve them.

Johnson said, 'Just what do you need to know?'

Lindsey turned to Latasha. She had lifted the bottom of her Black Bart T-shirt and was nursing her baby, watching it with a look of unreadable concentration. Lindsey said, 'I'm trying to find out something about Mr. McKinney. What kind of person he was; the life he led.'

Johnson said, 'I don't see why you need to know that to pay off his insurance.'

'He didn't have any insurance with our company. I thought I'd made that clear.

But if we can find some way to get benefits under the umbrella . . . '

Johnson frowned and said nothing.

Lindsey turned back to Latasha, willing her to talk to him. She said, 'My grandpa was a great man. He was a hero.' She looked away from Lindsey and back at her baby. Its eyes were closed but it was making little smacking sounds with its mouth. Lindsey lowered his eyes to his notepad.

'He was a war hero. He killed a whole machine-gun nest of Japs in the Philippines. And he saved two Americans. He was a pitcher, too. He should have been in the major leagues, but he never got a chance. And he ran a nightclub. He made people rich and famous and he never got nothin' for it.'

Lindsey was trying to keep track, jotting notes as fast as Latasha spoke. He wished he had a tape recorder. Maybe he'd buy one of those little portables and charge it to SPUDS. He said, 'Pardon me, but please slow down. You say your grandfather was a war hero?' He jotted, *Verify military service record — Dept.*

Veterans Affairs.

She carried her baby out of the room. While she was gone, Lindsey looked over his notes. Reverend Johnson said, 'How much is your company going to pay?'

'I don't know that we're going to pay anything. That's why I have to get all the facts.'

'This is a very needy family. I should think that a certain humane consideration would be involved.'

Latasha came back into the room, having left her baby elsewhere. She resumed her seat on the couch, looked past Lindsey, and fixed her eyes on the TV screen.

Lindsey said, 'About Mr. McKinney's military service . . .'

Latasha said, 'He was in the Marines. He fought all over the Pacific. He was at Iwo Jima; hurt his hand there. He was working in an ammunition bunker, and a Jap fire-grenade landed that would have blown up the ammunition and killed everybody. Grandpa grabbed the grenade and threw it back at the Japs; it wiped out a whole machine-gun nest of them, but it burned up his hand so bad, it was never any good again. It was so ugly, it was like a claw. I used to be afraid of it when I was little and I always made him cover it up when he came on my bed, or I'd start to scream.'

Lindsey said, 'I never heard of fire-grenades.'

'You don't know anything about it. My grandpa told me. He used to sit on my bed at night and tell me stories. After he hurt his hand, he still dragged two men to safety who would have died. He saved their lives. He was a hero.' She set her jaw angrily, but her mouth was quivering and her eyes looked wet.

'I wasn't suggesting — '

'I even have a picture of him. And a newspaper.' She brought a tattered San Francisco *Call-Bulletin* from the other room, and a yellowed snapshot with edges that looked as if they'd been made with a pair of pinking shears.

Lindsey said, 'May I take these with me? I'll photocopy them and return them to you.' He waited until she nodded absently and then he put the newspaper and the photograph in his attaché case. Latasha's eyes were fixed on the silent TV set. 'Do you have his Marine Corps discharge papers? Or any of his military records? Did he go to a veterans' hospital at any time? Was he receiving a disability pension?'

Latasha was staring at the TV screen. Even though the sound was turned off, she must have recognized the video they were showing because she was moving her lips silently to the unheard lyrics.

Lindsey looked questioningly at Reverend Johnson, who said, 'I asked Leroy about that. Many times. He never got anything from the government. There was some mix-up with his records. He never did get his discharge papers, disability payments, anything. He never got anything at all. I urged him to take it up with our congressman, but I could never get him to do it. He was a very embittered man. Well, he's in his glory now. Even if there's no justice in this world, there surely must be in the next, and Leroy is in his glory now.'

Latasha was still involved with her TV.

66

Lindsey said, 'I guess I'll be going now. I'll send back the newspaper and the photograph. Or maybe bring them.' He started for the door.

Reverend Johnson said, 'I was just leaving myself.'

4

Once they were outside the house, Reverend Johnson's mien brightened. Before they reached the sidewalk, he put his hand on Lindsey's elbow and stopped. 'Come on,' he said, 'let's stroll a bit. Maybe we can find the miscreants responsible for your wet jacket, and exchange a bit more information while we're at it.'

They walked to the corner and rounded it onto Nevin. A bar and a poolroom were in full action even though it was not yet noon. A cluster of young men standing outside the poolroom stirred at Lindsey and Johnson's approach. They were passing something around, which promptly disappeared amid murmurs of 'Rev, mornin', Rev.' Lindsey felt hot stares on the back of his neck as he and Johnson passed by.

'What about Latasha's story, Reverend?' Lindsey asked. 'The part about Mr. McKinney's being a baseball player?'

'I can only tell you that Leroy was very

convincing. I wasn't there; I didn't see the things he claimed to have done. But he told the same stories year after year.' He stood still, frowning. 'Wait a minute. He once showed me some old baseball programs when he visited me at the church. He was sorting through a batch of old papers and he found some scorecards or programs. He was very proud of them and was afraid they would be lost after he was gone, so I promised to keep them for him. I haven't even thought about them in years, but they must still be where I stored them for him.' Johnson stood facing Lindsey. 'Come with me. The church is nearby. Let's see if we can find those scorecards.'

They crossed Nevin and walked past a row of abandoned storefronts. Lindsey was worried, but Johnson read his mind. 'Don't be afraid, Mr. Lindsey. You aren't in any danger.'

Lindsey decided it was still a good idea to keep an eye out.

Johnson said, 'Yes, I was quite a baseball enthusiast in my day. Are you a baseball fan, Mr. Lindsey?'

Lindsey admitted that he didn't follow

the sport closely.

'Wonderful game, Mr. Lindsey. I was a shortstop once upon a time. You wouldn't believe it, would you?' He patted his ample paunch. 'That was before I received my calling, of course.'

He grinned ruefully. 'But Leroy McKinney, now — he used to tell wonderful baseball stories. He played in the old Negro National League. I suppose you've never heard of that, but we used to have our own teams, our own National and American Leagues, a Negro World Series and our own All-Star Games. I saw the Negro East-West Classic in 1948, Mr. Lindsey. I was there; observed the game from the upper deck of old Comiskey Park in Chicago. I was a very young man then, but it was a day I shall never forget.'

They had reached Johnson's church. It was better than a storefront, but not by much. The building stood on a small lot between a weed-covered field and a Chinese take-out restaurant. There was a single stained-glass window in the front wall of the church. The glass of the announcement board had been broken out and the letters rearranged to spell obscenities.

Johnson hurried Lindsey inside the building. It was musty inside. 'Let's see about those scorecards of Leroy's.'

The sacristy of the Reverend Johnson's church was a musty storeroom containing choir robes, battered hymnals, a stack of collection plates, and stacked corrugated boxes of files. Johnson riffled through the boxes, muttering and shoving cartons aside. Several minutes passed.

Lindsey said, 'Maybe you'd send them to me.'

Johnson looked up. 'I'm sure they're here. Just a minute.' Presently he said, 'Here they are!' There was a note of triumph in his voice. He waved a couple of five-by-seven sheets of light cardboard at Lindsey. '1942,' Johnson said. 'That was Leroy McKinney's last year as a ballplayer. After that he went into the service; and after the war, of course, he couldn't pitch anymore. Not with his injured hand.'

He spread the scorecards on the top of a cardboard file box. Someone had marked the scorecards with an old-style fountain pen and the ink had run and faded, but Lindsey could see the lineup printed in splotchy black ink. The team was the Cincinnati Buckeyes, and Leroy Mickinney was listed as a pitcher.

Mickinney. Not McKinney. Someone in 1942 had made a typographical error.

Lindsey found a dusty folding chair and sat down. He opened his attaché case and slipped the programs into the *Bessie Blue* International Surety folder. He said, 'It's really hard to understand, Reverend Johnson. I mean, with all the advocacy groups, veterans' organizations, and civil rights organizations, that Mr. McKinney never received any benefits.'

Johnson shook his head sadly. 'No benefits. No recognition. No appreciation. I don't think you quite understand what conditions were like, Mr. Lindsey.' He changed his direction. 'If you can do anything with those old documents — the newspaper, the photos, the baseball scorecards — please do so. But in any case, once you have made your copies, please make sure to return them. I'm certain that they will be precious mementos.'

'Sure.'

'If we were a wealthier congregation we'd have our own office facilities, including copying machines, but you can see that we serve the needy not the greedy.'

★ ★ ★

Lindsey thought of going home from Richmond and cleaning up, but instead he'd come to the office to catch up on paperwork.

Ms. Wilbur gaped. 'Bart, what happened to your jacket?'

He explained about the 12-year-old bandits and the water pistol.

Elmer Mueller had observed the exchange between Lindsey and Ms. Wilbur. He said, 'Harden and Richelieu have both been on the horn. I don't know which one is having a bigger fit. You better get back to 'em fast. You're really going to have your tail in the grinder after this fiasco, Hobie-boy.'

Lindsey ignored the name. He dialed out to SPUDS in Denver. Mrs. Blomquist put him through to Richelieu fast. Lindsey got as far as 'Mi — ' before Richelieu cut him off.

'Welcome to the hardball game,' Richelieu said. 'What have you done to contain this *Bessie Blue* matter?'

Lindsey started to tell him about visiting the airport, working with Lieutenant High, and interviewing Latasha Greene and Reverend Johnson.

'Are those airplanes in California yet?'

'I don't know. They were going to fly in today. I've been in Richmond all afternoon and — '

'I don't want an opera in five acts with full orchestra and chorus. Where are the airplanes? What's the status of that movie? We're standing in as de facto completion bond guarantor — and frankly, my dear, I don't give a damn if somebody whacks a janitor on the bean. I care about that movie getting made so we don't have to shell out millions of dollars.'

'Yes, sir.'

'Well, where are the airplanes?'

Lindsey swallowed hard. 'I don't know for sure.'

'You mean you don't know, period!'
Lindsey could imagine Richelieu twisting
his moustache, the high Colorado sunlight glancing off his rimless glasses. 'Get
into gear and report back to me in 24
hours, Lindsey. Good heavens, man, what
do you think we spent all the money to
train you for? What do you think we're
paying you for?'

Lindsey held the receiver away from his
ear, waiting for Richelieu to slam the
telephone down in Denver. All that came
over the line was a gentle click.

Lindsey laid the receiver in its cradle.

Elmer Mueller was grinning at him.
'Sounded like you handled that gink
pretty well, Hobie. Now it's time to chat
with Harden at Regional, right?'

Lindsey said, 'Harden at Regional
can — ' He stopped. He was not going to
lower himself to Elmer Mueller's level.
He breathed deeply until he'd calmed
himself, then he called home. Mrs.
Hernandez answered, and he asked after
his mother.

'She's just a little confused, Mr.
Lindsey. She's really all right. You can

come home now.'

When Lindsey got there, Mother was settled in front of the TV set watching one of her old movies, a cup of hot chocolate in her hand. She hardly noticed his arrival. He made his way to his room, showered and put on fresh clothing. Mrs. Hernandez reassured him that Mother was really doing all right; that her confusion had been a minor lapse. He thanked Mrs. Hernandez and she left for the day.

Lindsey stood watching the TV screen. Mother was completely absorbed in her old movie. Lindsey recognized the film. Mother hadn't even had to tinker with the TV controls; the movie was already in black and white. It was *Whatever Happened to Baby Jane*. Lindsey watched for several minutes. Davis and Crawford were either awfully wonderful or wonderfully awful, he couldn't tell which.

Mother set her cup on its saucer with a clash. She turned toward Lindsey, pointing back at the screen, at the frightening image of an elderly Bette Davis costumed as Baby Jane, prancing and singing, obviously mad. She said, 'You see,

Hobart? It's like that other one, like that one with Gloria Swanson. Only this one is different. Norma Desmond really thought it was long ago, but Baby Jane only wants it to be long ago. She wants to make it be long ago, but she can't do it.'

Lindsey didn't know what to make of it. What should he say?

★   ★   ★

Lieutenant High took Lindsey's call and told him that the DEA had approached the National Knights of the Air, and they had agreed to their aircraft and museum being searched, both of which had come up clean. 'Clean of drugs,' High added. 'The drug kiddies went in there with their dope-sniffing doggies and their little chemical analysis kits and they didn't turn up anything you could put up your nose or shoot in your veins and get a thrill from. But they found themselves a miniature zoo!'

'A what?'

'A zoo. Some of these old airplane people seem to have a fondness for rare animals. Uncle Sam has been getting down on illegal importers of endangered species. Mostly South American birds, a few primates, a couple of rare breeds of cats, even some snakes. It's quite a list. And you know what happens when you tell people they can't have something, whether it's dirty pictures or home atom bombs — that's what they want.'

Lindsey said, 'So are the planes in Oakland?'

'I don't know. There's no indication that they were planning to fly the animals out here on this jaunt. The people at the museum claim they didn't know anything about the illegal livestock. Some employee, whatever. They're quaking in their cowboy boots that Uncle Sam is going to bring a RICO action against 'em and seize their precious old warbirds.'

Lindsey held his head. 'You think that's going to happen?'

'I doubt it. But you can never tell with the Feds. Tell you what, I think your best bet is to ask Double Bee.'

High gave Lindsey Double Bee's local phone number without requiring a writ of mandamus.

Double Bee had taken a suite at the Pare Oakland Hotel, the glittery establishment on Broadway not far from police headquarters. It was their temporary office as well as the housing for their visiting personnel.

Lindsey expected to have to go out to the airport again to track down Ina Chandler, but to his surprise he was able to locate her by telephone at the Pare Oakland. After he'd explained his job to the production secretary a few times, he was put through to Mrs. Chandler.

She opened the conversation. Her voice was soft and her pronunciation sounded like Alabama, but her words were more postmodern career woman than southern belle. 'I'm very busy. This production is top priority. But we haven't even started shooting yet and we've already had a fatality, the airplanes aren't here, we're behind schedule and running up bills every hour, and you want to sell me life insurance. I don't know why that idiot put you through. The answer is no.'

Sensing she was about to hang up, Lindsey snapped, 'Shut up and listen to me. I'm from International Surety and I'm going to save your movie for you unless you stop me. And if you do, your ass is grass.'

'*What?*'

'The police are in charge of the murder but I'm in charge of the insurance, and I'm going to straighten this thing out and save your movie for you. You're in the Pare Oakland now. I'll be there in half an hour. Don't leave.'

'All right.'

He took the elevator up to the Double Bee suite. A dozen people lounged around looking miserable. Most of them wore plaid shirts and blue jeans. Lindsey spotted a couple of bright blue satin jackets with a *Bessie Blue* logo on the back. The logo featured a picture of a round-faced black woman in a beaded dress and feathered headband. Other than the jackets, there wasn't much of the Hollywood glamour that Lindsey had expected to find.

He located the production secretary and was directed to Ina Chandler. Despite her gray hair, Mrs. Chandler had the figure of a younger woman, and she obviously knew it and wanted others to notice. Either that, or someone in the laundry room had shrunk her shirt and jeans.

She was sitting at a wood-patterned table with a tray of donuts, a pot of coffee and a yellow pad. She took Lindsey's card and waved him to a straight-backed chair.

Ms. Wilbur had locked the *Bessie Blue* case folder in International Surety's office safe in Walnut Creek. Lindsey had finally read the file and had the salient data in his mind. And he didn't want to risk the documents that Latasha Greene and Reverend Johnson had loaned him.

She said, 'I thought Mueller was handling this for your company. What's the story?'

'Elmer works out of our local office. He authorizes payments for *legitimate* claims.' She didn't rise to the emphasis. 'I'm from Special Projects. I work out of Denver.'

Mrs. Chandler looked unimpressed, but she waited for him to continue.

'We'll be a lot happier if we don't have to pay off, and I don't mean we're trying to weasel out of our obligation. I mean,

81

I'm here to try and help you get your cart back on the track. If we can do that you'll be happier, and International Surety will save a load of dollars. Now, what's the story on your fleet of aircraft?'

'They're coming in tomorrow. At least, that's the plan. So we're two days behind schedule. And that's our best case.'

'Are you all set up with the airport? Tower controllers alerted? Oakland police informed? All cleared with the Feds?' She nodded. 'Lieutenant High didn't seem to know your plans.'

She said, 'I just got off the phone to him ten minutes ago. You know what happened in Texas?'

'The zoo?'

'First thing that happened, DEA wanted to wash their hands of the matter. Customs Service got involved, Department of Agriculture came snooping around, Environmental Protection sent a couple of their spooks, the local Humane Society got into the act. The Knights are going to be in and out of court for years on this thing.'

'But there's no RICO suit. The

airplanes can fly?'

'The airplanes can fly. They'll be leaving at dawn tomorrow.'

Lindsey said, 'Leroy McKinney was not employed by Double Bee. Is that correct?'

'That is correct.'

'You didn't know him. You and Mr. Crump found him when you arrived at the hangar yesterday. Is that correct?'

'That is correct.'

'What time was this?'

'Five-thirty a.m. It was early, but we thought the planes were coming in yesterday. We had a lot of work to do at the airport before they arrived. We work long hours in this business. Movies aren't all shiny cars and wild parties.'

'Was there anyone else in the hangar when you arrived?'

'No.'

'*Had* there been? Mr. McKinney was there — his body was. And whoever killed him had been there. Could you tell? Did whoever it was leave behind, oh, a sandwich wrapper or a coffee container or some cigarette butts?'

'Nothing. Oh, well the stove was going.

It was pretty low, but there were still some flames.'

'Right. It was still warm when I got there.' He frowned. 'What time do you expect the airplanes tomorrow?

'We want to film them arriving, and they fly at different speeds. So the slowest planes will leave Dallas first, and they'll time the other takeoffs so they'll assemble over San Jose and fly in the last 40 miles in formation. We're expecting them around four p.m.'

Lindsey jotted that down. 'Let's get back to yesterday. You and Mr. Crump got to the airport at five-thirty. What time did you leave the hotel?'

'Five o'clock.'

'Together?'

'Of course together. Why should we take two cars to drive from the hotel to the airport?'

'You were both staying here in the hotel?'

'Yes.' She frowned. 'I'd like to know why you're asking these questions. You claim you're here to handle the insurance side of *Bessie Blue*, but you must know that you're acting a hell of a lot like a dumb cop.'

'I'm not a cop, believe me. Okay. You left here together at five o'clock, morning of the day before yesterday. In whose car?'

'Double Bee company car.'

'Why didn't Mr. Crump just meet you there? The insurance file has him on the list of covered people. It indicates that he lives in San Jose.'

'Lawton Crump lives in Holy City. On Call of the Wild Road, no less.'

'Okay. Still, Crump would have to drive all the way *up* from San Jose or Holy City or wherever and then ride all the way *back* to the airport with you. Why not just meet at the airport?'

Mrs. Chandler exhaled in exasperation. 'He stayed here at the hotel the night before. Are you trying to stave off an insurance claim, or pry into people's personal lives? It's Lawton's business where he spent Wednesday night, not yours.'

The conversation was going nowhere. Lindsey said, 'When will you know if the planes are on time?'

'They'll be in frequent communication with ground controllers all along their flight path. This isn't any routine trip, you know.'

'I know. Where's Mr. Crump now?'

'Back in Holy City. Sorry to disappoint your prurient interest, if that's what it is. Nesting with Mrs. Nellie Crump, his bride and the companion of his life for the past 40-odd years, as he never misses a chance to remind me.'

On his way out of the suite, Lindsey stopped for a good look at the *Bessie Blue* logo on a young functionary's jacket. Lindsey said, 'I guess that's *Bessie Blue* herself, right? Was that her name?'

The young person shrugged. 'Not the foggiest.'

5

Lindsey phoned Lawton Crump's house from the lobby of the Pare Oakland. Mrs. Crump answered the phone and insisted on knowing Lindsey's identity and business before she'd put him through to her husband.

When Crump took the call he said, 'You'll forgive my wife. She gets protective. And after what happened to that poor fellow at the airport, I'm afraid I've been a little bit upset myself.'

Lindsey said, 'I understand. If I could have just a bit of your time, though . . . ' He left it there.

Crump said, 'All right. I presume you have credentials to prove your bona fides?'

'Of course.'

It was a relief to drive from Oakland to San Jose out of rush hour. The freeway passed between the Coliseum and the airport, and Lindsey flashed on the image of a bomber heading for the sports stadium and crashing into a deck full of spectators.

Holy City was southeast of downtown San Jose and difficult to find. The Crump house was one of several split-levels. The houses stood on large lots. The newly planted trees would take decades to provide any shade or beauty, or to support children's swings.

Lindsey pulled into the driveway behind a shiny Jeep Grand Wagoneer and a dark green Oldsmobile sedan. The sedan could have come straight from the showroom except for the traces of reddish dirt and the residue of oil that remained despite a recent washing.

The Crumps' lawn was immaculately edged and trimmed. An intricate pattern of red and yellow roses lined the front of the house. Lindsey felt a pang of guilt when he thought of his own casual landscaping in Walnut Creek.

Mrs. Crump admitted Lindsey. She wore a tan blouse and slacks, nearly the color of her skin. Her hair was only partially gray. She had to be close to her husband in age, but then if they'd been married for 40 years she'd have to be.

She led Lindsey into the living room, which was furnished in teak. The couch and chairs were covered with dark brown leather, there was a flagstone fireplace, and the walls were dark-stained wood. The room was decorated with pictures, including blowups of old group photos of men in uniform, many of them standing before World War Two aircraft.

Lawton Crump was there, wearing khaki trousers and a patterned sweater. He had an iron-gray moustache that extended beyond the edges of his mouth. He shook Lindsey's hand and offered him a seat. Lindsey had seen him at North Field being questioned along with Mrs. Chandler, but they had not actually met. Crump waited patiently while Lindsey showed his International Surety credentials. Mrs. Crump sat quietly, watching the men.

Lindsey said, 'You must be very excited about this film, Mr. Crump.'

Crump said, 'I *was* very excited. But Wednesday's incident has put a damper on it for me. Perhaps I'll regain my enthusiasm.'

Lindsey tried to explain his involvement in the case. If he could clear up the McKinney killing and get *Bessie Blue* back on track he'd save International Surety a lot of money, and that was his official task. Ina Chandler had hammered at him that he was not a cop, and she was right. But seeing Leroy McKinney flat on his back, the puddle of gore on his forehead, that frightening claw of a hand upraised, the old woodstove somehow connecting the empty hangar with another era, had all had an effect on Lindsey. He had to resolve the case for the sake of his own peace of mind.

'Are they going to cover your whole life, Mr. Crump?'

'Not a chance. The film isn't really about me anyway. I'm just an exemplar.' He grinned.

'You flew in the war, though. The Second World War.'

'I most certainly did. Best thing that ever happened to me. Going up into the air in 400-mile-an-hour machines and killing other men in 400-mile-an-hour machines for the sake of my country and the honor of my race. Escorting other men in giant machines carrying iron eggs full of TNT to drop over cities and blow up factories and schools and kill thousands of men and women and children. Very heroic.'

'But if we hadn't — I mean, if *you* hadn't, you and all the others — Hitler would have won the war.'

'Don't get me wrong; it certainly was necessary. I'd never deny that. And it was good for me. Very good. Still . . . '

Mrs. Crump stood up. 'Would you like a cup of tea, Lawton? Mr. Lindsey?' She left the room.

Crump gestured toward the mantel. Over it hung a painting of a young black man in officer's gear, circa 1945. A captain's twin silver bars glistened on his shoulders. His eyes were raised as if he were scanning the skies for approaching airplanes. He was standing in front of a bomber. Lindsey recognized it as a B-17. He wondered if it was *Bessie Blue*.

'Recognize me? Soon as I could afford

to, I had that painted. Artist used a photo for the background. I posed for him in my old uniform. Didn't look so different then than I had in Europe. You wouldn't recognize me now, would you?'

Lindsey said, 'I think I would.'

Mrs. Crump returned with a tray. There was tea and there were little rounds of melba toast.

Lindsey took out a notebook and his gold International Surety pencil. 'If you don't mind answering some questions, Mr. Crump . . . Let's start with Wednesday and work backwards. Will that be all right?'

'I answered Sergeant Finnerty's questions on Wednesday.'

'Yes, sir. Lieutenant High — he's Finnerty's boss — and I have cooperated before. He's providing me with information on this case. But I'd rather hear it directly from you. If you don't mind.'

Crump nodded. Lindsey saw his eyes flash to the military portrait before he spoke. 'Mrs. Chandler's company is paying me quite well for my services as technical advisor. They wanted me at the airport

92

early Wednesday, so I stayed in the Pare Oakland on Tuesday night. Mrs. Chandler and I drove out to the airport early Wednesday morning. She had a key to the hangar but the door was open when we got there. I thought that was strange. I insisted on entering first.'

Lindsey looked at Nellie Crump. She was listening intently.

'In I went. The hangar was dark and cold. There was a dying fire going in that old woodstove. I called out; I remember vividly. 'Anybody here? Anybody here?' I flicked on the lights — there was a switch near the door. And there he was, lying on his back. At first I thought he was just unconscious. Then I saw that his forehead was caved in. And I saw that claw, that deformed hand. The poor fellow. Just a janitor. He never had a chance.'

Lindsey said, 'I want to make sure of this. You didn't know the victim, didn't recognize him at all?'

'Never laid eyes on him before that moment.'

'All right. You'd breakfasted with Mrs. Chandler before leaving the Pare Oakland?'

'Restaurant wasn't open that early in the morning. Nor room service. We brewed up some instant java in the Double Bee suite. That was all the breakfast I had. After I saw the body I didn't have any appetite.'

Crump walked across the room and leaned against the mantelpiece, posing before the portrait of himself as he had been half a century ago. 'What else do you want to know?'

'Tell me about *Bessie Blue* and the Tuskegee Airmen.'

Crump rubbed his chin. 'How old are you, Lindsey?'

'I was born in 1953, sir.'

'Huh. You wouldn't remember what it was like, then. I'm a child of the old south. I was born in 1924.'

'I understand. They had segregation back then.' Lindsey was not going to go into his relationship with Marvia Plum. Not at this point.

'Segregation!' Crump roared. Lindsey saw Nellie Crump, watching and listening, tense. 'Segregation was nothing! I'm talking about lynchings, sonny boy!

Blacks hauled out of their beds in the middle of the night. Shot, hanged, burned at the stake! Black women at the mercy of white men. My mother used to make herself look stooped and ugly so white men wouldn't want her. Many of our beautiful women did that in those days. Negro families were broken apart by stresses you could not comprehend. Institutions wrecked or nipped in the bud to prevent their development.'

Lindsey said, 'But Tuskegee. The Air Corps.'

Crump strode back and picked up his tea cup. The act seemed to calm him. He said, 'United States Army Air Force! Let's get the designation right. The former US Army Air Corps became the Air Force on the 20th of June, 1941, well before I entered the service.'

Lindsey said, 'Air Force. Yes, sir.'

'Even the Air Force was far from color blind. That was why our units were entirely Negro at the lower ranks. The higher you got, the more white faces you encountered. You know what else they did? Any Negro soldier who could fight

— I mean with his fists . . . ' He held up his hands. They were heavy, strong, callused. Even at his age, Lawton Crump looked like a man who could hit like a piledriver. 'They summoned an assembly of Negro recruits and said they were going to put all the real fighters into a ring. We were to have a free-for-all. Tear each other to bits; they didn't care. They'd be all the happier for it. Last surviving man to get $50 and a weekend pass. The rest were confined to barracks.'

'What did you do?'

'I would have no part of it. Some of the others did. The carrot and the stick, Mr. Lindsey. You can get people to do anything.'

Lindsey nodded. 'My friend Eric Coffman talks about Jewish prisoners working in the crematoriums at Auschwitz. They knew that they would go eventually, but they could get another day of life that way. And another. Maybe they were hoping that the war would end and they'd still be alive.'

Crump said, 'But we made it. We had our own leaders, our own heroes. And we finally got our own commander. Did you ever hear of General Benjamin O. Davis? A great man. First Negro general in the US Army. And his son, Benjamin O. Davis, Junior. One of our first group of Negro pilots. He was a captain when he received his wings, Mr. Lindsey. By the time I knew him he was a major. In time he, too, won his stars. I worshipped that man. I would have flown into the jaws of hell for him!' Crump's face had a faraway look. Then he shook his head and said, 'I always loved airplanes. A fellow in our town owned a little puddle-jumper. You wouldn't remember; aviation was a very different matter back then. No jets, no radar, everything was smaller in scale and very informal.'

He smiled. 'I used to hang around this fellow's place. He kept the plane in an old barn. Flew out of a pasture. It was an old Consolidated PT-1. PT for primary trainer. He maintained the plane himself; he'd flown in the first war and he knew everything there was to know about flying machines. He let me hang around and watch him, hand him tools, run errands.'

'Was he a black man?'

'No, sir. He was a white man. Where would a Louisiana black get an airplane in 1930? I worked for that man for 12 years. Started when I was six years old. Worked for him 'til 1942. I learned how to maintain that airplane. And I learned to fly. That man never paid me a nickel, but I became an airplane mechanic and I learned how to fly and he never charged me anything for the lessons, either. So I guess I got a pretty good deal.'

Nellie Crump refilled their tea cups. Lindsey wondered how many times she'd heard her husband's story.

'Came the war,' Crump resumed, 'everything changed. People going into the service, people moving to the north and west to work in war plants. Everything changed. Recruiters. Everybody had to register for the draft. Most of the boys in town wound up going to boot camp, buck privates. Couple of them thought they'd outsmart the system, they went and joined the Navy instead. Didn't do them much good.

'Mr. Wagner — that was my mentor's

name — he went to bat for me. My home town was Reserve, Louisiana. Still there. But you'll need a good map to find it. Wagner took me up to Baton Rouge, talked to an Army Air Force recruiter. They were starting the Tuskegee Program and Mr. Wagner got me into it.' He nodded. 'Yes, sir. Tuskegee, Alabama. Some of those Negroes from the north, they didn't like going down south to train. Conditions were not ideal. Not much to do on base, and less off it. Most of our officers were blacks, though, which was quite a novelty. The higher you went, the smaller the percentage, but still it showed us that we could rise. They were delighted with me. I had to learn modern aircraft, of course, but they still thought I was hot. Here I was, a qualified mechanic, and I also knew how to fly a plane! Didn't have a pilot's license, but I could take a trainer up. We used PT-17s, Stearmans, good sturdy little biplanes. There are still a few of them around. I could take a ship up, fly around, bring her back and land her. That put me way, way ahead of the game.'

'I can imagine,' Lindsey said.

'It was truly wonderful. We went on to Texans. Those were the advanced trainers that we used. Sleek, metal-bodied monoplanes. Sweet aircraft. And after that, why, after that we moved on to fighters so we could travel to North Africa and thence to Europe. We were trained to become useful. We learned how to kill people.'

★ ★ ★

Lindsey left Holy City full of war stories. Listening to Lawton Crump was like spending the morning in a time warp. Was Crump another of those sad temporal nomads, a man whose glory days were long gone and whose present and future must be lived in the ever-fading glow of the receding past?

He got back to Walnut Creek and wrote up a progress report and faxed it to Richelieu in Denver. Ms. Wilbur and Elmer Mueller were both in the office, pointedly ignoring each other. No doubt about it, the old order was on its way out.

He phoned Lieutenant High's office and got Sergeant Finnerty, who had some information for him. The crime scene unit and the forensics gang had worked over the North Field hangar and learned a couple of things.

First, the monkey wrench with which Leroy McKinney had been killed was smeared. The wrench was covered with dirt and grease, and whoever had committed the crime had seen to it that no useful fingerprints remained.

Second, the contents of the woodstove had been carefully sifted and analyzed. They had consisted of wood and paper ash, some bits of metal that turned out to be staples or paper clips, a few lumps of a sticky, gummy substance, and the charred shreds of some kind of heavy fabric that had barely survived incineration. Forensics had determined that the gummy substance was rubber. Some rubber gloves had been tossed into the flames, had melted and partially burned. Some of the residue had remained unconsumed and had recongealed, producing the blackened sludge.

'Yeah. Looks like the killer really knew what he was doing. Put on a pair of rubber gloves, picked up the wrench and brained poor McKinney. Got the wrench thoroughly messed up, printwise. Dropped the weapon and burned up the gloves. Smart cookie.'

'Huh.' Lindsey pursed his lips.

Finnerty said, 'Listen, Mr. Lindsey, can I tell you something off the record?'

'Sure.'

'If you think you have a shot at unravelling this mess, I think you ought to go for it. We'll help as much as we can. But frankly, sir, just between you and me and the baseboard, I don't think OPD is going to do much more on this case.'

'Why not?'

'We only have less than a dozen investigators in this department. And this is a boom year for homicides in this town. I mean, just look at your morning paper. There's a big drug war going on. They're bringing 'em in in droves.

'So we're about ready to write off McKinney as an isolated incident. We'll put the folder in the permanent open file and see if anything comes to us. Sometimes you'll get a confession or an implication from some guy in a plea bargain. Can be years later. We never give up on a murder. But I don't think we're going to put much more manpower into this one. That's off the record, Mr. Lindsey. All right, sir?'

'No, I'm not so sure that it's all right at all. Maybe I ought to take this up with Lieutenant High.'

Finnerty hesitated. Then he said, 'Actually, sir, it was Lieutenant High who told me this.'

Lindsey phoned Marvia Plum's office and got a voicemail greeting. He asked her to call him back.

He wanted to talk this thing over, talk it out with someone he trusted. Eric Coffman was a possibility. He tried Coffman's office, but Eric was in Sacramento representing a client at a state commission meeting and wouldn't be back until late that night. Ms. Wilbur might understand, but the office tension was too severe to bother her right now, and of course Elmer Mueller was out of the question.

Lindsey went home and found Mother

preparing dinner. For once she didn't have the TV on. As he gave her a hug she said: 'Your father is dead, you know. He's been dead a very long time.'

Lindsey held Mother's hand until she pulled it away and concentrated on her task of preparing dinner.

What a difference. Lindsey was more grateful than ever. For years it had been a losing battle with her, one step forward and two steps back as she wandered slowly but steadily, ever deeper into her mental maze, seldom knowing what year it was, seldom knowing what world it was. But lately it had been two steps forward and one back. She still had her bad days, still slipped now and then; but the direction was toward reality, toward the present. If Lindsey had believed in miracles, he would have called this one.

Not that the meal was great, but Mother had actually put it together from scratch and placed it on the table, something she was increasingly capable of doing. Afterward, Lindsey helped her clean up and settled her in the living room. She was reading a copy of

Newsweek from April, 1973, paying more attention to the ads than the articles.

After his meeting with Lawton Crump, Lindsey could understand Mother's condition a little better. His own mind was filled with images of Mustangs and Thunderbolts, Messerschmitts and Focke-Wulfs. He hadn't lost his grip on time; he knew what year it was, and that World War Two had been fought half a century before.

His reverie was interrupted by the sound of the telephone. Marvia had gone from work directly to her parents' house on Bonita Street in Berkeley. She'd eaten with her parents and her son, Jamie, and then headed for home.

Lindsey told her about his day, about his visiting Mrs. Chandler at the Pare Oakland and Lawton Crump in Holy City. He asked if he could come to Oxford Street and talk it over with her.

* * *

They lay together listening to one of Marvia's vintage CDs. Rain was slashing against the windows. Marvia said, 'What about this case of yours that you're so excited about?'

'It's the man who found the body that interests me. An old-time fighter pilot. He found the body in a hangar out at Oakland North Field. He lives in Holy City, near San Jose. I spent part of today with him.'

Marvia waited for Lindsey to continue.

'I don't know if this is even going to tell me anything about the murder. I'm trying to understand the dead man, too. I visited his granddaughter yesterday, up in Richmond. But this old pilot, Lawton Crump. Did you ever hear of the Tuskegee Airmen?'

Marvia said, 'Teach your grandma to suck eggs.'

'Sorry. He told me about going up to Tuskegee. He was from Louisiana. How they trained him, sent him over to fight. He flew fighters in North Africa. Then they moved up to Italy and flew ground support, strafing, bomber escort into Germany. Some of his friends were killed. Some were shot down and he saw them again after the war. I asked him how

106

many German planes he shot down and he wasn't sure. Three or four, he said.'

'That was a long time ago. What did he do with the rest of his life?'

'He told me that he tried to go back after the war. He went back to Reserve, Louisiana, because that was home. His mother was still there. He had a brother, too. His brother was in the Navy. But he couldn't stay in the south. He wanted to keep flying, but he was mustered out of the Air Force and none of the airlines would hire him.'

'I know.'

'But he got a job as mechanic. First he went to college under the GI Bill, then he got a job as an airline mechanic. He worked for Pan Am. He worked for them for the next 40 years. Worked on everything from the old DC-4s to 747s. Wound up as a bigshot in their maintenance operation at SFO. They kept trying to retire him but he wouldn't go. When he was finally ready to retire, you know what happened? Company went belly up! Some fun.'

'And now he's going to be a movie star.'

'Well, almost.'

'How did he react to finding the body?'

'It was really hard to tell. He seemed, well, uncomfortable talking about it. He told me he'd lost his enthusiasm for the movie. For *Bessie Blue*. Oh, that was another thing. I asked him what that meant. He said that they named a B-17 after Bessie Smith — you remember, you were playing that music of hers for me. They didn't want to just call the airplane *Bessie Smith* — they thought that was too plain — so they called it *Bessie Blue*.'

6

Saturday. Sitting in Marvia Plum's bed, Lindsey phoned Mother. She was puttering happily around the house, instead of sitting zoned out in front of the TV, and was reading this morning's Contra Costa *Times*. Of course she would be all right. She had a lot of things to do. She didn't need him at home. A miracle!

Marvia pulled back the curtains. The storm front had passed. Another might be on course behind it, bringing in desperately needed rain from over the Pacific. For all you could tell, the storm had drenched the *Abraham Lincoln* and kept her jets and choppers, but at least for now the sky over California was a sparkling blue.

Lindsey phoned the Pare Oakland and reached Ina Chandler at the Double Bee suite. She told him that the air fleet had left Dallas-Fort Worth, the lone Flying Fortress first, then the smaller, faster planes: a twin-boomed Lightning, a rare mid-engine Airacobra, a stubby Thunderbolt, a sleek Warhawk, and the king of fighter aircraft, the Mustang.

The problems over the secret zoo and the illegally imported animals would take time to resolve, but the flight was going without a hitch. The Feds had not stopped the Knights of the Air from leaving the ground, which was all that Ina cared about.

The Flying Fortress had been designated *Bessie Blue*. Lindsey asked Ina Chandler whether it was the original *Bessie* or another B-17 redecorated for the movie. The Knights of the Air insisted that the bomber was the original. Mrs. Chandler was ready to take their word. And besides, with Lawton Crump to put his imprimatur on the production, that was all that mattered.

The ship was carrying a flight crew of Knights of the Air and a film crew from Double Bee. She had landed for refuelling at Sky Harbor in Phoenix even though *Bessie* had enough range, in theory, to fly non-stop from Dallas to

Oakland and back.

Double Bee had alerted the media along the way. Newspapers and TV stations sent up camera crews in helicopters to escort *Bessie Blue* and the fighters into Sky Harbor. On the ground, the airport was crowded with aviation buffs and curiosity seekers. There were interviews and photo ops. CNN was there. *USA Today* was there. It was a press agent's dream.

The fleet was expected at Oakland North Field by mid-afternoon. Double Bee would film the whole event. In addition to the camera crew aboard *Bessie Blue*, the old camera mounts in the fighter planes had been refitted with modern gear and the pilots had been rehearsed in getting good footage of the flight.

Lindsey said, 'I think I'd better be there, Mrs. Chandler.'

Mrs. Chandler didn't object to that.

'I hope it's all right if I bring a homicide officer with me.'

'Lieutenant High already knows about this. I expect he'll be there. I'm heading out to the airport myself, in a few minutes.'

'What about Mr. Crump? He going to be there?'

'You bet.'

'Okay. I'll see you at the airport.' He placed the telephone on its cradle and turned to Marvia. 'Want to see the air show on your day off?'

'Jamie would love it. Suppose we bring him?'

★ ★ ★

They took the Hyundai; more room than the Mustang. Double Bee had closed off the hangar and runway area at North Field. Lindsey flashed his International Surety credentials to get them in. Marvia didn't use her sergeant's badge. This was Oakland and she was Berkeley and off duty.

The Double Bee crew seemed to have multiplied. There were cameras on tripods, handheld cameras, lights, sound booms. Lindsey spotted Ina Chandler, surrounded by earnest-looking youngsters

112

with clipboards and walkie-talkies. The field might have been closed to the public, but several hundred aviation buffs had found ways to get in. The battery-powered camcorders outnumbered the professional cameras. Every distant droning, every bright reflection in the sky, caused a stir.

'Mr. Lindsey!' He whirled. There was Lawton Crump. No sign of Nellie. Lawton wore a leather jacket, bomber style, and his khaki trousers. A white baseball cap with the *Bessie Blue* logo and portrait on its front panel was cocked rakishly over his ear.

'That's Mr. Crump,' Lindsey told Marvia. 'He's their technical advisor. Was a Tuskegee Airman. Want to meet him?'

'Love it. And Jamie can learn something about the Tuskegee Airmen.' Jamie was holding her other hand, watching the crowd with suspicion.

Lindsey introduced them. 'Marvia Plum. Jamie Wilkerson, Junior — Marvia's son. Mr. Lawton Crump.'

The older man looked at Lindsey, then at Marvia, then at Jamie. He shook hands with Marvia, muttered 'How do you do,' squatted in front of Jamie, and stuck out his hand. Jamie shook hands solemnly with Lawton Crump.

Crump said, 'Fine boy. Wilkerson — ?'

'My ex,' Marvia explained.

'Ah.'

Lindsey said, 'Can you tell him about the Airmen?'

Crump nodded and said, 'Well, young man, this was all half a century ago. Before you were born.' He looked at Marvia. 'Before your mother was born.'

Crump started to tell Jamie about the Airmen, mostly information that he'd previously given to Lindsey. Suddenly a rustle went through the crowd, then a wave of pointing hands. Lawton Crump stood up, but Jamie had already transferred his free hand to Crump's. Lindsey saw a broad smile on the old man's face.

Sotto voce, Crump said, 'Mrs. Crump and I were never blessed with issue.'

Like spectators at a tennis match, the crowd swung to the right. If the air fleet had assembled over San Jose as planned, they would most likely have headed northwest to pass above San Francisco. That would provide more spectacular footage. A B-17 winging over the Transamerica Pyramid, a formation of glistening fighter planes circling the Coit Tower. Like some 1930s muralist, caught by the spirit of Futurism, capturing images for generations to come. They'd cross the bay and come in over water to approach the airport.

The first glint of sunlight bounced from aluminum or Plexiglass, and the crowd cheered like spectators at a baseball game. The B-17 appeared first. It was the largest plane in the fleet, four engines to the one or two of each of the others. The fighters boxed the B-17, above and below, ahead and behind, starboard and port.

As the airplanes passed over the runway, the formation strung out. The planes swung away, then approached a second time, then a third. The cameras ground; the spectators gaped.

Lindsey watched Lawton Crump and Jamie Wilkerson, Junior. Crump's eyes were fixed on the *Bessie Blue*. His jaw trembled and a tear fell. Jamie's mouth was open and his eyes were huge.

The flight circled the field still again, and on this approach the B-17 touched down, its wheels sending up clouds of dust as they hit the tarmac. The fighters swooped away.

The B-17 slowed, then veered ponderously off the runway, then rolled to a stop. A hatch opened in the lower fuselage and the pilot dropped to the ground. He turned toward the nearest camera crew and waved. He wore a leather jacket, helmet and flight gloves, and his goggles were pulled over his eyes. Lindsey wondered why he needed the goggles in a closed cockpit. It was hard to tell at this distance, but Lindsey was pretty sure that the pilot was white.

'That's where we cut to footage of Mr. Crump.'

Lindsey whirled. Ina Chandler was scurrying by. She winked at him. He said, 'Oh, right.'

Lawton Crump had pulled a handkerchief from his pocket. He wiped his eyes surreptitiously. He grinned proudly at the

Bessie Blue, then smiled down at Jamie Wilkerson, then back at the bomber. Jamie's mouth was open even wider and his eyes were bigger than ever

Lawton Crump bent and lifted Jamie so their faces were on the same level. Marvia looked happy. Lawton Crump pointed and Jamie followed his gesture.

The fighters were approaching the runway, still in formation. At the first pass of the fighters, a P-40 Warhawk touched down. A tiger's mouth and ferocious teeth were painted on its engine cowling. The pilot pulled the plane into a turn, revved the engine once and then cut it. He — no, she — bounded from the cockpit, waved cheerily to a camera, then slipped gracefully to the ground.

On the next pass the P-39 Airacobra set down on its tall, tripod-like landing gear. Lawton Crump offered a running commentary on the aircraft. The twin-boomed P-38 Lightning drew the biggest gasp of admiration, the massive P-47 Thunderbolt made the most impressive roar, the sleek P-51 Mustang drew a round of applause. Once the impromptu fighter squadron had landed, the remaining planes in the flotilla followed.

Lieutenant High of the Oakland Police Department touched Lindsey on the shoulder. 'Returning to the scene of the crime, Lindsey?'

'Uh — no. You know, ah, Sergeant Plum, Berkeley PD?'

High shook hands with Marvia. 'I've had the pleasure. Tried to romance her over to Oakland but she won't budge.'

High turned to Lawton Crump. 'See you've made a new friend there.'

Crump grinned. 'What a boy. I think he's learned a lot about these craft already. Absorbed everything I've told him.' He handed Jamie to Marvia. She lowered him to the ground.

'You were proud of your service, weren't you, Mr. Crump?'

Crump smiled. 'May I call you Marvia? Marvia, those were the greatest days. They were the best of times and they were the worst of times, but chiefly they were the best of times.'

★   ★   ★

118

The day's filming ended before sundown, and a chosen few were permitted onto the field to inspect the airplanes. Lindsey recognized the TV crews and the newspaper professionals by their gear and nonchalance. Another half-dozen amateurs were included, each one clutching a camcorder or still camera. They raced to the aircraft, jockeyed for position, scurried from plane to plane like a nest of ants confused by the sudden arrival of a honey rainstorm.

Ina Chandler appeared and laid her hand on Lawton Crump's arm. 'You're welcome on the field, Lawton. We'll have you set up for press interviews in a little while.'

Crump said, 'I'll try and give 'em what they need. Now, yes, I think I'll go take a peep. I want to see if that's really *Bessie* or just a reasonable facsimile.' He turned and said, 'Marvia, may I take young Jamie for a look-see?'

Jamie was clutching Crump's hand like a child clutching Santa's. An unafraid child.

'Of course.'

They headed across the tarmac.

Marvia said, 'We need more heroes like him. Kids like Jamie, especially, need more heroes.' She held Lindsey. 'Bart, I've been keeping something from you. Jamie's dad called me.'

'Captain Wilkerson?'

'Major now. He was into aviation when we were together in Germany. He's a helicopter pilot; was a hero in Desert Storm. Did something special at the battle of Basra, I don't know what, but he got a medal for it and a parade, the whole thing. You must have seen the news tapes. Personal handshake from Colin Powell.'

'I think I saw that.'

'Well, he got what he wanted. His career is assured. Good gosh, who knows what he's got his eyes set on now. Maybe he wants to be President of the United States.'

Lindsey couldn't figure out where Marvia was going with this. 'Good for him. I don't see what it has to do with us, though.'

'Well, he's coming out here.'

Lindsey tensed and looked away, and

saw Lawton Crump and Jamie Wilkerson, Junior standing beside the Flying Fortress. Crump was pointing at *Bessie Blue*, painting on the bomber's nose. He took off his white baseball cap, adjusted the plastic size strap and put the hat on Jamie's head.

Marvia said, 'James has remarried.'

Lindsey realized he'd been holding his breath. 'Then he doesn't want you back. I thought he wanted you back.'

'He did, for a while. He got over it.'

'Then what's he coming to California for?'

'Well, he has an excuse. He got interested in military aviation, American heritage, black heritage. He went out and learned how to fly some of the old warplanes. Claims he can fly a P-38 and he wants to watch them make this movie.'

Lindsey said, 'Surely he can't just walk in like that?'

'He's a black aviator, hero of the Gulf War. Don't tell me they'll turn him away. Not with press all over the place.'

Lindsey grunted. 'I guess it could make for a strained encounter. But we can get through it. Especially if he isn't trying to get you back.'

Crump lifted Jamie in his arms. Jamie twisted and waved to Marvia. Lindsey could make out his happy expression beneath the white cap's visor. Crump lifted Jamie into the airplane, then pulled himself in after the boy. He was a strong old guy, that he definitely was.

Marvia said, 'He doesn't want me, not with another wife in his bed. But he wants Jamie.'

'He can't have him! He didn't want him when he was born, you told me. All he wanted was to be rid of you both and get on with his career.'

'Times change, Bart. And people change. He's Jamie's dad. And he's a successful African American male, an Army officer, a decorated hero. Jamie needs a model. Living with his grandparents — '

'He's doing fine. Your parents are wonderful people. And you're a hero to him.'

She said, 'I know, but I have to think of my boy. He's a black child with a single mother, living with his grandparents. Do you know the odds that he'll ever see age 21? You know that the leading cause of death for black males under 25 is murder? That drugs are second? And AIDS is gaining fast? I don't particularly want Jamie to be an Army brat; I saw how those kids get packed around the world every couple of years. That's not such a good life either. But I want him alive.'

She dragged Lindsey with her, pacing the edge of the tarmac. They halted behind a temporary barrier. Lindsey heard a child's voice. Jamie Wilkerson, Junior was halfway out the waist-gunner's window midway on the fuselage of the Flying Fortress. He was waving. He looked very happy. Lawton Crump was holding on to him securely. Marvia managed a wobbly smile and waved back at her son.

On the way back to Berkeley, Jamie played happily in the backseat of the Hyundai. His *Bessie Blue* baseball cap was pulled low on his forehead. From some unknown source, Lawton Crump had produced a scale model B-17, complete with wartime insignia and *Bessie Blue* logo, and given it to Jamie. Maybe there was a secret stash of the models aboard the big airplane. Jamie was completely absorbed, flying the model through complicated maneuvers.

Marvia turned toward Lindsey. In a quiet voice she said, 'I thought you'd want me to give Jamie to his dad. You know, then we could be married. If you still want that.'

'I want that. But you *mustn't* give him up. He's your child.'

Marvia whispered, 'Thank you.' She pressed her head against his shoulder. He couldn't take his eyes off the road but he felt her body shuddering.

At Bonita Street, Marvia said, 'I want to be with my parents and with Jamie tonight. You won't mind, Bart, please?'

★ ★ ★

Lindsey sat in his makeshift study with the *Bessie Blue* file, making notes and studying documents. One thing about SPUDS, you didn't have to work from nine to five, Monday through Friday. No, lucky SPUDS got to work all hours of the day and night, every day of the week.

He didn't feel much closer to an answer in the death of Leroy McKinney. His last conversation with Finnerty had indicated that the Oakland Police Department wasn't going anywhere with the case; they weren't going to expend resources on it.

But Lindsey had to answer to International Surety and to his own conscience. His career might well rest on working this thing out. And so might his peace of mind.

Of course, Lieutenant High had turned up at North Field to watch the Knights of the Air land their flotilla, so OPD hadn't totally quit on the case. But Finnerty was right, Oakland was drowning in a sea of carnage. McKinney's death seemed unconnected to any other event.

The theory that McKinney was part of a smuggling ring — whether of cocaine or toucans — had fizzled. He didn't seem to be the victim of a serial killer; he didn't seem to be a casualty in a gang war. And the fact that he was an obscure janitor didn't do anything to bring attention to the case. The newspapers and the TV stations had already forgotten about Leroy McKinney. Why shouldn't the OPD?

Lindsey put down the file. He stood up and stretched. Mother had retired for the night. The house and the street outside were equally quiet.

He thought, *I've got to do something about Leroy McKinney.* He'd worked on two earlier cases involving murders, and he'd wound up, if not exactly solving the killings single-handed, at least making a big contribution. Two killers were behind bars now, thanks to him.

I'm not a professional detective, but I'm pretty good at learning about people. If I can learn enough about Leroy McKinney, I might get somewhere with this case.

* * *

Sunday morning he took Mother to the market and she did a full-scale shop for groceries. He gave her some cash; she handed the money to the cashier and counted her change, thanked the cashier, and walked with Lindsey back to the car.

A miracle.

At noon he took some copies of the Leroy McKinney snapshot that he'd blown up from the Oakland *Trib* and drove to Richmond. He parked near Latasha Greene's house but he didn't climb her steps. He was looking for another perspective on Leroy McKinney.

The streets were surprisingly empty for noontime on a bright spring Sunday. Maybe most of the neighborhood was still in church. He heard some of the bass thumping that passed for music coming from a tavern. The sign outside the place announced that it was called Fuzzy's #3. He'd somehow missed Fuzzy's #1 and #2.

He took a deep breath and squared his shoulders. You entered Fuzzy's #3 through a pair of heavy swinging doors with thick panes of dirty glass shaped like half-moons. The doors were covered in heavily padded, faded red leatherette decorated with hammered brass studs. The darkness hit him first, and while his eyes adjusted to it he took in the sour odor of the place and the music coming from an old-style jukebox.

If the bartender was Fuzzy he'd lost all of the fuzz from his head and added it to his chin, gray fuzz that spilled over the collar of his shirt. He was leaning on the bar, talking with a couple of customers. They all had glasses in front of them.

Half a dozen round-topped tables stood unoccupied, each with a couple of unmatched chairs resting upside down on the tabletop. Most of the illumination in the room came from neon beer signs mounted on the walls or against the backbar mirror. There was an old TV set above the bar that looked like something out of the Lyndon Johnson era. It was silent and dark.

Lindsey stood near the bar, looking at Fuzzy and the two customers. One of them wore a bandana on his head. The other wore an old-fashioned porkpie hat.

Fuzzy pushed himself away from the bar and looked at Lindsey. He said, 'What?'

The two customers looked up from

their drinks and observed Lindsey in the backbar mirror. Alerted by the bartender's response, they seemed accustomed to watching the world in that mirror.

Lindsey laid a copy of the Leroy McKinney photo on the bar. Fuzzy and the customers said nothing. Lindsey said, 'This man was killed last Wednesday in Oakland.'

Bandana said, 'Folks are killed in Oakland all the time.'

Lindsey laid an International Surety card on top of the photo. 'I'm an insurance adjuster. My company may have some money to pay out in Mr. McKinney's death. But we need more data before we can act.'

Bandana poked Porkpie Hat in the arm. 'You knowed Leroy. You was buddies with Leroy.'

Porkpie made eye contact with Lindsey in the mirror. Even at this distance his eyes were bloodshot and he looked as if he hadn't shaved for several days. From his odor, he'd probably been drinking right along.

Lindsey said, 'Can you tell me anything

about Mr. McKinney? His background?
His associations?'

Porkpie said, 'Maybe. I was one of his
associations. What's in it for me?'

Lindsey reached past Porkpie and
picked up the photo and his card. The
photo was copied on a plain sheet of
paper. It had been folded, then flattened
and smoothed on the bar. Lindsey
refolded it and slipped it into his pocket.

Porkpie swung around angrily on his
stool. 'I told you I knew that man. I'll tell
you a lot more, but it'll cost you. What
can you pay me?'

Lindsey said, 'How about a round for
the house?'

Fuzzy reached under the bar and
pulled out a bottle. He filled the glasses to
their rims before Lindsey could say
anything. He held out his hand.

Lindsey said, 'How much for the
drinks?'

Fuzzy growled, 'How much you got?'

Lindsey laid a twenty on the bar.

Fuzzy said, 'Just right.' He slipped the
bill into his pocket. There was a cash
register behind him.

Porkpie said, 'If that's all you got, I got nothing to say to you.'

'I have a little more cash. But if you provide useful information, International Surety will pay a lot more than I can give you.'

Porkpie took off his hat, wiped his face with a handkerchief, put the hat back on. He pulled it down to his ears. He picked up his drink and walked to one of the round-top tables. He said, 'Come on, insurance man.'

'Lindsey, Hobart Lindsey.'

'Okay, Lindsey-Hobart-Lindsey. Make yourself useful.' Porkpie removed one of the chairs and stood it on its feet. Lindsey lifted the remaining chair off, turned it over and put it down. He slipped into it opposite Porkpie, then took his notebook out of his pocket and ran out the lead on his gold International Surety pencil.

Porkpie said, 'You cross my palm with a double sawbuck and you pay for the refreshments, or I lose interest and wander off.'

Lindsey reached into his wallet and extracted a twenty. Porkpie whisked the bill out of Lindsey's fingers.

Lindsey said, 'Can I have your name, please, Mister — '

Porkpie grinned. 'Hasan Rahsaan Rasheed. You can call me Hasan, Lindsey-Hobart-Lindsey.' To Lindsey's astonishment, Hasan fumbled through his pockets and came up with a crumpled sheet of notepaper and a stubby pencil. He laboriously wrote out a receipt and handed it to Lindsey. 'There,' he said. 'You are dealing with an honest man.'

Lindsey said, 'Uh, why don't you just call me Bart. Is that your real name, Hasan Rahsaan Rasheed?'

'It is indeed.'

Lindsey jotted it down. 'You knew Leroy McKinney?'

'For 40 years. Man and boy. Well, old man and young man. I'm not so young myself no more. But Leroy McKinney wasn't his real name. His name was Abu Shabazz.'

'Abu Shabazz. Yes.' He wrote that down. 'How did you know him? His granddaughter said that he was in the Marine Corps in World War Two. Did you know him in the service?'

Hasan shook his head. He took a long drink from his glass. 'No, I never knew him in service. I only knew him after the war.' He tapped a fingernail against his nearly empty glass. 'You keep this full, I'll keep talking. It goes dry, so do my throat.'

Lindsey waved to Fuzzy. Fuzzy brought the bottle over and refilled Hasan's glass.

Lindsey said, 'Hasan, how did you meet, ah . . .' He consulted his notebook. ' . . . Abu Shabazz?'

Hasan rubbed his nose. 'What Latasha tell you about Abu?'

'She said that he'd been a baseball player, then was a hero in the Marine Corps, then became a nightclub manager.'

'Huh. Nightclub manager, Abu. Well, that's how I furst knowed him, before we was friends. Was after the war. Lot of Negroes moved up here during the war, you know. Come from the south. Georgia, Alabama, Mississippi, Louisiana. They was lots of good jobs here. I come from Mississippi myself. Biloxi. I think Abu say he from Louisiana. Some dinky little town with a funny name. Preserve — no, *Reserve*, Louisiana, that's it.'

Lindsey gave a start. Reserve, Louisiana. A flyspeck on the map! Lawton Crump was from Reserve, Lousiana. Leroy McKinney was from Reserve, Louisiana. And 50 years later and three thousand miles away, Crump found McKinney's murdered body.

Hasan was still talking. 'We used to build ships right here in Richmond. That's what I did in the war. I was a welder, and good at it. After the war, well, the shipyards closed down. Some of us was lucky, got jobs for the Navy in San Francisco, in Vallejo, different places. Some of us got jobs in Alameda. Most of us didn't get no more jobs — not no good, anyhow.'

Some more customers had wandered into Fuzzy's #3. Most of them slipped onto barstools. A few of them lifted chairs off tabletops and settled onto the seats. Fuzzy's business was picking up. Lindsey felt the pressure of eyes on him. He concentrated on his notebook and on Hasan Rahsaan Rasheed.

Lindsey said, 'But Leroy McKinney, ah, Abu Shabazz, was not a shipbuilder. Or was he?'

'No way.' Hasan tilted his glass. 'After the war, most of those Negroes didn't want to go back. So a lot of clubs opened. Abu, he was a musician, you know. He was a piano player. But he hurt his hand in the war. He tried to play but he couldn't play no more. But he didn't let it get him down. No way. He was a go-getter. He couldn't play no more so he opened a club. He was the best. He had his own place, couple places, and he worked at some of the best.'

Hasan paused. Fuzzy refilled his glass. Lindsey said, 'Leave the bottle.' They exchanged money for bottle.

Hasan smiled. 'You all right, Bart. I was a young blade then. You too young to know what a blade was. But I dressed sharp, talked smart. Danced like a snake. They called me Snake sometimes, I danced like one. Abu Shabazz, maybe they called him McKinney in the service but he became Abu Shabazz after. He worked at the Blackhawk, Jimbo's Bop

135

City. I 'member Jimbo's Bop City. Not there no more. Long time gone, long time gone. Owned by Jimbo Edwards, but Abu he run the place.'

The music from the jukebox stopped and in the distance Lindsey could hear a popping sound, a series of popping sounds, and then the keening of sirens. He looked around. Most of Fuzzy's customers were men but a few were women.

Hasan said, 'Yeah, that Jimbo a good man. But Abu, he my main man. Used to get me in free. Introduce me to the musicians. They blew good music. And they had good stuff, always plenty of good stuff.'

The popping sound came again, much closer, much louder. The half-moon glass in one of the doors of Fuzzy's #3 splintered. Someone fell against the door, swinging it open, and crashed to the floor. Lindsey flinched. The man thrashed around. Arterial blood spurted from a wound, spraying everywhere as the man writhed.

Lindsey heard sirens, brakes. A series of

blue-uniformed men and women crashed through the doors. The lead policeman bent from the waist and jammed a revolver against the skull of the man on the floor. The man stopped moving. The blood stopped spraying.

A second policeman — a policewoman, in fact — stood with her revolver drawn. She held it in two hands the way they all did it on TV these days, swiveling from side to side, covering the population of Fuzzy's #3.

Fuzzy's customers placed their hands flat on their tables. The ones sitting at the bar turned and held their hands in the air. They had the bored look of people who'd been through all this before.

That was how Lindsey wound up sharing a jail cell with Hasan Rahsaan Rasheed.

7

Lindsey had never been stood against a wall and patted down before. He didn't like it, or being locked up, either. It was only a holding cell, and he had his own clothing — minus shoe laces and belt, just like in the movies. And he had a receipt for his wristwatch and his wallet and his pocket change and keys. He wanted to hold on to his pocket notebook and his gold International Surety pencil, but they took those too.

At first, on the way to Police Headquarters, Lindsey had fruitlessly tried to find out what was going on. He'd find out shortly. Now keep still and be quiet. He was handcuffed, with his hands behind his back.

At headquarters they were locked up. They were told that somebody would be with them soon. Lindsey asked for his phone call.

The police officer told him, 'That's a

myth. Everybody thinks he's entitled to a phone call. But we'll let you make one pretty soon. There's too much going on right now. Take a load off your feet. Relax. Your buddy seems to have the right idea.'

Lindsey turned. Hasan Rahsaan Rasheed was sprawled on a cot, fingers laced behind his head. His eyes were closed. The police officer laughed and walked away.

Hasan opened one eye. He grinned. 'Take a load off your feet, Lindsey-Hobart-Lindsey.'

There was another cot in the cell. Lindsey lowered himself gingerly. 'Hasan, you been through this before?'

'Many, many times, Lindsey.'

'What happened back there? That man, the police. He was shot, wasn't he? Was he dead? Why were we arrested?'

'The walls have ears.' He closed his eyes. 'Relax, Bart.'

Lindsey realized he'd been holding his breath when he heard himself exhale loudly. 'I can't relax. What did I do?'

'Okay, we talk.' Hasan sat up on his cot.

'Maybe you can tell me more about

Leroy McKinney for a start.'

'Abu Shabazz.'

'Right.'

Hasan folded his hands behind his head and leaned back. 'I tell you 'bout them clubs and them musicians. That be interesting, that pass the time. That be all right with you, Lindsey-Hobart-Lindsey?'

'Go ahead. Tell me about the clubs that McKinney managed and the musicians who worked there.'

'Some of them good family men,' Hasan said. 'Some of them even women. I met Sarah Vaughan once. Sassy Vaughan, they call her. She a beautiful woman. She could sing, too. Mmmm. And the Lady. She on top then. Later on, they git her too.'

Lindsey merely nodded. This was one of those situations where the less he said, the more the other would tell him.

'Bessie Smith, she come one time. Empress of the Blues, they call her.' He shook his head. 'Big old woman, but could she ever sing. You close yo' eyes, she 20 years old and slim like a reed.

'Now these musicians, some of them

not so very nice. Miles, he a mean man. He play that horn like an angel. He close his eyes and they nobody else in the room, just him and the horn. But mean. *Whoosh!* Wouldn't talk to nobody, wouldn't smile at nobody, had this funny voice like he always whispering or something. Something the matter his throat, I don't know what. He always could play, but he couldn't hardly talk.'

Lindsey would have to remember what he'd said about Miles, and find out who Miles was. Marvia would know.

'Now Bird, he another story. Some folks think he a mean man, I don't think so. He not mean, he just crazy. He different from other people. He come and go, he miss gigs, he get mad. I saw him once, he mad at Abu. Bird, he always stoned on something, he don' care what. He gettin' ready to go on, he sittin' down, start to stand up and he fall down. He don' fall back on his chair, see, he fall down on the floor, you understan' me, Bart? Abu, he invite me over to meet this great Bird, and I seed this.'

Hasan blew out his cheeks. Lindsey

waited. Hasan said, 'I start to help Bird get back up but Abu he stop me, grab me with his good hand. Bird get up and pick up a fifth of gin and he throw it at Abu. Miss him, smash against the wall, glass all over. But he could blow. He could fly like a bird, that why they call him Bird, cause he fly like a bird.'

Marvia would know who Bird was.

'Now Monk, he the craziest one of them all. He talk to you, you never know what he gonna say. I talk to him one time. Abu invite me over. Was at the Blackhawk. They used to have a chicken-wire fence right down the middle of the club. So they can let kids in. Underage, you understand? They make all the kids sit on one side the fence, they sell them Cokes and stuff. Other side the fence, they serve liquor. You see?'

Lindsey said, 'I see.'

Hasan said, 'Abu he introduce me to Monk. He say, 'This be Mister Rasheed.' Monk, he say something so crazy, I never forget it. I tell you exactly what he say. I 'memers every word. He say, 'They an ocean floor. They a secret door. They a soul in yo' breast. They a pimento.' And when it time for him to play, I 'memers his band, Charlie Rouse, John Ore, Frankie Dunlop. They on the stage. Abu Shabazz, he had to lead Monk out and set him on the piano stool, and he play beautiful. That man a genius. But when he finish, Abu have to lead him away again.'

He shook his head. 'Oh, them was some days.' He opened his eyes and focused successfully on Lindsey. 'Abu Shabazz wrote music, you know. He could still write even when he couldn't play no more. He wrote a song for Monk. Called it fo' himself. Called it 'In Walk Abu.' Monk love that tune. Played it all the time. But he such a strange man, he fo'get the name. He call it 'In Walk Bud.' He thought it about Bud Powell. But that song really 'In Walk Abu.' Fo' Abu Shabazz.' He fell silent.

Lindsey said, 'I don't understand. If he was so successful, if he ran these clubs, wrote music, why was he living so poorly at the time of his death? And why was he working as a janitor?'

'They rob him, Lindsey-Hobart-Lindsey. They take everything, don' leave him nothing.'

The police officer rapped on the bars. 'You want that phone call, Lindsey?'

'You bet.' He jumped to his feet. As the officer unlocked the holding cell, Lindsey said, 'What about Mr. Rasheed?'

The officer ginned. 'He knows the drill. He'll be all right.'

Lindsey looked back as he walked to the telephone. Hasan Rahsaan Rasheed was stretched out on the cot, his eyes closed.

Eric Coffman took the call at his pool. Lindsey could hear the splashing and Coffman's daughters screaming. Coffman said, 'Happy Sunday. Eric here.'

Lindsey told him where he was and, briefly, what had happened.

Coffman said, 'Don't talk to anybody. Don't answer any questions. Wait till I get there. You'll make a criminal practitioner of me yet, won't you?'

'Please, Eric. Just get here.'

A very pleasant, very heavyset black lady wearing a pair of Reeboks and a maroon sweatsuit with a badge pinned to the shirt invited Lindsey into a plain room. She smiled at him. 'I'm Detective Hartley. And you are . . . ?'

Lindsey gave her his name.

'You're quite a fellow,' Detective Hartley said. 'Most white folks would be afraid to go into Fuzzy's. Most black folks would be afraid to go in there.' She reached behind her, found a clipboard, and started reading Lindsey his rights. Then she said, 'Did you understand all of that?' Lindsey nodded. 'If the answer is yes, please say yes. If the answer is no, say no.'

So they were taping. Lindsey said, 'Yes, I understand my rights. But I'm not going to answer any questions. I have the right to talk to a lawyer and to have him present during the questioning. I've already talked with my lawyer and he's on his way here now.'

Detective Hartley smiled. 'Would you mind signing a statement that you have been read your rights and that you understand them?' She handed him a ball-point pen and a card with his Miranda rights printed on it and indicated a place for him to sign. He signed.

'Now, about this little tiff at Fuzzy's . . . '

'I want my lawyer.'

Detective Hartley sighed and stood up and motioned to Lindsey. She led him back to the holding cell. Hasan Rahsaan Rasheed was no longer there. Lindsey sat on the cot and waited for Eric Coffman to arrive.

When he did, he was carrying his attaché case, the one that Lindsey knew contained a cellular phone and fax machine. A police officer opened the lock and rolled back the bars a couple of feet and Coffman squeezed into the cell.

Lindsey jumped up. 'Eric! Thanks a million. I was — '

Coffman said, 'Shut up!' He put his attaché case down and opened it, then started a tape recorder going. In a loud voice he said, 'This conversation between Hobart Lindsey, client, and Eric Coffman, counsel, taking place in the Richmond, California police headquarters at approximately four o'clock on Sunday afternoon — ' He paused to check a pocket calendar and add the date. ' — is fully protected under

146

existing rules of confidentiality and may not be used in any way, directly or indirectly, against aforesaid Hobart Lindsey.'

Lindsey said, 'Get me the hell out of here, Eric. I was just trying to get some information on a dead man, trying to do my job, and I'm treated like a criminal.'

Coffman said, 'Tell me everything you did today and how you wound up in the hoosegow, then.'

Lindsey went through a résumé of the Leroy McKinney investigation. When he got to the point about Oakland Homicide pretty much quitting on the case, Coffman held up his hand. 'And Sergeant Finnerty told you this was Lieutenant High's dictum?'

'Yes.'

Coffman rubbed his beard. 'Might be an interesting question. You could claim to be authorized by OPD. A new kind of deputization, without benefit of oath or badge. But let that be for now. You had no prior knowledge of Hasan Rahsaan Rasheed or of Fuzzy the bartender?'

'None.'

'What about the fellow who crashed

through the doorway?'

'I hardly got a look at him. I didn't recognize him, but I couldn't swear that I'd never met him.'

Coffman had Lindsey describe his encounter with Fuzzy, his conversation with Hasan and the exchange of cash and receipt, and the shooting. He closed up his attaché case and stood up. He said, 'Wait here. Don't say anything to anybody. I doubt that they'll bring Hasan back but they might put a mole in with you. Don't answer any question, however inconsequential. You understand me?'

Lindsey said, 'Yes.'

Coffman rapped a coin against the bars and was allowed out of the cell.

Hasan did not return, nor did they put anyone else in with Lindsey. Eventually, Coffman returned, accompanied by Detective Hartley. They went back to the interrogation room.

Hartley said, 'Your rights are still in effect. You understand that, sir?'

'Yes.'

Hartley laid a photo on the table. It was a standard mug shot, front and side, with the identification covered over. She said, 'Do you recognize this man, Mr. Lindsey?'

Coffman said, 'Go ahead. I'll stop you if she asks anything you don't have to answer.'

'I don't recognize him, no.'

'How about this man?' It was a Polaroid of a man lying on his back. Same man. His eyes were beginning to glaze. 'Is that the man who staggered into Fuzzy's?'

'I don't know. Looks like — it might be. I don't know.'

'How about this person?' She laid another photo on the table. It showed a child-size corpse riddled with holes and splattered with red. The corpse wore a Los Angeles Raiders jacket. Lindsey felt his stomach churn. Hartley said, 'Maybe this will help.' She laid another photo beside the one of the corpse. It was a close-up of a boy with African-looking features, light, almost albino skin, and freckles. The boy was dead. That was obvious.

Lindsey told Hartley that he recognized the boy. He told her about his encounter outside Latasha Greene's house with the boys and the squirt gun. She had him describe the other boys. He said, 'What happened?'

Hartley ignored his question. 'What did you say the boy's name was?'

Lindsey searched his memory. 'Uh — Ahmad Hope. That's what Latasha Greene told me.'

Hartley nodded. She laid a photo of Fuzzy on the table. Lindsey identified it. She laid a photo of Hasan Rahsaan Rasheed on the table. Lindsey identified it. She showed him the receipt that Hasan had given him and the twenty-dollar bill that he had given Hasan. He identified the receipt. 'I can't identify the twenty as mine, but I paid him with one.'

Hartley said, 'That's good enough.' She stood up. 'If you'll come with me and sign a statement that you were not beaten, tortured, threatened, offered a bribe or other payment, or otherwise mistreated or unduly influenced while in custody, we'll get your belongings and you can be on your way. Sorry to inconvenience you, sir. We may need to contact you again; I hope that will be all right.'

Lindsey said, 'Sure. Ah, what was that all about?'

Hartley said, 'You didn't recognize Hasan?'

'Not before today. But — that boy. He was just a child. I don't understand.'

Hartley said, 'That boy was a lookout. They pay them to serve as lookouts, runners, mules. He was just a casualty in a turf war. I know his grandma. I'll try and talk to her tonight. She's lost too many now.'

Lindsey said, 'He's dead.'

'Yes.'

Lindsey sat down and pulled his handkerchief from his pocket. They'd left him his handkerchief. He wiped his eyes. 'He was just a child.'

'Hasan Rahsaan Rasheed, of Richmond,' Hartley said. 'His real name is Luther Jones. The man who died at Fuzzy's had just killed the boy. He was working for Luther Jones; the boy was working for a rival of Luther's. Luther is absolutely clean. He was sitting in Fuzzy's talking with you when everything happened. You even gave us a receipt that he wrote for you for the money you paid him. You're his alibi, Mr. Lindsey.'

★ ★ ★

Desmond Richelieu wasn't as unhappy as Lindsey had expected. First thing Monday morning, Lindsey bit the bullet and phoned Richelieu in Denver. He'd learned less about the McKinney killing than he'd hoped to, and he was ready to get dressed down for lack of progress. But the movie was under way. That was International Surety's interest.

Lindsey pulled some more SPUDS work off the fax from Denver. Mostly these were problems for Legal and for Legislative Liaison, but SPUDS got involved too, and Lindsey found himself playing private eye, looking for lost relatives, tracking down inventories and depreciated values, and making sure that nobody was in collusion with Elmer Mueller to puff up their claims and split the profits. Either Mueller was clean, or he was too clever to get caught. Lindsey wasn't sure which. Mueller knew what Lindsey was doing and he was furious. He kicked it up to Harden at Regional. Harden took it up with Ducky Richelieu. Richelieu backed Lindsey.

It was nice to win that one. But now he knew he'd better never play poker with his back to the door.

And he couldn't clear his mind's eye of Leroy McKinney's face with the jelly puddle in the middle of his forehead. Or that other face — Ahmad Hope with his pale skin and his African features and the glazed look of death in his strangely pale, boy's eyes.

He phoned Eric Coffman and got a portable answering machine in Coffman's briefcase. The man never failed to amaze. Coffman called him back during a court recess.

Coffman said, 'Heard something from your friend Hartley?'

'No. Have you?'

'Not yet. I'm sure we will, though.'

'Eric, I — this thing is getting to me. Can I get hold of you for an hour, just to talk about it?'

'Is this International Surety talking, or

just Hobart Lindsey?'

'I don't know. No, it's not the Richmond thing. Or, only if it happens to connect up. It's the Leroy McKinney murder.'

'Oh, I see. You want me to play Nero to your Archie or Mycroft to your Sherlock?'

'I'd just like to talk to you friend to friend, if we can. But if you want to charge me for it, that's okay.'

'Huh, you drive a hard bargain! Tell you what, you still going with Marvia?'

'Yes.'

'She's never met Miriam and the girls. Why don't the two of you come out for dinner one night?'

'All right.'

'Oh — didn't you once tell me that Marvia has a youngster?'

'Jamie.'

'Bring him along.' Coffman hung up.

Lindsey ate dinner with Mother that night. She was able to discuss the day's news. She was taking an interest in the world now. Mrs. Hernandez had cut back to twice a week now, and acted more as Mother's housekeeper than the companion and de facto babysitter she had been for years.

After dinner, Mother made coffee and they sat in the living room with the TV turned off, talking. She said, 'Hobart, I've been thinking of getting a job. You're seldom home anymore. That's very nice. I like to see you on your own. You're a grown man now. So, why shouldn't I find work? You know, I used to work. When your father was alive.'

Lindsey studied her face. Her eyes were clear. She was making sense.

'I worked as a secretary. It would be nice to have a job. I'd have friends. I'd earn my own money. You wouldn't mind, would you? I get your father's little pension, and you earn a nice salary, but I'd feel better if I were earning money of my own.'

Lindsey put down his cup. He didn't know what to think. 'It's been so long, Mother. You don't know how to use a computer, a modem, a fax machine, even a copier. Everything has changed. You'd be competing with people 30 years younger.'

'I saw an article in the *Times*. There's a group for people like me. Late-entrant and re-entrant workers, that's what they call us. I'd be re-entrant. We get training to get us up to date. And they have a job placement service.'

Lindsey didn't say anything.

'I have to try this. Look at me.' She stood up. 'I gave birth at the age of 17, Hobart. I was a little girl. I'm 57 years old. I'm not ready to die. You don't need me, and I don't have a husband, and I am a healthy woman. I want to work for a living.'

★ ★ ★

Lindsey phoned Marvia. He told her about Coffman's invitation. She said that was fine, she'd be happy to visit Coffman's home. She'd bring Jamie. She hadn't heard anything further from Jamie's dad. Lindsey started to tell her about Latasha Greene and Hasan Rahsaan Rasheed but she asked him to save it until they were together.

★ ★ ★

Lindsey parked on Oxford Street and bounced up the stairs to Marvia's apartment. She'd already picked up Jamie at her parents' house on Bonita. She wore a blouse and skirt, tights and high heels. Lindsey couldn't remember seeing her dressed that way before. Jamie was decked out in his best superhero shirt and new jeans. Lindsey kissed Marvia and shook hands with Jamie.

They took Marvia's cream and tan Mustang. Even at age six, Jamie had a tight fit in the backseat, but he settled in with the B-17 model Lawton Crump had given him. Marvia said, 'He hasn't let that airplane out of his grip. And he won't stop talking about his friend Mr. Crump and his big bomber. He wants to know if Mr. Crump can take him flying.'

Lindsey said, 'Maybe he can.'

Marvia took them onto the freeway. She'd popped a cassette into the player; it was another of those wonderful blues singers Marvia played so often. *Cold-hearted papa*, this woman sang, *be on your merry way.* 'That's Issie Ringgold. Not very prominent, even in her day. Almost forgotten now. I like her, though.'

Lindsey said, 'I met this fellow Hasan

Rahsaan Rasheed. Rahsaan of Richmond, they called him.'

'You started to tell me about that. Where did you run into this character?'

'Uh, a — ' He looked over his shoulder. Jamie was absorbed in maneuvering his B-17.

Marvia said, 'You can say anything, Bart.'

'I met him in a saloon. In Richmond. Fuzzy's #3.'

Marvia laughed. 'Whoa! Have to stay on the road. Bless you, Bart, mad dogs and Englishmen go into Fuzzy's. You went into Fuzzy's when?'

'Last Sunday. Around noon.'

'What happened?'

'Well, there was some shooting and a couple of people were killed. The police came. In fact, they did some of the shooting. I spent a few hours in jail but Eric got me out. But I'm afraid I let Hasan use me. I didn't know what was going on.'

Marvia said, 'How did Luther use you?'

'You know who he really is?'

'Yep. Luther the Snake, Hasan of Richmond. I know.'

Lindsey told her about showing the photo of Leroy McKinney and Hasan's volunteering the information that McKinney was really Abu Shabazz, and the story of his career in the music business. As he wound up the story, Lindsey had an odd thought. 'Marvia, you told me that *Bessie Blue* was named for the blues singer Bessie Smith, right? When did she die?'

'1937. September the 26th.'

'Then how could she sing at a club in San Francisco after the Second World War? Hasan couldn't be mistaken? I mean, Bessie Smith. Smith, after all.'

'No way. Plenty of other Smiths. Mamie, Ida, Carrie, Trixie, Clara. But nobody who knows blues could ever mistake Bessie. She was the Empress of the Blues. If Luther Jones saw her, he knew it. If he says he saw her in 1945, '46, whenever — he's lying.'

'Okay. He lied about Bessie Smith. And if he was really Luther Jones, then maybe Abu Shabazz wasn't really Leroy McKinney. Or maybe he was.'

Marvia laughed. 'Luther is the biggest drug pusher in this area since Felix

Mitchell took a knife between the ribs.'

'I remember his funeral.'

The evenings were growing longer now. The sun had fallen behind the East Bay hills, and oncoming cars made a parade of headlights.

'I mean,' Lindsey said, 'if the part of Hasan's story about Bessie Smith was a lie, maybe his whole story was. Or maybe he knew I was interested in Bessie Smith, so he told me what I wanted to hear. I've come across that before.'

'Haven't we all.'

'How about those other people he told me about? Would you know them?'

Marvia said, 'Try me.'

'I didn't get to write this down. They took my notebook and my pencil from me. But I think he mentioned a priest and a bird. No. A monk and a bird. And Miles. Somebody named Miles. And the Lady. Somebody he just called the Lady.'

'Now that all rings true,' Marvia said. 'Miles was Miles Davis. Bird was Charlie Parker. And Thelonious Monk. Did he say anything particular about Monk?'

'He said he was very strange. He said

they had to lead him out to his piano and lead him away afterward. He said he told him some strange thing. I don't remember what.'

'I wish you did. Monk was a genius.'

'Hasan said the same thing.'

'The Lady could have been anybody. Probably Lady Day.'

'Doris Day?'

She gave him a strange look. 'I'm almost ready to tell you why I love you, Bart. Lady Day was Billie Holiday. I know you've heard her records with me. She died at age 44. Luther could have seen her after the war; she died in 1959.'

Lindsey said, 'I guess this is all important somehow, but I don't see how it ties in with Leroy McKinney.'

'I don't know whether it does. From everything you told me, I was ready to go along with Lieutenant High's theory. Just a random killing. Cops can sound pretty callous sometimes, but we have to focus our efforts. Some cases lead to big results, some lead nowhere.'

Jamie said, 'Mom, are we there yet?'

Marvia said, 'Almost, Jamie.'

'I have to pee.'

Marvia said, 'Very soon.' To Lindsey she said, 'Leroy McKinney wasn't leading High and Finnerty anywhere. But McKinney or Abu Shabazz was Latasha Greene's grandfather and they shared a house. And Hasan Rahsaan Rasheed a.k.a. Luther Jones sent a hitman to kill a little kid who was on the lookout at Latasha Greene's house. Rasheed's meeting you at Fuzzy's saloon and using you as an alibi is just one of those gorgeous ironies.'

Lindsey said, 'We are not amused.' Then he said, 'There's our exit.'

Jamie said, 'Mom, I have to pee.'

Marvia said, 'There's a gas station.'

They reached it in time.

8

Marvia pulled the Mustang onto the blacktop beside Eric Coffman's Mercury Topaz station wagon. Jamie brought his Flying Fortress with him. Coffman met them at the door. When Jamie was introduced, Coffman solemnly shook his hand.

The house was a modern split-level with flagstone floors and shag rugs. Lindsey knew Coffman's wife, Miriam, but Coffman insisted on a complete set of introductions. Miriam was taller than Marvia, and ample-figured, with honey-blond hair that she wore in braids. An old-fashioned, middle-aged woman.

The Coffmans' daughters were Sarah and Rebecca, one taller than Jamie, one shorter. Rebecca was holding a Barbie doll. The three children looked at each other shyly. Jamie leaned against Marvia, one hand on her hip, the other holding his Flying Fortress.

Sarah Coffman said, 'We have a Nintendo. You want to play?'

Jamie said, 'You have *Captain Skyhawk*? Or *Aquaman*?'

'Sorry, no,' Sarah said. 'I have *Mickey Mousecapade*. *Bugs Bunny Crazy Castle*. I have *Athena*. That's my favorite. We can play *Athena*.'

Jamie whined, '*Athena*'s for girls.'

Marvia said, scowling, 'Jamie, why don't you just try *Athena*. You might like it.'

'All right,' Jamie grumbled.

Sarah in the lead, Jamie following reluctantly, Rebecca trailing, they moved into the house.

Miriam said, 'Girls, dinner in 15 minutes.'

Eric led the way into the sunken living room. Polished mahogany bookcases occupied strategic positions, separated by elaborately framed paintings. The cases were crammed. Most of the shelves were open; a few were protected by glass covers.

'I didn't know you were a book collector, Eric,' Marvia commented. 'Are these law books?'

Coffman said, 'Those are in my office. These are my hobby. History, especially northern California history. The closer to home, the better I like it.'

'Isn't that a whole section on World War Two?'

'Yes, it is.' Eric walked away to serve drinks. Coming back, he said to Lindsey, 'I had a talk with your friend Hartley. And — Marvia, did your lunkheaded friend tell you about his scrape with the law?'

'He did.'

'I talked with Detective Hartley. I also had a most interesting little chat with a Contra Costa County assistant DA, and another with some federal personages. They kept trying to connect you with Luther Jones and his well-managed commercial enterprises.'

'But I'm not connected with him.'

'My dear friend, *I* know that. I had to convince *them* of it. Your conversation with Luther in your common cell didn't help.'

'But all we talked about was old

nightclubs and World War Two and jazz musicians. Mostly people I'd never heard of.'

'Right. Now, you and Mr. Jones have just been in the middle of a shootout, you get hauled into the pokey, locked in a cell . . . and you talk about defunct nightclubs and military history. Seems to me somebody suspected that the cell was bugged — it was — and that someone had something that he didn't want to talk about.'

Marvia said, 'Makes sense to me.'

Lindsey said, 'So if we talked about drug gangs and killing people that would prove we were criminals, and if we *didn't* talk about those things it still proves we're criminals!'

'That's why I prefer civil practice. Let me refresh those drinks.'

Lindsey told Coffman the story of the *Bessie Blue* project, the death of Leroy McKinney, and Lindsey's interview with Lawton Crump in Holy City.

Miriam returned from the kitchen. 'Thank you for setting the table, Eric. Now, would you check on the children? The food is almost ready, and besides, they're being quiet.'

Eric pushed himself out of his easy chair. 'She never trusts the girls when they're quiet.'

After a couple of minutes he returned, beaming. 'Marvia.' He held his finger to his lips and gestured with his other hand. She followed him.

They came back smiling. 'Completely absorbed,' Marvia said. 'Sarah and Jamie are playing Nintendo. Rebecca has her Barbie doll riding Jamie's B-17. This is the first time I've seen it out of his possession since Mr. Crump gave it to him.'

Miriam called, 'Dinner's ready. Everybody wash your hands before you come to the table.'

★　★　★

Lindsey was reaching for a towel, when he was gripped by a sudden realization.

'Reserve,' he whispered. So much had happened in the past 24 hours that he'd left Reserve, Louisiana somewhere in long-term parking. It was time to get it back and do something with it.

He ran from the bathroom and grabbed Marvia. She was already in the dining room, helping to settle the children. 'Marvia, listen! Hasan Rasheed — Luther Jones — told me that Leroy McKinney was from Reserve, Louisiana.'

'Never heard of it,' Eric said.

'Neither have I,' said Marvia.

Miriam brought in a huge teakwood bowl filled with green, leafy stuff and set it in the middle of the table. The handles of wooden implements stuck up. She said, 'Salad is good for young children. Full of minerals.'

Lindsey had opened his pocket notebook and was writing in it.

'You're acting very strange, Bart,' Marvia observed. 'You said Leroy McKinney was from Reserve, Louisiana. So what?'

'Lawton Crump is also from Reserve, Louisiana.'

Marvia whistled.

Miriam said, 'That doesn't exactly sound like a metropolis. They must know each other, yes?'

'Not anymore. One of them is dead.'

Eric said, 'He was a murder victim. We don't know anything about him. Or do we? Bart?'

'In fact, we know a lot about him. We just don't know how much of it's true. His granddaughter says he was a ball-player, a pitcher. Reverend Johnson gave me some old scorecards, so it looks as if that's true, anyway. Latasha says he was in the Marine Corps. I've put in a request through International Surety to verify that. Luther Jones says he was a nightclub manager and songwriter. I doubt if any of those clubs are still open after 40 years, but maybe we can find something out.'

'He hardly sounds like a mystery man,' said Miriam.

Marvia said, 'But from Lawton Crump's home town. Miriam, Eric, I don't think you know my boss, Lieutenant Dorothy Yamura. She always says that coincidences make her nervous. She says when things are connected, she likes to know why they're connected.'

Eric pointed a salad fork at Lindsey. 'What does that mean to you, old friend?'

Lindsey didn't say anything.

Eric added, 'I think it means you're going to Louisiana.'

'You're in that new SPUDS job now,' said Marvia. 'Doesn't that mean you can you just jump on a plane and go somewhere on I.S. business?'

Lindsey said, 'Yes.'

★ ★ ★

Lindsey expected the house to be quiet and Mother to be sound asleep when he got home. Instead he found her sitting in front of the TV watching *Royal Wedding*. In color.

Mother sensed his presence. She said, 'You took Marvia home? Is she all right?'

'She's fine, Mother. I may have to leave town for a while. Will you be okay by yourself? Should I ask Joanie Schorr to stay with you?'

She smiled at him. 'I'm going to see about a job. I'm going down to that training place. Maybe I can learn to work a word processor.'

'I'm sure you can, Mother. How's the movie?'

'I still like the ones with Ginger Rogers the best; but that Astaire, he's some dancer. Is he still alive?'

Lindsey shook his head. 'He died years ago. He was pretty old.'

She turned back to the screen. 'He could still dance.'

Mother never watched movies in color, except an occasional cartoon. Sometimes Lindsey reset the controls for color when he watched the late news and sometimes he forgot to reset them to black and white. Then Mother got very upset.

Now she was watching *Royal Wedding* in color.

★ ★ ★

Lindsey planned to phone Richelieu first thing on Monday, but Richelieu beat him to the punch. Lindsey was happy to see Ms. Wilbur still at her desk when he arrived at International Surety, and equally happy not to see Elmer Mueller.

Ms. Wilbur said, 'I've put in my papers. 30 days and I'll have my retirement.'

Lindsey sat at the desk that Elmer

Mueller had grudgingly authorized for his use on SPUDS business.

'Coffee's made.'

Lindsey filled his mug. It said SPUDS in gold leaf and *Bart Lindsey* in fancy script, and had an International Surety crest. The coffee was pretty good.

'You'd better call Ducky in Denver,' Ms Wilbur advised him. 'Apparently Elmer's been putting a bug in Harden's ear again. And Harden's been passing the dirt along to Ducky. Have you been in jail lately, Hobart?'

'A mistake. I was just in the wrong place at the wrong time. I wasn't charged. They even apologized for the whole thing.'

'Who's they?'

'Richmond PD. I was gathering some data up in Richmond on this *Bessie Blue* case.'

'Right. Anyhow, you'd better call Ducky back.'

9

'You know why I love you?' Marvia looked at Lindsey across the table. They'd finished their meal at a Thai seafood house on the Oakland Estuary. Spotlights illuminated the cabin cruisers moored a few yards from the window. 'You have nothing sour inside, Bart. There's no poison in you. You missed a lot of the good stuff, sure, but the germs didn't get into you either. I'm so lucky. I got in there first. I'll try never to poison you. I'll try to keep everybody else from poisoning you, but I don't know if I can do that.'

Lindsey settled their check. It was his turn.

They strolled on the pier afterwards, arms around each other. Marvia nestled her head against Lindsey. 'That's why I'm so frightened for Jamie.'

'I don't understand. Is it his father again?'

She nodded. 'I've had another letter.'

'I thought Wilkerson had given up custody. He must have some visitation rights — but he can't take Jamie from you.'

'That isn't the point, Bart!' She sounded angry. 'We can't choose our color. We can choose each other, you and I, but Jamie can't choose. He's a little boy. His dad offers him a black home, a black family. You and I can't. It isn't your fault, it isn't my fault, we can't change ourselves. I can't do that to him.'

He pulled her closer as they walked back on the pier. He said, 'You'll make the right decision. It will work out. I know it will.'

★   ★   ★

In bed, she said, 'Talk to me about something else.'

'Ducky Richelieu. He's backing me. He wants me to go to Reserve and see what the hell this is all about. I talked to Lieutenant High and he's keeping hands off, but I could tell he was pretty pleased. I talked to Eric about it again, and he just gave me his lawyer stuff. 'Be careful, don't sign anything, don't tread on the cops' toes down there.''

Marvia snuggled her head on his chest. He could have stayed like that forever. She said, 'Tell me some more.'

'I've got some homework to do before I go down there. See if I can get a lead on McKinney. See if there's a phone number for anybody named McKinney in Reserve, Louisiana. But even if there's a platoon of them, I can do some work on the phone and narrow it down.'

'How about Crumps?

'You bet. If I can find some McKinneys and some Crumps in the phone book I can start checking. And all the other things. High school yearbooks, check in with the local churches. Whatever.'

'You think you'll get a friendly reception?'

'You mean because I'm white?'

'White and from out of town. You'll talk funny. You'll represent a big institution. You might not get very far.'

'Someone black would do better.'

'I thought you'd never ask.'

'What about Jamie?'

'He'll be heartbroken. He gets aquarium magazines and he saw an article about the new aquarium in New Orleans. I can promise to bring him a souvenir.'

'You're willing to go with me? You can't be a cop down there, can you?'

'I'll take my badge. I won't take a gun. I won't be there officially, but if we talk to local cops I can show my badge and they'll probably be courteous.'

'Not like Rod Steiger and Sidney Poitier?'

'I don't think we'd have much trouble in New Orleans or Baton Rouge. We'll have to watch ourselves, watch out for some neighborhoods.' She laughed. 'That's no different from anywhere else. Do you know where Reserve, Louisiana is?'

'I checked. It's 30 miles west of New Orleans. In St. John the Baptist Parish.'

'Sounds like sugar cane country. A town like that. You and I together.'

'You think there'll be good old boys ready to tar and feather us?'

'No. I just don't want to take any foolish risks.'

'I could ask Aurora Delano to handle it. She was in my SPUDS class in Denver. Worked in the Eugene, Oregon branch, but she went back to New Orleans for SPUDS. Richelieu suggested having her check out Reserve. Save on air fare. But it's my case and I told him I was going to do it. But I don't want to ask you to come along if it's going to be dangerous for you.'

'A cop risks her life every day. We have to be careful, but we can't let the haters win, either.'

★   ★   ★

Their Southwest 737 touched down at New Orleans International in late afternoon. The airport looked just like the airports in Oakland, San Francisco, Denver, Los Angeles. The difference hit Lindsey like a giant boxing glove when he stepped out of the air-conditioned cabin, but it was only the steamy air. He'd travelled light, as had Marvia, so they were able to avoid the nightmare of baggage carousels and indifferent airport personnel.

They'd planned to take a cab into the city, but Lindsey spotted Aurora Delano waiting for them. She smiled. 'Nice to see you again.'

Lindsey introduced Aurora and Marvia. He watched them smile and shake hands and size each other up. That was something that would remain forever a mystery to the male race: the sizing up that women gave each other at first encounter.

Aurora said, 'I've got you a room in the French Quarter. Might as well see some local color while you're here. We need to go over this case before we go out to Reserve. You brought the file with you?'

'Right here.' Lindsey raised his attaché case.

'Marvia.' Woman to woman now. 'I don't mean to pry, but are you along purely on social grounds?'

'Did Bart tell you I'm a homicide officer?'

Aurora raised her eyebrows. 'Is this a police case?'

'I'm not here officially. Bart and I have cooperated a couple of times and it's worked out well.'

Lindsey said, 'We don't need to keep anything confidential.'

'All right. I just didn't want to spread this outside the company.'

Their hotel was on Rue Bienville, an old building with whitewashed masonry walls and wrought-iron balconies. Their accommodation was a third-floor suite. They settled in quickly, then convened over a stylish table in the sitting room. Room service had sent up a pot of chicory-flavored coffee and biscuits.

Lindsey laid out the papers relating to *Bessie Blue*. He showed Aurora a photo of Leroy McKinney, and another of Lawton Crump that he'd got from Ina Chandler at Double Bee. It took him almost an hour to get through the details of who Crump and McKinney were, the information he'd got from Latasha Greene and Reverend Johnson, and the whole Fuzzy's #3 incident.

Aurora leaned back with a low whistle. 'Okay. Lawton Crump, our small-town boy made good. He's our Mr. Clean. War hero, successful career, big house, nice wife, gives toy airplanes to little children.'

Lindsey said, 'That's him.'

'And Leroy McKinney is our Mr. Dirty. Leroy McKinney a.k.a. Abu Shabazz. Ex-ballplayer, nightclub manager, questionable associations with your friend Hasan Rasheed a.k.a. Luther Jones, shady character and reputed criminal bigshot. Who just happened to use you, Bart, as his alibi during a turf war shootout. Very nice people.' She sipped her coffee-and-chicory. 'And Leroy McKinney is also from Reserve. And thousands of miles away and decades after they left Reserve, Louisiana, the paths of these two men cross once more when Mr. Clean stumbles across the corpse of Mr. Dirty.'

'Right.'

'I don't like it. Did they know each other? Did Crump say that he recognized McKinney?'

Lindsey shook his head.

'That doesn't mean anything,' Marvia put in. 'If they never knew each other, you'd get that reaction. And if Crump *did* recognize McKinney and didn't want us to know it for some reason, you'd get the same reaction.'

Lindsey said, 'Either way I want to go out to Reserve and talk to the McKinneys. You did check that out for me, Aurora?'

She unfolded a sheet of computer paper and spread it on the table. 'I put everything into the machine. Only eight McKinneys in Reserve. I checked it through Tony Leroux, our local insurance agent. Very old Creole family.'

Marvia said, 'Creole.'

'Caramel brown. Could pass for white if he wanted to, or claim to be Panamanian or whatever. Chooses black. He handles International Surety business in Reserve. He knows everybody in that town. Immediately eliminated five McKinneys; they're white. Now, if you want to take this alone, Bart, it's your baby. But I think Marvia would get further than you would. But Reserve is not named lightly. It's a conservative town. And a mixed couple might meet some resistance. You won't be lynched or anything, but you just might not get any cooperation. I mean from the blacks as well as the whites.'

Lindsey said, 'So — ?'

'So I'm going to suggest that the four

of us go. You, Marvia, myself — and Tony Leroux.'

Lindsey walked away from the table. He stood looking out the tall window. It was getting dark outside. Old-fashioned gaslights flickered. Horse-drawn carriages moved down the cobbled roadway. Japanese tourists in Hawaiian shirts and baseball caps snapped pictures of each other.

'I don't know.' Lindsey turned back toward the others. 'I've done a lot of interviewing, and one-on-one usually works best. It's another Desmond Richelieu rule.'

'Right. But you can't have everything. Do the best you can with the resources you have. And Tony knows everybody in town. They're more likely to trust him than they are a stranger.'

★ ★ ★

The next morning Lindsey and Marvia met Aurora at the Café du Monde for coffee and beignets, then walked to her car and headed out on I-10 to Reserve. Aurora drove a Saab, still with

Oregon license plates on it.

The sugar mill still loomed over Reserve. There was a sickly sweet smell in the warm, close air, and not much else to identify the town: row of franchise stores, a laundromat, a couple of gasoline stations, a boarded-up movie theater. The storefront bore faded gilt lettering: 'Antoine Leroux — Real Estate and Insurance.' Aurora pulled the Saab to the curb and led the way inside. A black receptionist sat at a battered wooden desk studying a computer screen. There was no escaping the modern world.

Aurora said, 'Good morning, Martha. Morning, Antoine. You able to help us with that problem we talked about?'

Leroux stood up. He had khaki-colored skin, black wavy hair, a smile that showed brilliant white teeth, and an Adolphe Menjou moustache. He wore a light tan suit, a shirt like fresh snow and a narrow black knitted tie. He nodded and said, 'Of course. Won't you come into my private office?'

Aurora Delano introduced Marvia and Lindsey. Leroux extended his hand, touched his fingertips to Lindsey's, took Marvia's hand in both his and held it longer than he needed to. He said, 'Please do seat yourselves.' He opened a manila folder that lay on his desk. 'I have made a list of all the McKinneys in Reserve. And since you tell me the McKinney you are investigating is black, there is no need to bother with the five white McKinney households. That is correct?' He raised an eyebrow.

Lindsey said, 'Leroy McKinney was definitely black.'

'Very well. I have here the addresses. Might I suggest that we take my vehicle? It will draw less attention than Ms. Delano's. Citizens of Reserve prefer American automobiles and Louisiana license plates.'

On the way out Leroux stopped at the receptionist's desk. 'You'll hold down the fort, Miss Washington.' Martha Washington nodded.

Leroux drove a Chevy Caprice. Unlike his office, it was neither old nor shabby. He pulled up in front of a wooden house that looked as if it belonged in the poorer section of an Erskine Caldwell novel. The four of them stood on the porch. Leroux rapped his knuckles gently on the dry gray wood.

A black man opened the door a few inches, then waited for Leroux to speak. They exchanged a few words that Lindsey couldn't make out. Then the man opened the door further and Leroux gestured the others to follow him inside.

It took Lindsey a minute to figure out why the man looked odd. Then he realized that he had only one arm; the other had been neatly removed and the sleeve of his shirt stitched in place. It took a little longer to realize that he also had only one natural leg, that the other was a prosthetic.

Leroux said, 'This is Mr. Floyd McKinney. Miss Plum, Mrs. Delano, Mr. Lindsey.' They all exchanged nods. Floyd McKinney wore bib overalls, what looked like the top of age-yellowed long johns, and heavy shoes. You had to see him move to realize that one of the shoes was worn on an artificial foot. He pointed to chairs and grunted. They sat down.

Lindsey explained that they were looking for information on a Leroy McKinney who had once lived in Reserve.

Floyd McKinney said, 'I don't know him.'

Lindsey said, 'He left Reserve many years ago. He might or might not have returned. Are you sure you never met him? Might you even have heard of him? Could he be a relative, however distant?'

'Possibly. I haven't lived in Reserve all my life. Worked at the mill from age 14 'til I had my accident. Been on pension ever since. Missed the war because of it. I never heard of any Leroy McKinney.'

'Do you know the other McKinneys in Reserve?' Lindsey asked. 'In any town nearby? Could there be McKinneys who have moved away — I mean, other than Leroy?'

'What did Leroy do? Why do you want to find him?'

'We don't need to find him. He's dead. I'm sorry. But there's an insurance matter. If I could find out some facts about Mr. McKinney's background . . . ' Sure, it was an insurance matter. It was also a murder case, but Lindsey didn't need to talk about that.

'You don't want the white McKinneys, then. You just want us. Well, they're a few McKinneys hereabouts. Couple in Edgard. Two, no, three families of McKinneys in Lutcher. We're all distant cousins.'

'What about right here in Reserve?'

Aurora said, 'I tried to get something out of the old school records, but I couldn't find anything. Apparently when the courts made the local schools integrate, they just absorbed the black schools into the white schools. Nobody knows what happened to all the old records of the black schools.'

Floyd McKinney made a fist and brought it down softly on his real knee. 'Everybody *here* knows what happened. They burned them up. Threw away the sports trophies, burned up the old records, everything.'

Leroux started up. 'Well, I think we've taken too much of Mr. McKinney's time, perhaps, and we might — '

'Sit down, you,' said Floyd. He pointed a thick forefinger at Leroux. 'You going to bother everybody else about this?'

Lindsey said, 'If we could possibly — '

'Well, my boy is working at the mill. Don't know that there would be any point in your talking to him.'

Leroux said softly, 'That would be Claude William McKinney, Mr. Lindsey. Goes as C.W.'

'If I don't know this Leroy McKinney, Claude surely wouldn't either. You might want to talk to his Aunt Willa, though. That's my sister-in-law. The William in Claude William is in her honor.'

'Yes, if we could, please.'

'That would be Miz Willa McKinney. She's an old lady now. I don't mean old like me, I mean really old. My brother G.B. was her third husband. G.B. was 19 years older than I was. We came from a large family. He was the oldest and I was the youngest, and we had six sisters and seven brothers in between us. I'm the only one left. My mama bore 15 children in 19 years.' He took a deep breath. 'G.B. married Willa before I was born. He was younger than she was, a good deal younger. She had children from her other husbands, too, and I think she might have had one with G.B. before I was born.'

Lindsey was trying to keep up with this. He wasn't making notes. He didn't want to inhibit Floyd McKinney. He'd remember it now and write it down afterwards.

'I never knew my mama,' Floyd continued. 'Everybody said it killed her, having all those children and having to work to feed them. Once Mama died, we all got parcelled out, the ones too little to take care of themselves. I was raised in Napoleonville. There are no McKinneys left in that town.' He patted his knee with his hand nervously. 'I got married and my wife had one child and then she ran away, so I never knew if it would have hurt her to have more.'

Lindsey said, 'If we could talk with Mrs. McKinney — is she able to carry on a conversation?'

'Sure she is. She lives next door to me.' He jerked his thumb toward a window.

'Maybe we shouldn't bother her with so many people. Maybe if just Marvia and I visit her . . . ?'

Floyd McKinney grinned. 'You go right

189

on. She'll be up and around, cleaning her house and working. She says she'll never stop working till she dies, and maybe not then; she hasn't made up her mind about that. Just talk loud to her, that's all.'

Lindsey shook Floyd's hand. 'Thank you,' he said.

McKinney pointed at Antoine Leroux and Aurora Delano. 'You two stay right here. I'll entertain you while they visit my sister-in-law.'

Lindsey and Marvia went outside. Lindsey said, 'Did they do that with many schools? I mean, burn records, trash trophies?'

'I can believe it. There was a lot of resistance here, and a lot of resentment when the courts insisted. I never lived in the south, but we have to keep informed. I have heard of destroying trophies, so the other might be true too. And then the whites who could afford it started pulling their kids out and sending them to private schools, so the public schools are for poor whites and poor blacks. Ain't it grand?'

'Well, I guess we'd better try Willa McKinney.' He stood where Marvia would be seen first when Willa McKinney opened her front door, and knocked. They waited.

The door opened. Willa McKinney had a face like a walnut shell, brown and seamed. She was barely five feet tall, if that, and thin. Her wispy hair was the color of a gray cat. It was pulled into a bun at the nape of her neck. She wore a faded cotton house dress and had tied an even more faded apron over it. She wore tennis shoes with the toes cut out, and held a broom in one hand. Her eyes were very black and very bright; she peered at Marvia, then past her at Lindsey, then nodded and made a little crooning sound. She stepped back from the door and made a vague gesture.

Marvia stepped inside the house. Lindsey followed. He thought that if Floyd McKinney's house looked as if the furnishings hadn't been changed in 40 years, Willa McKinney's house looked as if it had been untouched for 60. He started to introduce himself, remembering to speak up.

Willa McKinney set her broom aside. 'Sit down, sit down.' When they complied she said, 'Tea? I have iced tea and lemonade in my house. Would you like some iced tea or lemonade?'

Lindsey felt Marvia's hand on his knee. There was a message in the touch. She said, 'That's lovely, Grandmother. Whichever is easier would be lovely.'

Willa made her crooning sound again. She turned and glided ghostlike through a doorway. Lindsey could see that the next room was a kitchen.

Marvia murmured, 'Let me, Bart.'

Willa returned carrying a tray with a sweating pitcher of lemonade and glasses. She set the tray on a wooden table with a crocheted cover. Slowly she filled two glasses of lemonade, set down the pitcher, then handed a glass to Lindsey and one to Marvia. Slowly she lowered herself onto an ancient chair.

Marvia sipped her lemonade, then set the glass down. 'Thank you, Grandmother. That's wonderful. Do you mind if I call you Grandmother?'

Willa turned her head from side to side. Marvia told Willa her own name and then Lindsey's. Willa leaned forward, her elbows on her knees, and took Marvia's hands. She peered into Marvia's face and said, 'You may call me Grandmother.'

'We're trying to find information about Leroy McKinney. Does that name mean anything to you? Is he a relative of yours?'

'I was married to my first husband in the year 1921,' Willa answered. 'I was 13 years of age. I had one child, born prior to my wedding. I was married to my second husband in the following year. I had one child with my second husband as well. I was married to my third husband in 1926. I had one child with my third husband. All three of my children were boys. I always wished I had a girl, but I only had but three boys.'

'Would you tell us their names?'

Willa nodded slowly. 'My first husband was Mr. James Crump. Our child's name was Lawton. All of my children were talented. Lawton was mechanically talented.' She nodded, smiling to herself, seeing the distant past more clearly than the drab present. 'My second husband was Jefferson King, Junior,' she resumed. 'Our child's name was also Jefferson King. He was musically talented. He played the organ for our church at the age of seven. He was blessed with a gift from the Almighty. He was Jefferson King the third. But his father was my second husband.'

Lindsey waited for the story to go on.

'My third husband was Mr. G.B. McKinney. Our child's name was Leroy. Leroy was athletically gifted. He became a professional baseball player at a very early age.'

Lindsey felt a shock. Before he could speak, Willa McKinney continued. She was still holding Marvia's hands. She said, 'You are very dark.' She shook her head sadly. 'Still, you're pretty enough. I always wanted a girl.'

'Are any of them still alive, Grandmother?' Marvia asked.

'All of my husbands are in the ground. All of my sons served their country. My oldest boy served in the Army. He learned to fly an airplane from Mr. Joseph Wagner right here in Reserve. Mr. Wagner is in the ground. My son flew an airplane in the war and dropped bombs on Adolf Hitler. He sends me money, and has been

194

to visit with his wife. My younger sons were in the United States Navy. One of them was killed in the war. I don't know if the other is alive or in the ground.'

'Lawton Crump is your son?'

'He is.'

'And your second son, Jefferson King, was killed while he was in the Navy?'

'No,' Willa said. 'Not Jefferson. I don't know where Jefferson is.'

'I don't understand.'

Lindsey was taking it all in, like a witness at a fantastic ceremony, an audience of one at a play he only remotely understood.

'Leroy McKinney died in the Navy,' Willa said. 'I received a telegram from the government. Mr. Joseph Wagner came to my house and read the telegram to me. I never learned to read or write. The telegram said that the Secretary of the Navy regretted to inform me that my son Leroy McKinney had been killed in the service of his country.'

Lindsey said, 'You're sure? You're sure it was Leroy?'

Willa ignored him. She said to Marvia, 'Leroy and Jefferson were both members of the United States Navy. Leroy gave his life in the service of his country.'

'Do you know the date?' Marvia asked.

'Mr. Joseph Wagner told me that the date of the telegram was the 18th day of July in the year 1944. I received a check from the United States of America, and Mr. Joseph Wagner helped me to deposit it in the Dixie Savings Bank of Reserve, Louisiana. It's still there.'

'Do you have any papers, Grandmother? The telegram, anything else? Do you have your bankbook?'

Willa released Marvia's hands and slowly stood. She walked to an ancient chest of drawers. An oval mirror mounted on gimbals stood on top of the chest. Lindsey could see Willa's patient walnut face in the mirror. She opened a drawer, rooted through things that Lindsey could not see, removed a small envelope from the drawer, closed the drawer, then turned and glided with her ghostlike walk back to Marvia. All in silent slow motion.

Marvia opened the bankbook. She said, so Lindsey could hear, 'This hasn't been updated since 1949. Does your brother-in-law Floyd know about this?'

'I don't know. We seldom discuss financial matters. I do not think it would be seemly.'

'I'll take this to him, if I may. Is that all right, Grandmother?'

Willa considered for a while. 'I suppose it will be all right.'

'Can Floyd read and write, Grandmother?'

With pride in her soft voice, Willa said, 'Floyd and Claude William can both read and write and can do sums. Claude William was named for me, you know.'

Marvia stood up. 'Thank you, Grandmother.'

Willa took Marvia's face in her hands. Lindsey watched. It was something that he had done. He saw Willa look into Marvia's face. She kissed her on one cheek, then on the other. She said, 'You are very dark, but you are still a pretty child.'

Outside on the porch Marvia turned away. Lindsey waited, saying nothing. After a minute Marvia turned back and took Lindsey's hand. He saw that she had

Willa's bankbook in the other.

During the very short walk back to Floyd McKinney's house, Marvia said, '48 years' worth of compound interest. What do you think this thing is worth?'

'Floyd will have to track down the bank. Chances are it's long since disappeared into some giant 'glom.'

'I'll have Aurora Delano stay in touch with Floyd and Willa. I don't trust Mr. Antoine Leroux.'

★ ★ ★

Back at Antoine Leroux, Real Estate and Insurance, Martha Washington looked up from her keyboard and said, 'Your appointment is waiting, Mr. Leroux.'

Leroux shook his head. 'They're early. If I can move that old boarding house I'll buy champagne for all.' He shook hands hastily with Lindsey, with Marvia and Aurora Delano.

Martha Washington grimaced behind Leroux's back. She said, 'I'll put up the closed sign when I take my lunch.'

Lindsey said, 'Is there anyplace here to

get a light meal? Nothing fancy.'

She nodded. 'I'm just going for a sandwich.'

Lindsey looked at the others. 'That all right with you?'

Marvia and Aurora agreed.

Martha Washington led them to a luncheonette with faded red and green lettering on a sign that had once said 'Walter's Fine Food Grille.' They found a booth and slid into it, Lindsey facing Marvia, Aurora Delano beside him facing Martha Washington. It had not been planned.

They ordered from the menu. Walter's Fine Food Grille had one waitress. Stitched on the pocket of her uniform was the name Rita. She exchanged a few words with Martha Washington. Clearly, Martha was a regular at Walter's.

By the time the food arrived Lindsey was talking about the Double Bee project. Aurora Delano was interested from a SPUDS perspective, quoting Ducky Richelieu at every opportunity. Martha Washington knew enough about International Surety to offer a comment from time to time.

Rita set Lindsey's sandwich on the wooden tabletop. Amazing. Lindsey was talking about *Bessie Blue* and about the Tuskegee Airmen and Double Bee Enterprises. Rita had no qualms about joining the conversation. She said, 'I'll bet little Walter knows all about that.'

'Who's little Walter?' Lindsey asked.

'Little Walter Scoggins. This place has been in the Scoggins family for four generations. Little Walter, he studies at Southern U up in Baton Rouge, but he's home now for a while. He always comes in to help out. He's in the kitchen now.'

'And he knows about the Tuskegee Airmen?'

'He's studying our people's history. He says he's going to be a teacher. Big Walter says he'll have to take over the business. I don't know what he'll do.'

Lindsey nodded. He took a bite of his sandwich.

'You really making a movie about the Airmen?' Rita asked.

'Well, I'm working with the people making the movie.'

'Little Walter would like to hear about

that. Okay I send him out?'

'Sure.'

Little Walter Scoggins was big. He wiped his hands on his white apron before he shook hands with Lindsey. He made a little bow to Aurora and to Marvia, then gave Martha Washington a kiss on the cheek. She moved sideways and Walter slid into the booth beside her. It made for a little crowding but no one complained.

'You know about the Airmen?' Walter asked.

'I've been talking with one of them,' Lindsey replied. 'Lawton Crump. He comes from Reserve.'

'You know your stuff. I'd like to meet Lawton, but we don't see him around here. He tell you some stories?'

'He seems to think it was the best time in his life. He was taught to fly by a man here in Reserve, a Joseph Wagner.'

'Those Airmen, they really were heroes. They fought against all the odds to get the training they needed and to get into combat. I don't want to pose as a memory expert, but I happen to remember some of this. They graduated 992 pilots. They flew 1,578 missions in North Africa and Europe, destroyed 261 enemy aircraft, damaged or destroyed gun emplacements, radar installations, trains, ammunition dumps. Even sank a German destroyer in the Mediterranean. They won a Legion of Merit, a Silver Star, and hundreds of other medals. And 147 of them gave their lives for their country.'

Lindsey nodded, impressed.

'It's about time they were remembered,' Scoggins added. 'I'll go and see your film, Mr. Lindsey.' He slid from the booth. 'I have to get back to work. Pop will skin me if the gumbo isn't ready by dinnertime.'

Martha Washington waited until he had disappeared into the kitchen. Then she said, 'I'm going to marry that man.'

Marvia said, 'Does he know that?

'I haven't told him yet.'

★ ★ ★

The drive back to New Orleans only took half an hour. Aurora Delano said, 'I have desk space at the I.S. office. You can use that, use the phone, fax, whatever. It's just mid-afternoon in Denver.'

'No thanks,' said Lindsey. 'I'm not ready to report to Richelieu just yet.' Then to Marvia, 'The trip was worth it. Marvia, you saved the day. As far as Willa was concerned, I wasn't even there.'

'I'm glad I met her. She was born so long ago, her father grew up in slavery.'

'I'll have to sit down and work this out when I get back to California,' said Lindsey. 'It's very peculiar.'

Aurora shook her head. She'd penned her hair since Denver. New job, new hairdo, new life. She'd parked the Saab and accompanied Lindsey and Marvia Plum into their hotel. They were sitting in the brick courtyard. 'Are you headed back to California, then?' she asked. 'I mean, right away?'

'If I can get Marvia to stay another day or two, I will. I'll need to phone home, but if Mother is all right, and if Marvia can stay, that's what I want.'

'Well, call me if you need anything. At I.S. or at home. Enjoy your stay.'

They got some advice from Aurora

before she left. They strolled through the French Quarter and along Decatur Street, and made their way to the old French Market. Marvia bought a black T-shirt with a golden saxophone on it for her brother, a purse for her mother, and an alligator-skin belt for her dad. She dropped her purchases at their hotel on Bienville, and they took a taxi out of the Quarter to another restaurant that Aurora had recommended.

Marvia phoned Berkeley from their hotel. She was using vacation days, but Lieutenant Yamura said that things were under control. There were no more problems than usual in Berkeley.

Lindsey said, 'You were crying, weren't you? On Mrs. McKinney's porch. When you turned away.'

She nodded. 'It's the history, Bart. Being that close to it — it must be like Eric Coffman. He says his interest in history is casual; he pretends it's just a hobby. But those books on World War Two . . . You must have seen how he changed the subject when I asked him about them. If I were Jewish I'd feel that way about the Holocaust, the way I feel about slavery and everything that came after. It still isn't over.' She shook her head as if she could shake off the feeling. 'Tomorrow's our last day. Can we go to the aquarium? I want to get some souvenirs for Jamie.'

'Maybe we can come here again. To New Orleans. And bring Jamie. He'd love this town. We could go to the aquarium, to the zoo . . . '

Marvia reached across the table and put her hand on his.

He said, 'Like a real family. I don't think you should let his father take him, Marvia. I understand what you told me about his having a black home. But I think I could be a good father to him. I want to try.'

'Where would we live? What about your mother?'

'She's getting better. That's the fantastic thing. All the years that I had no one else, no outside life, she couldn't get over the idea that I was her little boy. I think that was part of what was making her crazy. The more I took care of her, I think

I was harming her, too.'

She frowned. 'I doubt that.'

'Ever since I've been with you, been away from her a lot of the time, she's been getting better and better. She's taking some course now for older women who want to get into the job market.'

Marvia pressed her hand against her eyes. 'I don't know, Bart. I'm just confused.'

They took a cab back to Rue Bienville and sat by the fountain for an hour, then went to bed.

In the morning they rode a streetcar along the waterfront to the aquarium and spent half the day there. Marvia said, 'We have to bring Jamie here. The rainforest was wonderful, but those white alligators were just astonishing. Did you get a good look at them?'

'I got eye to eye with one fellow. I could almost read his mind. He was thinking, 'If only I could get through this glass, that thing would make a lovely little meal.''

But Willa McKinney would not give them peace. 'I keep thinking about her,' Marvia said. They were back at Decatur

Street now, sipping cold concoctions at an outdoor bistro while a jazz trio serenaded the tourists with old music.

'Is it the history again?'

'No. It's what she said about her sons.'

'I've got that in my notebook now. I'll follow it up when we get home.'

'Why did Lawton Crump say that Leroy McKinney was a stranger to him if they were brothers? Half-brothers, anyway. If Willa McKinney is Lawton Crump's mother — '

'I believe that. Crump told me the same story about Mr. Wagner and the flying lessons that Mrs. McKinney told you. It was a wild shot but it wasn't completely wild. Crump admitted that he was from Reserve. Well, he didn't exactly admit it. It's just part of his biography. The whole story about Joseph Wagner and the flying lessons. But why did he leave out the McKinney family and his connection to it? He must have known we'd find out.'

Marvia shook her head. 'Maybe, maybe not. Did he say he didn't know Leroy McKinney, or that he didn't know the dead man at North Field?'

'I'm trying to remember. As far as I can recall, he just said that he didn't know the dead man. He didn't say the name Leroy McKinney. But what's the difference?'

'Willa McKinney said that Leroy was killed in 1944. Joseph Wagner brought the telegram to her house and read it to her because she didn't know how to read.'

'Right.'

'So how could Leroy McKinney have died last week at North Field in Oakland, if he died in 1944? In the war. In the Navy.'

They spent a last night in New Orleans, a last night in the four-poster bed in the hotel on Rue Bienville. They promised each other not to think about the McKinneys, about murder, about International Surety.

When their 737 was an hour from Oakland, Lindsey used the in-flight telephone to call Eric Coffman. It was Marvia's idea, and Coffman agreed. They would bring Jamie again, and he could play with Sarah and Rebecca. Marvia and Lindsey would consult Coffman, not about law but about history. Coffman said he'd promised Miriam dinner out tonight, but they could come tomorrow.

When the plane touched down, Lindsey phoned Mother, or tried to. Mrs. Hernandez answered the phone. True to her word, Mother was out of the house.

He spent the next day catching up on SPUDS work, including Double Bee. Ina Chandler had told him they'd been shooting in Oakland. The terrain was suitable, the airport management was cooperative, and the foundation that was funding the project had pressed them to use Oakland as their home base. They didn't have the budget to shoot in North Africa, Italy, or Germany.

Lindsey had balked at that point. 'If the planes are based in Texas and the action took place in Alabama and then in Europe and North Africa during the war, it still doesn't make sense to me. I mean, that they're going to shoot this film here.'

Ina Chandler's response had been brief. 'Money talks.'

Lindsey had asked her how Double Bee had got the Knights of the Air to relinquish control of their precious airplanes.

'They flew the planes up from Texas

and they'll fly them back when the shooting is finished. They'll do all the flying except when we're actually shooting Lawton Crump. And when he takes up the *Bessie Blue* there will be a flight crew of Knights with him.'

* * *

Lieutenant High took Lindsey's call at Oakland police headquarters and told him that OPD had contacted the Pentagon for verification of Leroy McKinney's identity. Lindsey sat up straight and grabbed a pencil. Ms. Wilbur and Elmer Mueller were both in the office for once, and they both stared at Lindsey.

High said, 'We got our reply this morning.'

'All right, what did they say?'

'Well, first of all, they couldn't verify Mr. McKinney's fingerprints. The military fingerprints all their new inductees nowadays. They have for many years now. But back during World War Two things weren't so well organized, and a lot of records have got lost or destroyed over the years. Warehouse fires, floods, packing and moving records.'

'Okay, that's the bad news. What's the good news?'

'Well, I wouldn't call it that, but it is information.'

'Okay. What?'

'Well, they did have a record of a Floyd McKinney. I thought there might be more than one person with that name. Maybe you can help me with that angle.'

'Was he born in Reserve, Louisiana?'

'That's what the Pentagon says. All right, then we've probably got the right man. Ah — or maybe not. You see, the Pentagon says that their Floyd McKinney was killed in 1944. And our Floyd McKinney just died. How could that be? Father and son, do you think?'

Before Lindsey could say anything, High said, 'No, scrub that. The medical examiner indicated that our victim was a man of about 70. That would jibe with a young serviceman in World War Two. But how could a young man, maybe even a teenager, die in 1944 and die again almost half a century later?'

'I thought you folks were going to soft-pedal this case to concentrate on the drug gangs and the turf wars.'

'Well, yes. I heard about your little escapade in Richmond. You certainly have a way of putting your foot into it, Mr. Lindsey. So I'll say that my interest in McKinney has picked up once again. Just a little bit.'

'What was McKinney's date of death?' Lindsey asked. 'His first date of death.'

'That was July 17th, 1944. He was a Navy man, a seaman first class, assigned to the U.S. Naval Barracks, Port Chicago, California. You've heard of that? Little town up on the Sacramento River right where it flows into San Francisco Bay. The town doesn't even exist anymore. But it was up near Concord, right where the Concord Naval Weapons Station is.'

Lindsey was writing fast.

'How does that sound to you? You have any information that would jibe with?'

Lindsey gave High a rundown of his interview with Willa McKinney. Of Marvia's interview. He finished with the arrival of the telegram from the Secretary of the Navy and Joseph Wagner's reading it to Willa.

High whistled. 'Sounds like our man, all right. But we've got a bigger mystery now than we had before. And the part about Lawton Crump being the half-brother of Floyd McKinney. I'm going to review Sergeant Finnerty's file on Mr. Crump and then have a chat with Mr. Crump myself.'

'Keep me posted, will you?'

'Now I'm not so sure. You know how we feel about private eyes messing around in homicides.'

'You know I'm not a P.I.'

'Right, thanks for reminding me. If you were, I could threaten you with having your license lifted. Just be careful, Lindsey.'

10

Marvia Plum parked her Mustang at Lindsey's house in Walnut Creek. Lindsey opened the car door for her. She climbed out of the car and he put his arms around her and gave her a warm kiss.

'Wow! You're turning into a real Romeo.'

'You do that to me.'

Jamie swung open the passenger door and bounded out. He still had the Flying Fortress in his hand. He said, 'I flew in the Flying Fortress. Mr. Crump took me up.'

Lindsey looked at Marvia. 'Is that true?'

She nodded. 'They're doing footage of Lawton Crump flying the B-17. Mrs. Chandler said they could have used bluescreen, whatever that is. But he wouldn't do it. He said he'd been trained to fly a 17 and by God he was going to fly one. He's been up almost every day, out over the ocean, out to the Farralones and back.'

'But — was he really a bomber pilot?'

'You might want to talk to him about that. I went to the library, and there's a book on the Tuskegee Airmen. They flew fighters in North Africa and Europe. Must be the same book little Walter Scoggins memorized. Has all that info in it, that Walter was quoting. They were training to fly four-engine bombers. Once the war ended in Europe, the Army brought them home and started training them for bombing missions in the Pacific.'

'I don't recall Crump mentioning that.'

'The war ended before they got into combat in the Pacific. But they'd had training. Crump knows how to fly a B-17. And remember, he was in the airline business for another 30 years. He knows about big airplanes.'

'And he took Jamie up?'

Jamie said, 'Sure he did. Mom said I could go.'

'Jamie brought his scale model to school and showed everybody,' Marvia told him. 'His teacher phoned Double

Bee and they took the whole class out to North Field. Everybody loved it.'

'And all the kids got to ride in the Fortress?'

'Just me!' Jamie was circling Lindsey and Marvia, flying his B-17 and making engine sounds.

'Come on in the house for a minute,' Lindsey invited them.

'Good idea. Jamie can use a pit stop. So can his mom.'

Lindsey's mother was home from her class. She told Marvia about learning to use a computer. 'Our teacher's a wonderful colored girl — no, we don't say that anymore. I have to remember. She's a wonderful young woman; works for one of those computer companies and they give her time off to teach our class.'

'You didn't have any trouble getting accustomed to the computer?'

Mother hesitated. 'At first. I didn't know how to turn it on. But she won't let anyone be embarrassed. And I'm catching on. I won't go back. I will *not* go back.'

Lindsey took Mother's hand. 'I'm proud of you.'

Mother said, 'Miss Reilly — Doris Reilly — she says we all come from someplace and she won't let any of us go back. She's such a wonderful girl. She says she's black Irish. That's why her name is Reilly.'

Jamie came back from the bathroom and Marvia excused herself. He spotted Lindsey's own computer and said, 'Do you have any games, Mr. Lindsey?'

'You can call me Bart, Jamie. No, I'm sorry. I only use it for business. No games. But we'll be at Sarah and Rebecca's house in a little while.'

'Nintendo!' Jamie exclaimed.

Mother took Lindsey by the hand and led him into the kitchen. She nodded back toward the living room. 'He's just a little boy.'

'He's seven years old.'

'But I see them on the news. These gangs. All the killing.' She made an anguished gesture. 'And your friend Marvia is his mother. And Miss Reilly, my teacher. What makes them change?'

'I don't know, Mother. Look, why don't you come along with us to the Coffmans'?

You're invited for dinner, too.'

'Not yet. Please, Hobart. Later.'

'I understand, Mother. When you're ready. All right.'

'Bart?' Marvia called from the living room. 'Let's not be late at the Coffmans'.'

They left the Mustang in the driveway in Walnut Creek and took the Hyundai to Concord.

Sarah and Rebecca did not have to capture Jamie and drag him off to play Nintendo. Even before they left the foyer they were negotiating over which game to play.

Lindsey told Eric about the McKinney family of Reserve, Louisiana, and the story of the 1944 telegram. Then he said, 'Lieutenant High at OPD got a fax back from the Pentagon, confirming Leroy McKinney's Navy service at Port Chicago, and his death in July of 1944. So we still have to figure out who really died in the hangar at North Field. If it was Leroy McKinney, then who died in 1944? Or if McKinney really died in '44, who got bashed in the forehead in Oakland?'

Coffman walked to a bookcase and

reached into his pocket for a pair of gold-rimmed glasses. He pulled down a couple of books. 'Marvia, how much do you know about the Port Chicago disaster and the mutiny?'

'Some. It's a painful chapter.'

He laid out the books on the cocktail table. 'You can borrow these, Bart, if you want to.'

'I know those books,' Marvia said. 'Pearson blames the mutineers. Allen exonerates them and blames the Navy.'

Eric nodded. 'You want to give Bart a fill-in, Marvia, or shall I?'

'I'd like to hear your take on it.'

Eric plumped his bulk into an over-stuffed chair, then leaned forward. Lindsey decided that he knew who he looked like. If Sidney Greenstreet in *The Maltese Falcon* had been 20 years younger and had grown a reddish-brown beard, he would have been Eric Coffman.

'During the Second World War,' Eric began, 'the armed services were under pressure to grant equal treatment to racial minorities, particularly to blacks. *Negroes*, that was the accepted term then. The Navy was by far the most hidebound service — they would say, tradition-bound — on that score. There was a lot of ethnic harassment. Those old war movies about the tough Italian kid and the Iowa farmboy and the scholarly Chinese fellow with the glasses, all getting together in the name of freedom and democracy — '

'I've seen a hundred of those,' Lindsey said.

' — they were more propaganda than reality.' Light glinted off Eric's glasses. 'That was the ideal. There were more barracks tussles and teeth knocked loose than you can imagine. The blacks had it the worst. All they could do in the Navy was work as mess-boys. Waiters and dishwashers for the brass. And the Jews didn't have it much better. We were fighting to stop Hitler's Holocaust, but we weren't much better off right here. But the blacks had it the worst.'

He paused to catch his breath. 'Okay. Port Chicago was the major supply depot for the Pacific Theater. Right here in Contra Costa County. Thousands of tons of supplies and ammunition went through there. The Navy would bring in Liberty ships or Victory ships. Big, slow-moving freighters. The ammunition came in by rail. They had a rail spur running right out onto the pier. They'd bring empty ships up, sometimes two at a time, one on each side of the pier, and start winching ammunition onto the ships and filling the holds.'

Shrieks erupted from the Coffman Nintendo parlor. Eric paused, then resumed. 'Apparently the Navy had more Negroes than they needed for mess duty, and there was this heavy stevedoring work to be done, so they formed up labor battalions and set them to work at Port Chicago. Marvia, do I have it right?'

'That's the version I've learned.'

'All right. Now, Allen's book is the more recent and seems to be the better informed of the two. He says these stevedores had no special training. They worked 24 hours a day, seven days a week. They were handling dangerous materials. Most of the men were black; some of the petty officers were black but the higher they rose the more were white, and all of the commissioned officers were white. There were some pretty vicious, pretty nasty individuals involved.

'On the night of July 17th, 1944, there was a disaster. Something set off a huge explosion. There were two ships tied up at the pier, one nearly full, one completely empty. They were vaporized. There was an ammunition train on the pier. The pier was completely demolished. The train disappeared. Later on they found it sunk in the mud where the pier had been. The engineer was still in the cab.'

Lindsey shivered.

'If you read the newspapers from 1944, they saw the flash and felt the tremor for miles around. There are still old-timers who'll tell you what it was like. Nobody knew what had happened at the time. Some thought it was an earthquake, some thought it was a Japanese bomb attack. It was a huge explosion. At least 320 people were confirmed dead. Most of them were black stevedores. The explosion was estimated at ten megatons. Ten million tons of TNT.'

'Wait a minute,' Lindsey said. 'That's

atom-bomb size. That's impossible.'

'Yes and no. Yes, ten megatons would be half the power of the Hiroshima bomb. And no, it's not impossible. Some people have suggested that the Port Chicago explosion was nuclear. That there was a small bomb loaded in the *E.A. Bryan*. That was one of the ships that blew up, the fully loaded one. Allen discounts that, but the question is still open. There's even a paranoid theory that the explosion was deliberate, a damage test. I don't buy that.'

Marvia said, 'Me neither.'

'What a tragedy,' Lindsey mused.

'That was just the beginning,' Marvia said.

'You take over for a while, Marvia,' Eric urged her. 'I'm getting dry. I'm going to see if Miriam needs a hand in the kitchen. And I want to check on the kids.'

Marvia turned on the couch so she was facing Lindsey. 'After the explosion came the mutiny. The sailors claimed they hadn't been trained in loading explosives. They had a lot of other grievances, too. Tommy Morris, a friend of my dad's, was

223

a Port Chicago sailor. He told me there was a little mutiny even before the explosion. The white officers were pretty hard on the sailors. There were some black petty officers, who were in charge of work crews. One white officer in particular was really riding them. He started chewing out the petty officers and insulting them.'

Eric popped his head into the room. 'Dinner's just about ready.' He disappeared again. Shrill voices rose, complaining about the interruption of their Nintendo game.

Marvia continued, 'The crew chief pulled his men off the job. They settled that one, smoothed it over. But after the explosion, some of the men refused to load ammunition again.'

'Mutiny.'

'Technically. There were hundreds of men involved. The whole situation was an awful muddle. The Navy picked out 50 men and tried them for mutiny. They were convicted, but there was such a scandal that the brass didn't dare impose serious penalties. So they kind of shuffled them around for a while, held some of them on ships but didn't give them any work to do. Finally they discharged them.'

Miriam called them to dinner. She served pasta and a green salad.

Over the meal, Lindsey said, 'And Leroy McKinney was one of the 320 men who were killed.'

'That would jibe with Willa's story,' Marvia said.

'And it would jibe with Lieutenant High's Pentagon fax.'

Eric said, 'But it wouldn't jibe with the body at the airport.'

'No, it wouldn't,' Lindsey agreed. 'I think I'd better talk with Lawton Crump again. I want to find out a little more about the Tuskegee Airmen.'

'I've got a book on them, too,' Eric said.

'Right. But there's no substitute for talking to somebody who was there. Marvia, I might want to meet Tommy Morris, if you can arrange it. But I really want to talk with Mr. Crump.'

The children seemed uninterested in the adult conversation, but somehow the topic had seeped across the generational barrier. Jamie was telling Sarah and

Rebecca about his flight on the *Bessie Blue*. The girls reacted with disbelief at first, but when Jamie persisted and added details, they gradually swung around to admiration, then envy.

Sarah tugged at Eric's sleeve until he focused on her. 'Father, may Rebecca and I go on the airplane with Jamie and his friend Mr. Crump?'

'I don't know. Marvia, Bart — what do you think?'

Lindsey said, 'If it's all right with you and Miriam, we'll see about it.'

'Bart, I want to get back to this McKinney killing,' Eric said. 'If you think the answer lies in the Port Chicago disaster, why do you need to talk with Crump again? Wasn't he at Tuskegee? Or, by the summer of '44, he would have been in North Africa or Italy, flying fighter escort missions.'

'Crump and McKinney were both from Reserve; they were half-brothers. I want to talk to Crump about that. But I think there's more to it than that. I think it involves the Tuskegee Airmen *and* the Port Chicago Mutineers. Look, these

Negro servicemen were trying to serve their country and to improve their own lot at the same time. Somehow the Navy gave them a chance.'

'Pretty grudgingly.'

'No quarrel there. But they did get a chance. And they won their share of glory, to say the least. And the Navy stuck their black recruits in Port Chicago doing stevedore work, and then came the explosion, the mutiny . . . It was tragic.'

Marvia said, 'So far, I follow you. But what does it have to do with North Field?'

'I don't really know. It just seems to me that we're looking at two sides of the same coin. One group got a chance to prove themselves and wound up as decorated heroes, and the other group were squashed down and wound up branded as mutineers.' He looked around. 'And now, 50 years later, these two roads that were created 50 years ago . . . for some reason, they've crossed. Lawton Crump and Leroy McKinney were half-brothers. Born in Louisiana, in the 1920s. By the 1940s they're young men. Crump becomes a

Tuskegee Airman and gets to fly in Africa and Europe. He comes home a hero. McKinney becomes a Port Chicago stevedore and — dies.

'But did he die in 1944, or just last month? Dead by violence in either case. His head smashed with a monkey wrench? Or was he vaporized by the explosion in 1944? Or did he survive that? Was he one of the mutineers? Why isn't his name in the record? Did he avoid the mutiny, or at least the trial, and stay in the Navy? Then what?'

Marvia said, 'You're leaving someone out of this, Bart. What happened to Jefferson King the third? Willa McKinney's middle son?'

It was getting late and the children were getting cranky, so Lindsey and Marvia Plum and Jamie took their leave.

★　★　★

Nellie Crump answered the phone and told Lindsey that her husband was taking a nap, but she'd have him call back later; or if Lindsey preferred, he could just see him at North Field the next day. They were shooting more footage, and he was going to be there in his leather flying helmet and his heated flight suit. Lindsey agreed.

Lindsey had called from Marvia's apartment. Afterwards he flipped the pages of the two books dealing with the Port Chicago mutiny that Eric Coffman had loaned him. He found a list of the 320 men killed in the explosion, black and white, civilian and military. The list was broken down by status and assignment. He pointed to the page and said, 'Marvia, look at this.'

She whistled. 'Leroy McKinney. Listed under bodies recovered and identified. So Willa told the truth.'

'And that's why he never tried for veteran's benefits; why he was so evasive about his service record. Reverend Johnson told me that Leroy never wanted to pursue any kind of government claim, even though everybody thought he was entitled to something. He wouldn't do it. He couldn't. Not if he was dead.'

Marvia snorted.

'Wait,' Lindsey continued. 'If Leroy McKinney was dead, then who was living under that name all these years? Who died at North Field and was buried under the name Leroy McKinney?'

'Let me have a look at that book.' Marvia ran her finger down the page, turned the leaf, and stopped. 'Look at that.'

The heading ran: *Unidentified Dead — men who were on the ships and pier and presumed dead after the explosion.* The list was four pages long, broken down into naval groupings and civilian employees. The biggest group was headed: *Enlisted Personnel — U.S. Naval Barracks*. Names number 108, 109, and 110 were *King, Calvin, King, Clifton*, and *King, Jefferson III*.

Lindsey said, 'I think Jefferson King the third was not killed in the explosion. I've suspected that for a while, but I thought he might have been one of the mutineers. Now I don't think so. I think he became Leroy McKinney. He didn't like the Navy; he didn't want to go back to loading ammunition. Who can blame him? But if he deserted and turned up under his own name, they'd drag him back and throw him in the brig.'

Outside Marvia's apartment, somewhere in the night, a Berkeley police car sounded its siren.

Lindsey said, 'He could just have made up a name, but he took Leroy McKinney's instead. His half-brother. If anybody ever questioned him, ever checked out his story, he knew all about Leroy McKinney. They even had the same mother. They were both from Reserve, both went through Navy boot camp. Nobody would bother to find out if McKinney was alive or dead if he was standing there talking to them.'

'But he could never apply for benefits. If he ever did, they would discover that he wasn't who he claimed he was. His real identity might come out, and then they'd have him for desertion.'

Lindsey rubbed his chin. 'So that accounts for the baseball story and the music story. Leroy was really a ballplayer, you know. Johnson showed me the scorecards. And Jefferson — Jefferson King who became the false Leroy McKinney — really was a musician. If his hand was ruined in the Port Chicago explosion . . . ' He shook his head sadly. 'Damn!' he whispered.

'What's the matter?

'The damned fool! When the explosion happened, July of 1944 — if Jefferson King's hand was so badly injured, he could have gone to the hospital. He *should* have gone to the hospital! He couldn't possibly have reported for duty. He wouldn't have had to join the mutiny and he didn't have to run away. He didn't have to end up in a janitor's coveralls with a hole in the middle of his forehead.'

He slid the two Port Chicago books away and picked up the book on the Tuskegee Airmen, and looked for Lawton Crump in the index.

★ ★ ★

On the North Field runway, The B-17's engines fired up, one by one, coughing a cloud of black smoke before settling down to its steady drone. The morning fog had burned off and the sun glinted off the airplane's aluminum skin. The only paint on the Flying Fortress's exterior was its identifying data, its World War Two Air Force insignia, and the huge portrait of Bessie Smith with the *Bessie Blue* logo in bright blue lettering on the airplane's nose.

A camera crew rode on a motorized dolly near the airplane's wing tip, slowly rolling past the engines and toward the cockpit.

Lindsey stood in the mouth of the Double Bee hangar with Ina Chandler and Lawton Crump. Crump sipped coffee from a steaming paper cup. Behind them a catering table had been set up for the aircrew and the Double Bee staff.

Lindsey watched the camera crew at work. 'I hope they know those propellers are dangerous.'

Ina Chandler laughed. 'Ever the insurance man, aren't you?'

'There *have* been cases, you know. People not watching themselves, stepping into a propeller. What a mess. And what a claim.'

The camera dolly rolled safely past the outboard engine.

'Not that jets are any safer.' He smiled. 'We've had to pay a couple of those claims. Instead of getting chopped up, you get sucked in. *Whoosh!* And then when they get airborne, a window blows out or a door opens, or a hole in the roof. People zoom out of the aircraft. Remember that one in Hawaii? Never found the body. And then you get a case like D.B. Cooper. Of course that wasn't an accident, so there was no claim to pay, but what a story!'

Lawton Crump said, 'You're certainly tuned in to disasters today, Mr. Lindsey.'

'Just my job. I heard about you giving young Jamie Wilkerson a ride.'

Crump smiled broadly. 'Great kid. Put him in the co-pilot's seat and took him for a little excursion. Ina had a cameraman with us, of course.'

'I thought there had to be a Knights of the Air crew on every flight.'

'We got around that. By gosh, the old Fort was a great plane. One man can fly it. They had to, sometimes, coming home from missions full of flak and fighter fire.'

Ina Chandler said, 'You should see the

dailies. That kid has a million-dollar face. The airplane shots were fine but we've got lots of those now. But that boy will have offers from every producer in Hollywood. Not that he'll be in our film, just in the outtakes. But what a face.'

'Did you say anything about that to his mother?'

'Not yet. She'll hear.'

Lindsey said, 'Mr. Crump, there are a couple of things I'd like to talk over with you, if you don't mind.'

Crump frowned. 'You were down in Holy City. I thought you got what you needed.'

'Pretty much. There were just a few more questions, though.'

Somehow the leather jacket and the soft helmet made Crump look 20 years younger and 30 pounds lighter.

Lindsey said, 'I just wanted to ask you a little more about Tuskegee and your experiences in the Army. And a couple of other questions.' He'd get to Reserve and Willa Crump and her three talented sons in time.

Crump looked at Ina. 'How soon you

going to want me again?'

Ina studied her clipboard, put the walkie-talkie to her mouth and muttered into it. She jotted something on the board. 'Be about half an hour. Don't go far.'

Crump inclined his head toward the catering table. 'Come on, then. Help yourself to some java. Treat's on Mrs. Chandler.' He strolled into the hangar.

Lindsey helped himself to a cup. He didn't really want any coffee, but he'd found that people talk better over shared food and drinks.

Crump said, 'Come on, let's borrow an office. It isn't fancy but it beats standing.'

They sat in the same room where Lindsey had seen Crump and Ina Chandler being interviewed by Sergeant Finnerty on the day of the murder. Lindsey ran his gaze back into the hangar. His eye found a stain on the floor where he thought Leroy McKinney had lain. Somebody had tried to clean away the stain, and a greasy copy of the Oakland *Trib* lay where it had been abandoned.

Lindsey said, 'Little Jamie really enjoyed his flight.'

Crump nodded.

'You sure it was completely safe? I mean, our coverage is only intended for the movie.'

Crump growled. 'I'll tell you something, Mr. Lindsey. The B-17 was one of the safest aircraft ever built. She was one of the first airplanes that ever had a redundant control system. Fortresses were forgiving airplanes. Some of 'em came home with holes in 'em, engines gone, pieces knocked off the tail. It was remarkable.'

'Even so, do you think a little boy — '

'Or are you challenging my ability as a pilot? I'm still FAA certified, you know.'

'Nothing like that, no. But, you know, there's always a risk. The crowded skies, and so forth.'

'Oh.' Crump took a sip from his cup. 'We've got splendid cooperation from the tower. Outstanding. And I'll tell you something else. That B-17 is safer with Lawton Crump at the controls than a car is on the freeway in the hands of an expert driver. Has young Wilkerson ever ridden in your car? What kind of car do you drive, anyway?'

'A Hyundai.'

'Hyundai!' Crump roared. 'Asian-built tin cans, that's what those cars are! Why don't you buy American? What's the matter with people nowadays? Japanese are buying up the whole country. Germans are the boss of Europe. What did we fight that war for?'

This interview was not going the way Lindsey had intended. He sipped his coffee and tried to think fast, to get back out ahead of Lawton Crump.

Crump was still rolling. 'That's what this picture is going to do, if I have anything to say about it. Get some pride back in our people, get some backbone back in America. We were strong in my day. We had to struggle for everything we got. I was a poor boy fresh out of a very small town. You know that already. I got nothing for nothing. I — '

Lindsey held up his hand. 'That was what I meant to ask you about. You flew fighters in Europe, right?'

'North Africa and Europe.'

'Yes. Single-engine aircraft.'

'Some twins. The P-38 was a twin-engine. You know how they taught us to fly those? Of course we'd qualified in single-engine fighters, everything from the old 39s and 40s up through the 51s. So when some 38s came in — you never knew what was coming in, you might be flying Warhawks on Monday and Thunderbolts on Tuesday — when the 38s came in, they led us out to the flightline and handed us each a manual. They said, 'Climb in the cockpit. Read the manual. Handle the controls. When you figure you've got it under your helmet, start the engines and fly.'' He nodded in agreement with himself.

Lindsey looked at him, astonished.

Crump said, 'That was how we did it. Lost a lot of pilots and a lot of aircraft, but by golly we learned to fly. I'm the living proof of that.'

'I understood, yes. Yes. But how did you learn to fly the B-17? And what's the story of *Bessie Blue*?'

Crump swung around in his chair. Lindsey could peer through the hangar door and see the Flying Fortress still on

239

the flightline, its propellers spinning, its engines idling. Obviously, Crump could see it too. That showed in his eyes. He was dreaming of 1944, reliving his glory days. Lindsey expected to see Dean Jagger stride into the hangar with a clipboard in his hand, but it was only Ina Chandler.

She stuck her head into the little office. 'Everything okay?'

Crump said, 'Just fine.'

'Few more minutes, then.

'Once Hitler was whipped,' Crump resumed, 'they sent us back home. Loaded us on ships. The Atlantic was safe then. It was frightening, shipping out there. Subs all around us, or so they warned us. Could be torpedoed at any moment.

'We got back to Tuskegee; nobody knew what was going to happen. They were still turning out new pilots and gunners and mechanics, then they set up conversion training to turn us into bomber crews. We trained in the Mitchell for a while. That was a sweet plane to fly. Noisy son of a gun, but it handled beautifully.'

'But the B-17?'

'I was in the 332nd fighter group, 99th

squadron. Those were the Tuskegee Airmen. Man, were we ever proud. Then they sent us home and formed up the 447th bombardment group. That was going to be a B-17 unit out in the Pacific. Matter of fact, by the time we got there the 17 would have been ready for retirement.' Crump's eyes had a faraway look. 'Boys were flying the 29 by then. The Superfortress. Pressurized fuselage, warm air. Not like the little Fort.'

Ina was back. She stood in the doorway with her clipboard in hand.

Crump said, 'We got to name our planes, of course. I was designated pilot and aircraft commander of a B-17F. Even as a 17 she was kind of old and outmoded. They changed the design a little with the G model, put the Cheyenne tail turret on 'em and put that extra gun mount under the bombardier's station. Called it a chin turret. A few Fs had that, but old *Bessie Blue* didn't.'

Ina said, 'Gotta get airborne, Lawton.'

Crump pushed himself to his feet. To Lindsey he said, 'The B-17 was the greatest bomber ever built. Don't let

241

anyone tell you otherwise, sonny. You know they flew in Korea? You know the Israelis used 'em in '48, in their war of independence? You know Uncle Sam even painted some of them flat black and used 'em for secret night missions in Vietnam? No sir, don't you tell me about the wonders of the jet age, the wonders of the stealth age. B-17 was the greatest bomber ever built.'

11

Lindsey started to follow Crump and Ina back toward the runway, but the phone on the borrowed desk rang. Something made him pick it up.

'High here. That you, Lindsey?'

'How did you know where I was?'

'An old Gypsy woman gave me the power to divine your whereabouts. I hear you're still pushing the McKinney thing. What have you got to share with me? Think we ought to get together over lunch?'

Lindsey said okay. Outside the hangar he could see the silvery B-17 still in position. The Double Bee people and the Knights of the Air had sent up a couple of camera craft. A new-looking Bell helicopter was hovering above the B-17, a daredevil camera jockey standing on the Bell's landing skid, pointing a camera straight down at the bomber.

Lawton Crump was visible through the cockpit window of the B-17. He'd donned his soft leather helmet and he did look like a youngster barely out of his teens. Ina stood just beyond the 17's wingtip. Crump gave her the thumbs-up sign, four Wright Cyclones roared and the plane rolled forward.

As Lindsey headed up Hegenberger Road toward the freeway, he heard a droning and looked up. There was the *Bessie Blue*. The old bomber climbed and banked back toward North Field.

At Oakland Police Headquarters, Lieutenant High was awaiting his arrival. He suggested a nearby Mexican restaurant. They settled into a booth. After they'd placed their orders, they both pulled out pocket notebooks and pencils.

High said, 'All right, what have you got for me? Bring me up to date.'

Lindsey described his visit to Reserve, Louisiana, and the information he had derived from Marvia's interview with Willa McKinney.

High jotted notes, gesturing with his free hand for Lindsey to keep the facts flowing. When Lindsey finished, High said, 'That's wonderful! If I had an expense account

I'd buy you this lunch to celebrate.'

Lindsey said, 'That isn't all. I was out at Eric Coffman's house — Marvia and I were out there, and — ' He broke off as the waitress brought their food.

High crunched a taco. Around it he said, 'Yep. I know Coffman. Didn't he rescue you from my clutches once or twice?'

'You put it so elegantly. You know, Coffman is a history buff and he's got an impressive reference library.'

'So what?'

'So he heard the story of Willa McKinney's three talented sons and their exploits in World War Two, and he put them together so they almost make sense.'

'Almost?'

'I just think it'll take a little more work to sift out the truth from the lies or distortions. Eric loaned me his reference books, and I spent a while with them at Marvia's place. I think I need to talk with Latasha Greene again. And maybe with Mr. Luther Jones.'

'Yep.' High loaded his fork with rice and refried beans. 'Yep, I've been following your exploits in the wonderful City of

245

Richmond, too. You certainly get around, Hobart. I love having Richmond nearby. Makes me realize I'm better off working here.'

Lindsey said, 'Do you know if Jones is still in jail?'

'I can check. It's odds-on he's been sprung, though. You want me to phone up to Richmond and ask 'em? Who was the tech you talked to up there?'

'Hartley.'

'Okay. Soon as we get back to the shop. No point in using a pay phone when I can charge it to the taxpayers.' He downed another bite of taco. 'So what do you make of the three McKinney brothers? Well — only one McKinney, right? One mom, three dads, so we have a McKinney, a Crump and a King. How do you put them together?'

'The thing that tripped us up was the connection between Leroy McKinney and Jefferson King. Apparently they joined the Navy together and were both serving at Port Chicago in 1944. Leroy McKinney was a Negro league ballplayer before the war, and Jefferson King was a musician. Had been a church organist; was getting started as a professional.'

'I follow that.'

'It's the night of the explosion, July 17th '44. Leroy McKinney and Jefferson King are both at Port Chicago. Leroy is on duty, loading the *Bryan*. His half-brother, Jefferson King, is off duty, sound asleep in his bunk. When the ships go up, Leroy is killed outright. Jefferson King survives but he's injured, maybe badly burned. Again, the books say that the men actually on the ships or working on the pier were wiped out. Those a little further away from the explosion received varying degrees of damage. The blast shattered the window glass and sent slivers all through the barracks. The unlucky ones were blinded for life.'

High winced.

'All right.' Lindsey took a sip of water. 'Jefferson King's right hand was ruined. He was finished as a musician. And he deserted. He could have reported to sick bay — he probably would have been hospitalized until they could discharge him and send him home with a disability pension — but instead he panicked.'

'Poor guy.'

'He didn't want to turn himself in. He could be charged with AWOL or even desertion. Not a light matter in wartime. He couldn't keep his own identity because he'd already been listed as missing, presumed dead, in the explosion. There were stories in all the local newspapers, in the Oakland and San Francisco papers. But King's half-brother Leroy McKinney had been identified as dead. His body had been found. So King took McKinney's name. He was safe as long as he kept his head down, but if he applied for any kind of benefits they'd nab him. And that was how he lived for the next 50 years.'

High said, 'Let's go back upstairs. You pick up the check.'

Once at Homicide, High phoned Richmond. He put his call to Detective Hartley on the speakerphone. Lindsey identified himself, then asked, 'Do you still have Luther Jones there?'

'Sorry, Mr. Lindsey. We had to release him — thanks to you furnishing him with an ironclad alibi. Not that it was your fault, but it would have been nice to pin him for the Ahmad Hope killing.'

'Did you get an identity for the man who was shot at Fuzzy's #3?'

'The dead man was Andrew Hope, young Ahmad's uncle. Really tough on Mrs. Hope, losing her nephew and her son the same day. But at least she won't have to see 'em go to trial.'

Lindsey heard a ringing in his ears. His hands felt cold. He sat down quickly and waited for the feeling to pass.

High said, 'You okay, Mr. Lindsey?'

'Just . . . just give me a minute.' Lindsey heard Detective Hartley's voice coming over the speakerphone from Richmond.

'Lieutenant High, you still there?'

'Everything's all right,' High said. 'Mr. Lindsey just felt a little faint.'

★   ★   ★

An hour later Lindsey was in the Hyundai, headed up the freeway to Richmond. He parked on 23rd Street and walked to Fuzzy's #3. The shattered half-moon glass in the padded door had been covered over with a sheet of brown cardboard. Inside the saloon Lindsey hovered for a moment while his eyes adjusted to the darkness and his ears to the blues blasting from the jukebox. When he could see again he spotted Fuzzy behind the bar.

Fuzzy stared at Lindsey.

The saloon was more full than empty. Every bar stool was occupied, as were the majority of the tables. The place reeked of cigarette smoke. Lindsey pulled his handkerchief from his trousers pocket and wiped his eyes.

A familiar voice said, 'Looky here, if it isn't Mister Lindsey-Hobart-Lindsey.'

Luther Jones was seated at a table. There was a bottle of beer in front of him. A cigar smoldered in an ashtray. Jones wore a black shirt closed with shining black buttons. A fine gold chain circled his neck, supporting a golden religious ornament. He gestured to an empty chair. 'Won't you deign to honor me?'

Lindsey edged toward the table and slid gingerly into the chair. 'Hello, Luther.'

'What's that?'

'I said, 'Hello, Luther.' Luther Jones, isn't it?'

The only sign of displeasure was a momentary narrowing of the eyes. 'I prefer my name as a free man. I don't use my slave name.'

Lindsey waited for him to say more.

'Luther was a preacher, anyhow, and I'm no preacher. And a Jones is a bad habit. Maybe you didn't know that. A Jones is a bad thing. So you see, I don't like Luther and I don't like Jones. Preaching a bad habit. Heh-heh. But you can call me Hasan or Rahsaan, or you can call me Mr. Rasheed, whatever you need.'

Lindsey said, 'I need some more information about Leroy McKinney.'

'You don't scare easy, do you, Lindsey-Hobart-Lindsey? Would you like a brew, courtesy of Rasheed?' He signaled Fuzzy.

Fuzzy brought Lindsey a beer. He didn't wait to be paid.

Rasheed said, 'You helped Rasheed in an hour of need. Enjoy your brew, and what can I do?'

'I need some more information about Leroy McKinney.'

'For an insurance man, Lindsey, you sure act a lot like a cop. What do you want to know about Leroy?'

'Was that his real identity? I have reason to believe that he was really someone else. That Leroy McKinney has been dead for many years, and that the man you knew as Leroy McKinney took his identity.' He picked up his beer, examined the lip of the bottle and sipped.

Rasheed said, 'Far as I know, Leroy McKinney was Leroy McKinney.'

'How long did you know him? When did you first meet him?'

'Christmas time. I remember it clearly. All the news was coming from Europe. Our boys thought the war was all won. Ike was the big noise over there. Then the Germans started to push back. Caught our side by surprise.'

Lindsey nodded, willing Rasheed to continue.

'They called it the Battle of the Bulge. I 'member I was working in the shipyard. All the stores was full of Christmas decorations, radio was playing all Christmas music, the newspapers was all full of the Battle of the Bulge. I met Leroy in a saloon. I 'member I took one look at that awful claw hand of his and I couldn't look at it no more. I was a young, young man at that time. A blade.'

'And his name was definitely Leroy McKinney?'

'He was just out of the Marine Corps.'

Lindsey grunted.

'That's what he told me. I wasn't gon' ask him no difference. He told me he'd got that claw out in the Solomon Islands someplace. Picked up a white phosphorus grenade, he told me. Throwed it out a bunker. Saved his whole squad, but it burned the shit out of that hand. Ruined his career. He been a musician afores the war.'

'So he spent the rest of his life managing nightclubs.'

Rasheed nodded.

'Then why was he working as a janitor?'

Rasheed leaned forward. 'You know what, Lindsey? I kidded you. He wasn't never no club manager. He wasn't never no nothing but jes' a janitor. He worked in those places, all right. He saw those greats. Bird and Miles and Monk. But not from behind no microphone. No. He saw them from behind a wet mop. Leroy wasn't no goddamned bigshot. Wasn't nothing but a goddamned floor-swamper, toilet-swabber, puke-scrubber janitor. And he was a goddamned liar. Probably wasn't no goddamned war hero, neither.'

★   ★   ★

The faded stucco front of Latasha Greene's house had fresh bullet holes in it. A few scraps of yellow plastic fluttered from the house or lay in the overgrown front yard. Lindsey picked up a strip that had wrapped itself around a brown weed. The black lettering said: IME SCENE — DO NOT CRO.

Lindsey knocked on the door. The man who opened it very nearly filled the doorway. His skin was very black, as were his trousers and narrow bow tie. His shirt was white, the sleeves rolled above his elbows. The wooden grip of a black metal revolver protruded from his trousers. It made a dent in his belly.

Lindsey said, 'I came to talk with Latasha Greene. Is she at home?'

The huge man looked down at Lindsey. 'Why?'

Lindsey reached for his pocket. He could see the huge man's eyes follow his hand; see heavy muscles tense beneath his skin. Lindsey extended his card.

The huge man looked at it without moving to take it. He repeated, 'Why?'

'My company has insured the *Bessie Blue* project out at Oakland Airport. Latasha's grandfather worked there and he died.'

The huge man blinked at the word *died*.

'I'm trying to learn about Mr. McKinney and the circumstances of his death. I am not a police officer. I am concerned solely with the insurance aspects of the event. We may be able to pay some benefits in Mr. McKinney's death, which would probably accrue to Ms. Greene.'

The huge man wrinkled his brow and moved aside. Lindsey heard him close the door behind him as he stepped inside the house. He felt his presence behind him as he crossed the living room.

Latasha Greene sat on the tattered couch wearing what seemed to be the same T-shirt and jeans she had worn the last time Lindsey was in the house. She was nursing her baby. The TV set was turned on, tuned silently once again to a rap video.

Lindsey laid his attaché case across his knees. He unsnapped the clasps and extracted the old *Call-Bulletin* clipping. 'I've made a couple of photocopies for you, on good paper.'

Latasha extended a long, slim brown hand and took the papers. She didn't say anything. Lindsey had studied the photo and its caption. It showed a group of American Marines in combat gear, brandishing their weapons. They were surrounded by tropical vegetation. The caption indicated that they were celebrating a victory over Japanese defenders on Tarawa. No names were given, and the faces were blurred and faded. Somebody, long ago, had drawn a heavy circle around one of the Marines. The Marine Corps wasn't integrated during World War Two.

Not according to everything Lindsey had been told about that war. But it wasn't for him to judge.

He said, 'I'm sorry if this is painful for you, Latasha, but please try to answer my questions. You could be a big help. Do you know if your grandfather had any dealings with a man named Luther Jones, also known as Hasan Rahsaan Rasheed?'

Latasha shook her head.

'The little boy who was killed, Ahmad Hope — '

'I knowed Ahmad.'

'The police say that he was killed by his own uncle, Andrew Hope. Then Andrew was killed in a running shoot-out with the police. The same day. Do you — '

'I knowed Ahmad. I din't know Andrew. If he kill Ahmad, it's a good thing he's dead.' She turned her face away, lifted the edge of her T-shirt and used it to wipe her eyes. When she turned back her cheeks and her upper lip were wet. Lindsey decided to try another tack.

'Your grandfather was Leroy McKinney. Do you know if he ever used any other name? Would you remember a name such as Abu Shabazz? Jefferson King? Or Lawton Crump?'

Latasha shook her head very slowly from side to side.

'Did your grandfather ever speak of his childhood? Did he ever mention a town named Reserve, Louisiana?'

Latasha turned her face from Lindsey, bending down to her baby. She moved the baby from one breast to the other, pulling one side of her T-shirt down and the other up.

Before Lindsey could ask another question, he felt a vise close on his shoulder. The lid of his attaché case slapped shut as he was lifted to his feet and steered toward the front door of the house. The door slammed behind him with a sound like a howitzer.

Lindsey left his car in front of Latasha's house on 23rd Street. If anything was going to happen to it, it would happen. He retraced the path he'd taken with the Reverend Johnson the day of his first interview with Latasha. He might as well return the Negro League scorecards while he was at it. And he might learn something further from the minister. He certainly couldn't accomplish any less than he had with Latasha.

The minister was in his office when Lindsey arrived at the church. The front door of the building was unlocked. Lindsey heard the sound of voices and followed it until he saw the door of the reverend's study. It was open a crack.

Lindsey waited. At length the study door opened fully and a young couple emerged, followed by the Reverend Johnson. The boy couldn't have been more than 12 or 13. He made eye contact with Lindsey for a fraction of second. Lindsey wasn't sure but he thought the boy was one of Ahmad Hope's former playmates. The girl looked even younger than the boy, and even skinnier. She was obviously pregnant. She avoided Lindsey's eyes.

Lindsey watched the minister guide the two youngsters to the door. He embraced the girl, shook hands solemnly with the boy, and watched them leave the church. He closed the door behind them. Then he walked back toward Lindsey, shaking his head.

'Did you know that our school district actually went bankrupt a couple of years ago? No money for sex education. And half the community doesn't want it anyway. Claims it will lead to the deterioration of the morals of our youth.'

'What are they going to do?'

Johnson shook his head. 'I don't want to depress you, Mr. Lindsey. Come into my study and sit down. What can I do for you today?'

In Johnson's study Lindsey found a seat and opened his attaché case. He looked up to see Johnson lifting a bottle from a lower drawer in his desk. A couple of glasses followed.

Lindsey returned the Negro League scorecards to Johnson. He said, 'I've been learning a good deal about Leroy McKinney, Reverend. Maybe some things that will be useful. I thought I'd share them with you and see if you could offer any help.'

Johnson nodded. 'Some mineral water, Mr. Lindsey?

Lindsey accepted a glass.

Johnson said, 'I buried Mr. McKinney.

I've tried to counsel his granddaughter. There seems to be no other family, at least in the area. Latasha's mother was Mr. McKinney's daughter. She has been deceased for a decade at least. No one seems to know anything about Latasha's father, only that his name was Greene. Even for that, we have only the word of Latasha. What more can I do, Mr. Lindsey?'

Lindsey said, 'I hope you didn't spend too much for the tombstone.'

Johnson's eyebrows flew up. 'There was no money to pay for a monument or for the funeral. The church paid for everything. If you're that concerned, perhaps you could see your way clear to make a contribution.'

Lindsey dug his wallet out of his trousers. He had $150 in cash. He took a breath, extracted $100 and laid it on Johnson's desk.

Johnson picked up the bills and dropped them into the top drawer of his desk. He laid a book of business forms on his desk and carefully made out a receipt and handed it to Lindsey. 'Thank you very much, sir.'

Lindsey said, 'If you'd erected a marker with McKinney on it, you might have to take it back down. His name was Jefferson King the third.'

'What are you talking about?'

'I'm talking about two young sailors from Louisiana. Two half-brothers who served at Port Chicago. One was Leroy McKinney, the other was Jefferson King. McKinney was killed in the disastrous explosion of July, 1944. King was injured in the same explosion but ran away. He deserted and took his half-brother's identity. The man you buried as Leroy McKinney was actually Jefferson King. The real Leroy McKinney died in 1944. In all likelihood, he was completely vaporized when the *Bryan* went up.'

Johnson tossed off his mineral water and refilled his glass. 'What did you say about Louisiana?'

'Both McKinney and King were from a small town in Louisiana. There was a third brother — half-brother. He's the only one still alive. His name is Lawton Crump and he is a retired airline employee. He lives near San Jose.'

Johnson leaned forward eagerly. 'Perhaps he could help Latasha and her child. What is his financial condition? He would be Latasha's, ah, I'll have to check the rules of genealogy. I think he would be her half-great-uncle. At any rate, I shall impress upon him the nature of his obligations as Latasha's only possible hope in this cruel world.' He found a sheaf of scratch paper and picked up his pen. 'You say this Crump lives in San Jose?'

'Actually, Holy City.'

'An aptly named community, I pray.'

'I don't know that he'll be able to help much. He was on the retired role of Pan American, and they went belly-up. I don't know what becomes of their pensioners. I'm sure he gets Social Security, and maybe some veteran's benefit.'

Johnson pursed his lips. 'We'll have to look into this.'

Lindsey asked, 'Did your Leroy McKinney ever say or do anything that made you think there was something odd going on? Something that he kept concealed?'

'Leroy wasn't a regular church-goer. In fact, he wasn't a member of my congregation, nor of any that I know of. But I consider it my duty to visit the homes of all those in the community who are in need, even the unchurched, and I visited his home from time to time. Mainly, I worked with Miss Greene. She did attend services now and then, and I was able to baptize both her and her baby.'

'Did King ever travel? Disappear for a few days at a time, or longer? Did he ever turn up with large amounts of unexplained cash?'

'I recall a few such incidents,' Johnson said. 'Just once I can recall Latasha coming to see me. She must have been little more than six years old. I remember she was just learning to read. She could read her name and a few other words.

'She showed me a postcard. She had read the name on it; it was addressed to her. She asked me to help her read the rest of it. I asked why she didn't show it to her mother and ask her to help. She told me that she was afraid of her mother and afraid to show her the postcard. I thought that was a shame. I wish I had intervened at the time, but you know we try to regard family relationships as sacrosanct. Still, I wish I had intervened.'

'What did the postcard say?'

'I really can't recall. It was just a greeting, to the effect of, 'Having fun down here but I miss my girl.' Quite innocuous. It was signed, 'Grandpa'.'

'Certainly sounds harmless. It was a picture postcard? What was the picture?'

'As I recall, it was a Mardi Gras scene. A picture of a black marcher made up as some exotic figure with sequins and feathers and such folderol.'

'Did you notice the postmark?'

'I did not, but if the card was from New Orleans, I imagine it was postmarked there. Or somewhere in Louisiana. At any rate, when Leroy returned, he seemed to have some extra money. Yes, I believe he actually made a contribution to the church, even though he was not a member. As you are aware, we have no prohibition on receiving contributions from persons who are not members of the church. We believe that doing good works in this world is as worthy an act as that of prayer or praise.' He sent a message with his eyes.

Lindsey sighed and reached for his wallet and his remaining $50.

12

Mother was seated at Lindsey's computer, giving him a demonstration of the skills she had picked up at Miss Reilly's class. Lindsey watched her insert a disk, boot up the system and access a file. He still hadn't got over it.

She didn't know it, but she had been within one anguished decision on the part of her son of being sent to a nursing home or a mental hospital, from which she would probably not have emerged. And now she was shopping and cooking meals, attending classes, running a computer, and preparing to apply for a job.

Lindsey put his arm around her shoulders and said, 'I'm really proud of you.'

The phone rang. He picked it up and heard Marvia Plum's voice say, 'He's here. James is here. With his bride. They just checked into their hotel and he wants to have a meeting and he wants to see Jamie.'

'When? When does he want this meeting? What did you tell him?'

'Tomorrow after work. I'm back at work now and I'm not going to let the taxpayers down and the killers go on killing. I'm not going to take another vacation day to talk to those two.'

'Where are they staying?'

'Nothing but the best for Major and Mrs. James Wilkerson. The Pare Oakland, my dear.'

'Oh, boy. I wonder if they'll run into the Double Bee gang. Don't see how they can miss them, the way they've taken over that hotel.'

'I expect that's why they picked it. James can strut around and tell his Desert Storm stories, you know, 'How I Won the Battle of Basra Single-Handed,' while wifey worships him from a respectful distance and the movie people beg for his autograph. He says he wants to go out to North Field and see what they've got, anyhow.'

'You're going to see him, then. You're not going to stonewall him.'

'I can't. Not Jamie's father.' Her anger was tangible. 'But I haven't promised he could see Jamie. I haven't decided how I'm going to handle that.'

'Is there anything you want me to do?'

'I want you to come with me. Will you?'

'Absolutely. I'll pick you up at your house. What time are you going to meet him? What time should I come by?'

She told him. He said, 'Okay, I'll see you, then, tomorrow night.'

He talked with Mother for a while, then settled in his recliner and watched the late news on television. He couldn't contemplate going to bed just yet.

The local news led with a story from right here in Contra Costa County. Someone in Richmond had set a fire or planted a bomb or thrown a grenade, or maybe a gas line had developed a leak, or maybe the Saturnian Squid People had switched on their Interplanetary Explode-O Ray; nobody was quite sure.

Anyway, there had been an explosion in a mixed business and residential neighborhood in Richmond. The blast had flattened a neighborhood tavern, a longtime community institution called Fuzzy's #3. Deaths included the proprietor Fuzzy Quinn, and several customers including a self-styled community leader and reputed gang figure, one Luther Jones a.k.a. Hasan Rahsaan Rasheed.

★   ★   ★

Marvia was in a sweatshirt and jeans when Lindsey arrived at her apartment. He wore a suit. She peeled off her shirt and jeans and said, 'Do I look so bad?'

He said, 'You look wonderful. You look beautiful. Come on, let's fly to Reno and get married and phone the s.o.b. from there.'

'What if I said yes?'

He didn't hesitate. 'Let's do it. I really mean it.'

'I have to do this, but thank you for saying that and thank you for going with me. I don't want to go up one against two and I didn't want to bring my daddy or my brother.'

She opened a dresser drawer and pulled out a pair of slacks and pulled them on. They were black and tight. From another drawer came a filmy gold-orange blouse. She pulled it on and adjusted the bodice to expose her cleavage.

Lindsey said, 'Nice.'

'This will show the bastard!' She put on a thin golden chain with a tiny, vaguely Egyptian charm.

Lindsey said, 'Are you sure you wouldn't rather fly to Reno?'

On the short drive to Oakland he asked, 'Where are we supposed to meet them?'

'We're going to have dinner. There's a fancy restaurant right in the hotel.'

When they got to the hotel Lindsey let the top-hatted and gloved valet take his Hyundai. The valet's sneer was clearly audible. Walking into the lobby, Lindsey felt Marvia grab his hand.

The Wilkersons had arrived first. Lindsey asked for their table, but he spotted them at once. At least, there was only one man in the room in an army officer's uniform.

Wilkerson stood up when Marvia and Lindsey approached. He looked like Wesley Snipes with a short haircut and a thin moustache. He smiled and twitched forward enough to suggest a bow without looking silly. His wife sat next to him. She didn't move. Lindsey felt Marvia dig her fingernails into his wrist.

Wilkerson reached across the table toward Marvia. She offered him her free hand. The metal on his uniform glittered: major's oak leaves on his epaulets, gleaming U.S. and branch insignia on his lapels, combat infantryman's badge, paratrooper's badge, pilot's wings. Among the ribbons over his pocket Lindsey recognized an Air Medal and the colors of Desert Storm.

'Marvia, you look wonderful!' Lindsey saw Wilkerson's eyes dart to the cleavage unconcealed by Marvia's orange blouse. 'You look younger and lovelier than ever.'

Marvia said, 'James.'

Wilkerson released Marvia's hand with one of his own. He took his companion's hand and raised it a few inches, like a referee raising the hand of the winner and new champ. 'My darling wife, Claudia. My ex, Marvia.'

Lindsey smelled the ozone that crackled between the women. They barely touched fingertips.

Marvia said, 'This is my friend, Hobart Lindsey.'

Lindsey shook hands with Wilkerson. 'Major.' He nodded. 'Mrs. Wilkerson.'

'Ferré. Ms. Claudia E. Ferré. I exchanged vows with Major Wilkinson, and rings. Not names.'

Waiters swirled around the table. Lindsey watched one of them hold a chair for Marvia. Then he felt a pressure on the back of his knees and found himself seated beside her.

Wilkerson said, 'It's been a long time.'

'Six years.'

'And you've been a police officer all this time. Well, good for you. I'm just a trifle disappointed that you didn't bring James Junior along. But I suppose it's a little late for him.'

'Jamie has homework.'

Lindsey watched Claudia Ferré taking in the conversation. She wore a maroon suit with huge white buttons. The jacket closed at her neck. Her skin was lighter than Marvia's, closer to the color of her husband's. She wore her hair long. A tiny rectangular purse lay on the linen near her wrist.

A hovering waiter asked if they would

like a beverage before dinner. Four mineral waters.

Lindsey said, 'Uh, have you and Major Wilkerson been married very long, Mrs., uh, Ms. Ferré?'

'Three months.'

'Well, ah, congratulations. You're practically on your honeymoon.'

She said, 'Hardly. I'm visiting my firm's local affiliate. Ferré, Borden, Squires, Ferré, Quaid. Corporate and estate work.'

Lindsey was impressed. 'You're a partner already? Pardon me, but you look very young.'

'The first Ferré was my grandfather. Founder of the firm. We keep his name for its historical value. He was our first attorney in our county. The second Ferré is my father.'

Lindsey shot a look at Marvia. Major Wilkerson was telling a Desert Storm story.

Ms. Claudia E. Ferré was gazing at her husband as if she'd never heard the story before, as if she were suffering the vertigo of love at first sight.

The waiter hovered behind Major

Wilkerson, oversized menus tucked under his arm, waiting for his chance to pass them around. But Wilkerson was busy.

Ms. Claudia E. Ferré was still gazing at her husband. At last Lindsey identified the look. It was the Politician's Spouse's Stare. Major James Wilkerson, Senior, was running for office.

When the major paused, the waiter inserted four menus into their hands. Wilkerson asked for a recommendation. The waiter suggested the sea bass. Wilkerson ordered a steak. His wife ordered Coquilles St. Jacques. Lindsey ordered sea bass. Marvia ordered an endive salad.

Claudia E. Ferré said, 'Tell me, Mr. Lindsey, what do you do?'

Lindsey told her.

She said, 'Oh, how fascinating. And how do you find International Surety as an employer?'

'They could pay more, but they're all right.'

By the time the food was half-consumed, Wilkerson brought up the topic of Jamie again. 'I know you mean well for him, Marvia, but do you really think this is the best environment? Living with an invalid grandfather and a grandmother who is out of the house all day, earning a living?'

'Invalid? What gave you that idea?'

'I thought you told me your father had a disability retirement.'

'He caught asbestosis from his work. He's going to die of it someday. But for now he's still strong and capable. He does a wonderful job.'

Claudia put her hand on Marvia's wrist. Lindsey saw Marvia flinch. Claudia said, 'But don't you think Jamie would be better off with a real father and mother, not living with grandparents? And what happens when your father . . . ' The sentence faded into the air like a hint of subtle perfume.

'I see him every chance I get. I see him two or three times a week.'

'Whenever your police duties permit, I'm sure. But is that truly as good as having a real home?'

'He has a real home.'

Wilkerson said, 'Don't you see, Marvia, what would be best for Jamie? And he's my son, too. Don't forget that.'

Angrily, Marvia said, 'You signed away all rights. Or don't you remember? An officer getting a little female MP pregnant! I did everything for you, everything to save your career. And you were thrilled to be rid of us. Of Jamie and me. Get me out of Germany, out of the Army, get us both out of your life. And now you're remarried, well good for you. I hope you're both very happy. But you're not taking Jamie back.'

Claudia said, 'But the child needs — '

'Marvia and I are going to be married,' Lindsey interrupted. 'We're going to make a home for Jamie. He is going to be our son.'

No one said a word. Lindsey could feel Wilkerson's and Ferré's eyes shifting from his face to Marvia's. Marvia grabbed his hand. Her touch was like ice.

Finally, Claudia Ferré said, 'I guess that's that. James, call for the bill.' She started to stand but he pulled her back to her chair. He looked furious. Lindsey wasn't sure with whom.

Wilkerson said, 'I'll be out at the airport the next few days. I've already talked with the Double Bee people, with that Chandler woman. And with some of the pilots handling those old aircraft. They're from Texas. I'm at Fort Hood now, near home. It doesn't hurt to have connections like that for later on.'

Marvia said, 'What later on is that?'

'James is planning to resign his commission,' Claudia announced. 'He is going to be a Congressman.'

'Now I see,' Marvia said.

Wilkerson said, 'You see nothing. Most of those airplane people are from Texas, except for the old geezer.'

'You mean Lawton Crump?' Lindsey asked. 'He was one of the original Tuskegee Airmen.'

Claudia said, 'How remarkable, Mr. Lindsey. Have you been studying African American history?'

'I've been studying American history.'

Wilkerson said, 'I'll be flying a P-38 this week, Marvia. The least you could do is let James Junior see me; let him know who his father is and what he's accomplished in this world.'

On the way back to Oxford Street, Marvia said, 'Thank you.'

Lindsey said, 'For what?'

'What a horrible encounter. What a horrible woman. 'Grandfather was our founder. James is going to be our next congressman.' Do you think that's truly best for the child?''

'At least it stopped short of a food fight.'

Marvia managed a feeble laugh. 'Not by much,' she said. 'If I'd had a plate of spaghetti I think I would have let her have it.' She reached over and touched his face with her hand. 'Anyway, thank you.'

'Well then, what about getting married?'

She inhaled sharply and leaned her head on his shoulder.

Lindsey said, 'But you know, they were using the same arguments for taking Jamie you've used for why you can't marry me.'

'I know that. Hearing it from them — hearing it from them was a good thing. It made me understand better.'

'You don't think she'll make trouble? She's a lawyer.'

Marvia said, 'I don't know. But I'll never give Jamie up. They can't make me and I won't do it.'

* * *

Lindsey drove to Holy City first thing in the morning. The Jeep Grand Wagoneer stood clean and sparkling on the blacktop. There was plenty of room beside it, where a dark green Oldsmobile had stood during Lindsey's last visit.

Nellie Crump was kneeling in front of a rose bush. When Lindsey climbed from his Hyundai and closed the door, she stood up and turned around. Frowning, she said, 'Mr. — Lindsey, isn't it?'

'Yes, ma'am.'

'Mr. Crump isn't home. He's up in Oakland working on the movie. You really should have telephoned.'

'Yes, ma'am. But I just thought I'd drop in. Since Mr. Crump isn't here, I thought maybe you could help me out a little.'

'I can't imagine what I could possibly tell you. You know my husband found that poor man in the airport. He answered all your questions. What more can you want to ask? And why me?'

'We're still working on the insurance aspect, Mrs. Crump. I know you've been married to Mr. Crump for a very long time. Maybe you could provide the information I need and save me another trip down here, or pestering Mr. Crump out at the airport.'

She looked regretfully at her roses. 'I suppose that would be all right. Come inside.'

She opened the door — it wasn't locked — and followed him inside. She laid her pruning shears and gloves on a wooden stand, pulled off her bonnet and laid it on top of them. 'Suppose we sit in here.' She led the way into the kitchen and gestured Lindsey to a chair. 'Would you like some tea, Mr. Lindsey? Some iced tea?'

He nodded and she poured for them both. He said, 'I'm trying to learn about Mr. Crump's life over the years. I suppose

281

this may sound a little odd — how could it possibly be connected with the, ah, unfortunate death of Leroy McKinney, eh? I don't expect it will, but I have to do my job, don't you see.'

Nellie frowned. 'Well, you can ask away, I suppose, but I don't really grasp your point. Mr. Crump discovered this unfortunate person, but he was a perfect stranger. How could there be any connection?'

Lindsey studied his pocket organizer. He said, 'You met Mr. Crump during World War Two, is that right?'

'Yes. I was a USO girl. I'd been a student at Tuskegee before the war, and I just stayed. I was what they called a townie girl. You know, town and gown.'

Lindsey nodded.

Nellie continued, 'Well, when the Air Corps came, suddenly there were all these wonderful young men just flooding into Tuskegee. Nobody knew how all the young cadets were going to spend their free time. Not that they had very much; but when they got a weekend pass, what were they going to do?'

'So the community leaders, they organized parties and dances and the like. We got bands to come and play. The cadets looked so handsome in their uniforms. And we knew they were going off to fight in the war, flying those big airplanes, and that some of them would never come back. It was easy to get carried away.'

She smiled distantly. 'The Army tried to discourage those training-camp marriages, but there were still quite a few of them. And some, well, let's say that some of the girls got into trouble, too. It was sad. And a lot of romances blossomed with the promise that couples would be married after the war. I don't suppose you've ever been through anything like that.'

'My father was in the Korean War. My parents were married just before he left. My mother didn't know she was pregnant. My father was killed in the war; he was in the Navy. I never met him.'

'I suppose you can understand, then. Well, Lawton and I were married. It's been nearly 50 years. We're looking forward to our golden wedding anniversary.'

'You were from Alabama and Mr. Crump was from Louisiana, is that right?'

'That's right.'

'He visited your home, he met your family in Tuskegee?'

'Oh, yes. My parents were very concerned. They kept an eye on us. I had a brother and a sister. My brother served in the Army. He lived until two years ago. I have a niece and nephew, his children. And I have a sister. She never married. She stayed with our parents all their lives, and she still lives in our old house back in Alabama.'

'What about Mr. Crump's family? Did he talk about them much? Did you ever meet them? Did you ever visit Reserve?'

She smiled. 'Reserve, Louisiana. Oh my, yes. But Reserve was just a dirt-poor, ugly, isolated place. I loved Lawton's mother, though. What a strong woman. I don't think I could have done what she did. Willa McKinney — ' A strange look appeared on her face. 'Leroy McKinney.'

'That's right,' Lindsey said. 'Are you

telling me that you never put that together, Mrs. Crump?'

'I didn't, no.' She shook her head. 'I'm so stupid! I never thought — '

'There's no reason you should have. You never saw the body.' He didn't want to call her on it. He couldn't prove she was lying, and if he held back from accusing, he might get more out of her. He continued, 'You never met Leroy — or did you? Was he in Reserve when your husband took you there to visit? Did Willa ever say anything about him to you? Or about her other son, Jefferson King?'

'He only took me to Reserve that once, to meet his mother. He thought she was a heroic woman, and she was. Still is, isn't she? He never talks about his family. He sends her money, but he never talks about his family and we've never gone back to Reserve, not once in all these years. And now with the Pan Am bankruptcy, I don't know what's going to happen.'

Lindsey thought, *He sends her money.* Willa hadn't said anything about that, and neither had her crippled brother-in-law, Floyd McKinney. Leroy — the false

Leroy — had returned to Louisiana at least once. Lindsey was certain of that. Leroy had sent a postcard to his granddaughter, Latasha Greene. But nobody ever said anything about Lawton Crump's sending money.

'Did he send checks? Would there be cancelled checks or stubs?'

'Check stubs, yes.'

'I hate to pry, but do you think I could have a look at those stubs?'

Nellie stood up. She had still not recovered from the realization of who the dead man was — or was supposed to be. But she was turning reluctant again. 'I don't see what it has to do with this. And you are not the police.'

'No, ma'am, I'm not. But the police will want to know, eventually. And if you won't help me — and maybe I can help you — you'll have to show it to them.'

She looked at him angrily, then said, 'Come along. Let's take a look.'

The checkbook was kept in Lawton Crump's desk and the desk was in his study. Nellie unlocked the desk and took out an oversized checkbook. She opened the book, ran her finger down a page of check stubs, turned the page, and stopped. 'There it is.'

Lindsey read Lawton Crump's strong writing, the stub made out to the United States Postal Service for a money order. The amount was very substantial.

'Were the checks always that large? That's a lot of money.' *And it certainly hasn't shown up in Willa McKinney's way of life*, Lindsey thought.

'They've increased over the years. At first, when we weren't making much money, of course they were smaller. As Lawton rose in the world and our income increased, so did the amounts he sent to his mother.'

'He always did it that way? Never actually wrote a check to Willa McKinney?'

'Never. He always used money orders.'

'Did you actually see the address on the envelopes when he sent the money orders?'

She shook her head. 'He always kept that to himself.'

Lindsey said, 'Did you know that Lawton had two half-brothers? Did Willa tell you that, or did Lawton ever talk about them? About their serving in the Navy, and that one of them died in the war?'

'He had such a big family. And he never liked to talk about them very much. Just his mother.'

She locked the checkbook back in the desk and escorted Lindsey from the murky study back to the sunshine-filled kitchen. She said, 'I'll tell Lawton that you were here. Shall I have him telephone you?'

'Thank you for helping me out. Mr. Crump needn't call me, I'll call him.'

She pulled her bonnet over her hair, slipped on her gloves and picked up her pruning shears. She said, 'I'll get back to my gardening, then.'

13

Lindsey phoned Marvia from International Surety in Walnut Creek. She was at her desk, catching up on her paperwork. She told him that James Wilkerson, Senior had contacted her at home last night.

'I asked him if he wasn't keeping his bride awake and he said he was calling from the hotel lobby. He wants to take Jamie out to the airport today. After school. He wants to show him what a wonderful dad he has. I don't like the idea, but I don't feel I can stop him.'

'Sure you can. He signed away all his parental rights.'

Marvia sounded weary. 'I mean, I don't think it's fair to Jamie. He *is* entitled to know his dad.'

Lindsey wanted to ask where he himself came into this picture, but he didn't say anything.

Marvia continued, 'So I'm signing out

early and I'm going to pick Jamie up after school. I don't want James picking him up. I don't want him going with strangers.'

'Okay. Do you want me to come along? You and Jamie and I?'

'Not with us; it could be too confrontational. I don't think James liked you very much.'

'I don't think Claudia liked me at all.'

'Her! Patronizing bitch. I don't really hate James, but if I did I would gloat over his marriage to her.'

'Is she going to be at the airport?'

'No. She has to visit her daddy's firm in San Francisco. So, if you could do this for me . . .'

'If I could do what for you? I thought you didn't want me there.'

'No, I just don't think you and Jamie and I should arrive together. And I don't want James picking him up at school, or even at his grandparents' house. But Jamie knows you. If you could pick him up at my house, maybe take him for a treat, maybe stop at his favorite hot dog stand, and then arrive at the airport together — I'll meet you there. Is that too much, Bart?'

'I'll be there,' he said. 'I'll meet you at Oxford Street. Don't worry about it. We'll get through this.'

'Thank you, Bart.'

Lindsey sighed deeply, then picked up the phone again and dialed Double Bee in Oakland. Someone might pick up the call at the Pare Oakland, or it might go through to North Field.

Before a word was spoken, Lindsey could tell from the echoing sounds of engines that someone had picked up the phone in the hangar at North Field. After a couple of minutes he was able to get patched through to Ina Chandler.

'Everything's going wonderfully,' she said. 'The flying's been great, the shooting's been great. Looks like we're going to wrap in a couple of days. And what can I do for you?'

'I wondered if Lawton Crump is there today. And Major Wilkerson. Have you been in touch with him?'

'In fact Mr. Crump will be flying tonight. He isn't here yet but I expect him any minute. I heard from Major Wilkerson. He's sitting in the P-38 now, getting the feel of the controls. He's quite an airman, isn't he? Must be the pride of the Air Force.'

'Army,' Lindsey said. 'He flew a chopper in Kuwait. He was a big hero. I'm surprised he didn't tell you all about it.'

Ina snorted. 'He tried to. I couldn't get rid of him until I got him into the cockpit, then I just walked away. Is there anything else, Mr. Lindsey? I'm glad you called. I want to make sure that umbrella policy covers Major Wilkerson.'

'Only if he's affiliated with Double Bee in some capacity. I suggest you write out a personal services contract. Make him a consultant at a dollar a day. Don't let him fly until you do that.'

'Right, will do. Anything else?'

'I'll be out there in a few hours. Good idea if you make that agreement in triplicate. One for Wilkerson, one for Double Bee, one for International Surety.'

He dunked the handset onto its base and turned to his former secretary.

'How's about lunch, Ms. Wilbur? On me. You can set that thing for voicemail until Uncle Elmer gets back.'

★ ★ ★

Jamie and Marvia were in the living room when Lindsey arrived. He picked Jamie up, then hugged Marvia with the boy squeezed between them. Jamie didn't seem to mind. Clutching his Flying Fortress in one hand, he said, 'Hello, Mr. Lindsey.'

'I thought we'd agreed to call each other Jamie and Bart.'

'Okay. Can we go to Mr. Harry's?'

'Mr. Harry runs Kasper's,' Marvia explained. 'Telegraph and 45th. It's been there for years. You can have a hot dog with anything there.'

Lindsey said, 'Okay with me. And then we'll head out to North Field. Then what?'

'I'll get there before you do. Take your cue from me, okay?' She gave Jamie a hug and kiss. Lindsey could see that she was shaky. He touched her, then took Jamie and led him to the Hyundai.

Lindsey and Jamie finished their hot dogs and slid off their stools. As they headed for the exit a young customer called, 'Bye, Jamie.'

'Bye, Ken,' Jamie replied.

The young man said, 'Nice to see you. Say hello to your uncle Tyrone for me.'

Outside, they climbed into the Hyundai. Lindsey had parked outside Kasper's. He said, 'You have a lot of friends, don't you, Jamie?'

'Yep.' Jamie was flying his B-17.

Lindsey said, 'Jamie, you love your mom a lot, don't you?'

'Yep.'

'You like living with your grandma and grandpa?'

'Yep.'

'But would you rather live with your mom?'

Jamie put the B-17 through a difficult bank-and-roll. Lindsey waited tensely for him to answer. Finally he said, 'I guess so.'

'Would it be all right if I lived with you? I mean, with you and your mom?'

Jamie said, 'Sure.'
Lindsey's heart started to work again.

* * *

Lindsey pulled onto the oiled dirt parking lot at North Field. He recognized the Crumps' Jeep Grand Wagoneer parked among the usual work vehicles and the Double Bee film vans. There was also a flashy Ford Probe, nail-polish red, parked at an angle that didn't quite block anyone else but that would draw attention from anyone else arriving or leaving. The Probe had rental indicia on its dashboard. One guess whose car it was.

Marvia's Mustang was nowhere to be seen. Lindsey checked his watch. She should have arrived by now.

Bessie Blue sat on the runway surrounded by smaller aircraft. She looked like a queen bee encircled by busy workers and idle drones.

Good as Ina Chandler's word, Lawton Crump had arrived before Lindsey. He was standing with Major James Wilkerson in front of the hangar. Ina hovered nervously nearby. The big hangar doors were open and the P-47 Thunderbolt had been rolled inside for servicing. Crump and Wilkerson were deep in conversation, comrades in arms, fellow airmen with shared experiences. They were really into it. Crump had his elbows raised, his hands palm down at eye-level, illustrating a bombing run. At closer range, Lindsey could hear his vocalizations.

James Wilkerson, Senior was obviously more interested in telling his own Gulf War stories than in hearing about Lawton Crump's long-ago exploits. Lindsey imagined that he could hardly care less about this relic.

Crump looked away from Wilkerson and locked eyes with Lindsey. Lindsey could see Crump gesturing dismissively at Wilkerson. He stalked toward Lindsey, looking angry. He said, 'I want to talk to you.'

Lindsey was surprised. He relaxed his grip on Jamie's hand and the boy slipped away. Lindsey saw Wilkerson Senior flash a look at Jamie, then at Lindsey. He moved toward the boy. Jamie looked confused.

Before Lindsey could act, Crump reached him. He grabbed him by the lapel and steered him toward the hangar. Lindsey looked behind him. He could see Major Wilkerson and Mrs. Chandler and Jamie standing together. Mrs. Chandler squatted in front of Jamie and began to talk to him. Wilkerson looked after Lindsey and Crump, then rejoined Mrs. Chandler and Jamie.

Without missing a beat, Crump dragged Lindsey into the hangar and into the little office that seemed to have been designated a Double Bee conference room. Lindsey tried to protest. Jamie seemed in no danger, but he didn't want to leave the boy with two strangers. And where was Marvia? Everything was turning into a shambles.

Crump slammed Lindsey into a hard metal chair and plunged himself into the swivel chair behind the desk. Even seated, Crump was inches taller than Lindsey, and despite the difference in their ages he was an intimidating presence.

'Why did you go to my house?'

Lindsey said, 'You can't do this to me.

I'm responsible for that boy. I have to — '

'He's safe with Ina and Wilkerson. You can go back out there as soon as you answer my questions.'

'What questions?'

'My wife told me you went there to snoop. Who the hell do you think you are, mister? You're a puny little insurance adjuster, that's who. I welcomed you into my home and treated you with courtesy, and as soon as I turn my back you sneak back there and harass my wife. You rifle my desk and stick your nose into my private papers. And you've been spying on my family. You went to Reserve, didn't you? Don't deny it. I've been checking on you too, mister. I still have connections in Louisiana. I have family and friends. How dare you intrude on my mother and torment her with questions? She's an old, old woman. She's suffered. She's lost most of her family. You think a long life is a blessing, don't you, insurance man? But it isn't when you have to bury your loved ones, one after another.'

He shook his head like an angry bull, ready to lower his horns and charge. But he still wasn't finished. 'I want an explanation from you right now, and it had better be something good!'

Lindsey thought, *A good offense is the best defense.* He hadn't harassed Nellie Crump; he'd questioned her politely, almost diffidently. He hadn't rifled Crump's desk; Nellie had shown him the checkbook after only a little prodding. He hadn't tormented Willa McKinney; Marvia Plum had drawn her out gently, lovingly, and left the old woman happy.

'Why did you lie to me?' Lindsey demanded. 'More importantly, Mr. Crump, why did you lie to the police? Sergeant Finnerty and Lieutenant High are going to be very upset with you.'

'Lie!' If Crump had been angry before, now he was furious. 'What in hell are you talking about?'

'Leroy McKinney.'

'What about him?'

'Or should I say, Jefferson King the third?'

Crump grabbed Lindsey by the lapel once again. 'Tell me what you know!'

'I know that you had two half-brothers,

Jefferson King and Leroy McKinney. Your mother had three husbands, and she had a son with each.'

Breath was hissing like steam through Lawton Crump's nostrils.

'I know that both of your brothers served in the Navy during World War Two. They served at the same time you were in the Air Corps. I know that both your brothers — half-brothers — were Navy stevedores involved in the Port Chicago disaster. One of them was killed outright. The other was injured — his hand was ruined — but he recovered. He ran away, and to avoid getting picked up as a deserter he took the dead brother's name.'

Crump said, 'More.'

'Leroy McKinney was the brother who was killed. Jefferson King took his name and used that name — or Abu Shabazz — until he was murdered in this hangar. As Abu Shabazz he was mixed up with a drug ring in Richmond. Did you have anything to do with that? I don't know. But I think you were paying your half-brother all these years to avoid a family scandal.'

Every time Lindsey paused for breath, Lawton Crump shook him by the lapels.

'All those check stubs that you used to buy money orders — they weren't for Willa McKinney. They were for Jefferson King. Why was it so important to keep King's desertion secret, Lawton? Tell me that.'

Crump said, 'Figure it out.'

'You were a poor kid from the south at a time when a Negro hardly had a chance in this country. But you'd gone against all odds. With Joe Wagner's help you'd made it in the Air Corps. You didn't want to be dragged back down. You were afraid that if they knew your brother was a deserter it would smear you as well. You couldn't bear to give up your rank, your officer's uniform. After the war you made a good career with the airlines. But you were always afraid. Always afraid. So you kept on paying. You didn't want a family scandal. You didn't want your brother to go down and drag you with him.'

'And what did Jeff do with the money?' Crump asked.

'I don't know. Lived on it. He didn't

live well but he got along.'

Crump had released one of Lindsey's lapels but he was still clutching the other. 'I thought he was living on it. Sometimes I guess he was. But he wanted a big payoff. I wormed it out of him. I found out why he needed the big payoff. It was that Richmond business. It was that Rasheed gang. I doubt that I would have paid him anyway, but with Pan Am belly-up, I was frightened. That's a nice house we have, two big cars. You don't know what that means. I couldn't risk losing that. So I said I'd meet him here and pay him off.'

Lindsey started to reach for the telephone to call Oakland Homicide. He glanced toward the telephone and so he barely saw Lawton Crump's fist — his onetime sugar mill hand's, onetime fighter's, onetime mechanic's iron fist — fill the world.

Blinding white light burned through Lindsey's brain. As his lapel pulled free of Crump's other hand, he felt himself rotate toward the cement floor, and saw a final shower of sparks as the back of his head smashed against the cement. Then came blackness.

* * *

Lindsey opened his eyes and the world was still mostly black, with only an edge of light somehow forcing its way through a narrow crack. He was crumpled up like an empty sack. He tried to get to his feet, and found that he was in a metallic enclosure that smelled of oil. There were heavy machine parts in the enclosure. One of them was digging into Lindsey's back.

Bracing his elbows against the sides of the enclosure, he succeeded in standing up. Some hot, sticky stuff was smeared on his face. He felt toward the edge of light and discovered that it was seeping between a pair of metal doors. There was no latch on the inside of the enclosure. He tried to call for help but his voice was so feeble, he doubted that anyone could hear him.

He tried pounding on the doors, then kicking at them. He yelled for help. On each successive attempt his voice grew stronger. When he heard someone say, 'What the heck's going on in there?' he renewed his kicking and banging.

The metal doors swung open and Ina Chandler stood gaping at him. He slumped forward and she dropped her clipboard and reached to catch him. She helped him to a chair — the same one Lawton Crump had put him in. With aching eyes Lindsey could see the stubby, single-engined *Lady Day* gleaming under brilliant work lamps. The permanent hangar lights cast a pale illumination over the rest of the building.

Ina yelled, 'Somebody get the first aid kit!' She looked at Lindsey. 'What happened to you? Did Lawton Crump do this to you? I saw you come in here together, then he came out alone.' She reached toward his face, then drew back her hand. 'Mercy, how could that gentle person — '

Somebody in a Double Bee jacket clattered a first aid kit onto a work bench and opened it. Ina reached for a sterile package of gauze pads. To the Double Bee person she said, 'Go fetch Marvia Plum.'

She opened a bottle of hydrogen peroxide and soaked the gauze in it and started to swab Lindsey's face. He sat dazed, helping hands and concerned faces moving in and out of his field of vision. Beyond the hands and faces, beyond the massive P-47, he could see that the big doors had been rolled back. Cold night air had crept into the hangar.

Outside, the runway was illuminated by huge electric lights. The sky was black. A damp, heavy mist had moved in from San Francisco Bay, and all the exterior lights were surrounded by ghostly haloes. The bright moon's edges were blurred.

Lindsey didn't know how long he'd lain unconscious before that. He remembered that it was full daylight when Lawton Crump had dragged him into the hangar, so it must have been two or three hours at least. He tried to stand up but hands held him in the chair.

Marvia Plum ran toward him. She said, 'Bart! What happened to you? Where have you been?'

He pushed the restraining hands aside

and staggered to his feet, then stumbled toward Marvia. He caught a glimpse of his reflection in the airplane's polished metal skin. He looked like Robert DeNiro in his Jake LaMotta makeup, after taking a thrashing from Rocky Graziano.

Marvia touched him. He winced away from the pain. He was getting his equilibrium back, getting his eyes and his mind into focus. He said, 'Where's Jamie? Where's Wilkerson?'

'Jamie is with Lawton Crump,' Marvia told him.

'Crump? No! He killed McKinney. Only he wasn't really McKinney. He was Jefferson King.' Marvia had been with him in Reserve — she knew the story of Willa's sons; she would know what he was talking about.

She yelled at Ina Chandler: 'Get OPD. Dial 911. Try to get High or Finnerty here, but get someone from Homicide.' She drew her breath and clapped her hands to her cheeks. 'Jamie! Jamie's in the B-17 with Crump!'

Behind her, the runway was empty. The fighters had been towed to the edges of the tarmac, clearing a takeoff path for *Bessie Blue*. The Flying Fortress was gone.

Lindsey could see James Wilkerson, Senior trotting toward himself and Marvia. He was decked out in full flying regalia. Except for his burnished skin, he looked like a Chesterfield ad on the back cover of a 1943 *Life* magazine.

Marvia said, 'Lawton Crump took Jamie.'

Wilkerson nodded. 'I know that.'

'He killed McKinney,' she added. 'He knows he's been found out. He clouted Bart and he's taken Jamie.'

'This doesn't make sense. It's a night sequence. There are choppers up there with the Fort; the plane has extra lights on it for filming. It's a thrill for Jamie. I let him go with Crump. It's just the two of them in the bomber.'

Lindsey snarled, 'You don't understand. Crump smashed a man's forehead in with a wrench. He'd been paying him for years and he wanted a final payoff and Crump killed him. I confronted him and he did this to me.' He knew his face was a ruin.

Ina came running from the hangar. 'He won't come down. They finished the scene and the 'copters are heading back — but Mr. Crump won't come back!'

Lindsey said, 'Wasn't he supposed to have a flight crew with him? From the Knights of the Air?'

'Yes, he was supposed to. But he doesn't.'

'You mean one man can fly that giant plane?'

'It's not a giant plane. Maybe the old movies made it seem big, but it actually isn't much bigger than a DC-3. Those crews were mainly gunners and bombardiers. The actual flight crew was only three or four people — pilot and co-pilot, navigator and flight engineer. One man can fly a B-17, and he's doing it.'

Lindsey's breath hissed. 'Did Crump say anything? Did he talk to you or to the control tower?'

Ina shook her head. 'I don't understand what he was talking about. Something about making history. Something about the war. He didn't say which war.'

Wilkerson said, 'I'm going after him.'

He turned and ran toward the P-38.

Lindsey shuffled after him. Marvia easily caught up with him. She said, 'That plane holds two. I'm Jamie's mother. I'm going.'

'You're not. Crump and I know each other. I'm going to talk him out of it. I'm going to talk him down.'

'But you're not a hostage negotiator. We need — '

Lindsey took her by the arms. He glared at her. He knew that his eyes were red. Literally bright red, with broken blood vessels from Lawton Crump's smashing blow. He knew that his face was bloody and swollen and that his nose was broken.

He was in control of himself and yet he had no control; it was if a higher self had stepped in and said, *Just this once, Lindsey, and just for this moment.* He said, 'There's no time to get a hostage negotiator here. And I'm Jamie's dad and he needs me. My life for my boy's, that's an easy trade.'

Marvia looked stunned.

Lindsey sprinted after Wilkerson. Alone.

Wilkerson had climbed onto the short wing segment beside the cockpit of the P-38. The Plexiglass canopy was open and Wilkerson was climbing into place. The area behind the pilot's seat had been cleared of hardware and fitted as a cramped jump seat.

As Lindsey clambered onto the wing he said, 'I can talk to Crump.' Wilkerson nodded and shoved Lindsey into the jump seat

Wilkerson hit the starter. The Lightning's twin Allison in-lines coughed into life. Wilkerson was already on the radio, talking to Oakland International Control. They cleared the P-38 for takeoff. He muttered, 'Damned Air Force stand-down, they should have scrambled by now but all of a sudden it's love-thine-enemy time.'

Lindsey said, 'Can we catch them? Can we find them?'

'Let's just hope. If there's radio contact we can home in on them. And there's radar. Everybody's looking for them.'

'Where are they going?'

Wilkerson muttered into the cockpit

radio. The jump seat was fitted with a headset as well, a pair of modern-looking earphones and a bead mike. Lindsey slipped the rig onto his head. Now he could hear Wilkerson and the tower.

The tower said, 'P-38, subject plane has headed due west. They're in radio contact with us. They've passed the Farralones and they're still going.'

Lindsey said, 'How far can they fly?'

Tower replied, 'We've got a log here on 17Fs. The book says they had a range of four-four-two-oh miles at one-six-oh MPH cruising speed, top speed of three-two-five MPH. Pilot seems to be proceeding at cruising speed. You should have no problem overtaking.'

'That's for sure,' Wilkerson said. 'We can cruise at 300 and catch them okay. Tower, what's the traffic?'

'We're clearing everything. Commercial flights to and from Hawaii either delayed or diverted. We think he's headed for Hawaii. We've alerted Alameda Naval Air Station. They're going to patch the *Abraham Lincoln* into our net. There's a naval flotilla out there. If they can match

Bessie Blue's route, they might be able to lend some help.'

Wilkerson said, 'What can they do?'

'Alameda's not sure. Listen, my contact is Commander Jarrold. Let's get him on here.'

A new voice came over Lindsey's earphones. 'Jarrold here. Who's up there in that 38? ID yourselves.'

Wilkerson and Lindsey gave their names.

Jarrold said, 'What's Crump up to?'

Lindsey said, 'I think he's fighting World War Two. He was a fighter pilot in Europe; he came back to the U.S. and he was training to fly bombers in the Pacific when the war ended.'

Wilkerson muttered, 'The old fool. He's flipped out.'

'It was his glory time. It was his Desert Storm, Major. He never let go of it. Now he's afraid. He's killed a man, and he wants it to be 1945 again so he can be a war hero instead of a murderer.'

Jarrold cut in. He had the authoritative manner of a career officer. 'We've got the *Abraham Lincoln* steaming to intersect *Bessie Blue's* course. She can send up aircraft to escort *Bessie Blue* ahead to Hawaii.'

Wilkerson said, 'I don't think *Bessie Blue* can make it. That range was based on maximum fuel load. I think they kept her light for those filming flights.'

Jarrold uttered a sailor's oath.

Lindsey said, 'Can Crump land that bomber on the *Abraham Lincoln*?'

There was a pause. Lindsey could imagine Jarrold searching for a pencil and scribbling numbers on a yellow pad. 'It might just be possible,' Jarrold said. 'Major Wilkerson, what's the landing speed of a 17?'

'17s didn't stall out till about 50 knots, Commander.'

Jarrold moaned. 'If we can put the *Lincoln* under *Bessie Blue*, headed west at her top speed . . . Flight deck is almost exactly 1,000 feet . . . It might be possible. Just barely possible. Take a hell of a pilot to keep his wingtip over the edge of the flight deck, land with his wheels barely on deck.'

Wilkerson said, 'At least it's worth a try.'

Jarrold asked, 'What kind of brakes does the 17 have, Major?'

'Wing-mounted air brakes and wheel brakes. Trouble is, he should still use the arrestor cables to stop his aircraft. He wouldn't have a tailhook.'

'Hard enough even with one. Without, he's in big trouble.' Jarrold paused. 'Still, it looks like the only chance. The *Lincoln* can launch rescue choppers in case Crump has to ditch.'

'Let's try it, sir.'

'One other thing might help a little, Major. Oakland Tower tells me Crump has your boy with him. It never hurts to pray.'

Oakland Tower said, 'We're following you on radar, P-38. And we've got a fix on the B-17. Here's your course.' The tower gave Wilkerson a course correction. Lindsey squinted over Wilkerson's shoulder. He could see the illuminated instruments, and could feel the plane respond when Wilkerson adjusted her course.

The plane banked. Lindsey was shoved sideways in the jump seat. Through the Plexiglass canopy he could see the stars and the bright moon. The P-38 had climbed quickly above the clouds. They were already past the Golden Gate, over the Pacific. This was nothing like flying in a commercial jet. There was no sense of enclosure in a machine. The Lightning seemed like part of himself and of Wilkerson. They were separated from the sky only by a layer of curved plastic. He was suddenly aware that they were several miles off the ground. Without warning, he was trembling with the cold.

The radio crackled again. Oakland Control said, 'You're going to have more company, P-38. The rest of the National Knights squadron is following you.'

Wilkerson said, 'What do they think they can do?'

Control said, 'They say that *Bessie Blue* is their aircraft and they're going after it. Maybe they can force it to turn around. I can order them back, Major.'

'No, let them follow. They might be able to help.'

Lindsey was shivering and sweating at the same time. Wilkerson sensed his discomfort. 'These planes didn't have much in the way of creature comforts, Hobart. Just hang on.' Then he said, 'Tower, can you patch me through to them?'

A few seconds later Lindsey heard Lawton Crump's gruff old man's voice. 'What is it?'

Wilkerson said, '*Bessie Blue*, this is *Rainy Mama*. This is your fighter escort. How are you doing?'

'Everything's under control. No bandits. No flak. Pure milk run.' His voice sounded strange to Lindsey. In a matter of seconds it had changed. Crump sounded like a young man. He even pronounced his words differently. He sounded a little like Willa McKinney's younger brother Floyd.

Wilkerson said, '*Bessie Blue*, I think you should turn back to Oakland International. This flight is dangerous and unnecessary.'

'Dangerous, yes. But it *is* necessary, brother. The wide blue yonder is no place for the fainthearted.'

Good God, he was starting to sound like John Wayne.

Lindsey said, 'Captain Crump?'

There was a pause. Then Crump said, 'Who is this, please?'

Lindsey's mind raced. Who was the top commander of the Tuskegee Airmen? Crump had spoken of him in Holy City, and he'd been all through the Eric Coffman's book.

Lindsey said, 'Captain Crump, this is General Benjamin Davis. Do you — ' What was that slang they used in all the war movies? ' — do you read me, Captain Crump?'

Crump sounded startled. 'Captain? It's Lieutenant Crump, sir.'

'It's Captain now.'

'Yes, sir.' He sounded happy. Lindsey thought, *He's snapped. He's all the way back in 1945. He wants to be a hero.*

'Captain Crump, I want you to check your aircraft for a stowaway.'

'Yes, sir.'

Wilkerson moved his hand on the controls. He said, 'Radio off, Lindsey. What's going on? That's my son he's got on that plane. He — '

'Look — look — is that *Bessie Blue*?' Ahead of them, brilliant lights glaring on its polished skin, Lindsey could see the four-engined bomber.

Wilkerson said, 'That's it.'

The P-38 was well above the bomber. Here above the Pacific cloud layer, the bomber was illuminated by the brightness of the moon as well as by its own exterior lights.

A new voice crackled in Lindsey's headphones. '*Chippie's Hips* here, *Rainy Mama*. *Chippie's Hips*. Do you read me?'

Wilkerson said, 'I read you, *Chippie*. Position?'

'Five o'clock, climbing above you.'

Wilkerson turned. Lindsey followed his glance. Above and behind the P-38 he saw a streamlined, silvery, single-engined airplane. It gleamed in the moonlight like a Christmas decoration.

'We're all here, *Mama*. Do you have visual?'

Wilkerson said, 'With *Bessie Blue* and with you, *Chippie*.'

'The rest are strung out behind me. Form up, Knights!'

Wilkerson had turned back to the controls. Lindsey turned to watch *Chippie*. Now he could see a formation assembling in an unbalanced vee with

Chippie's Hips at its point. Lindsey tried to identify the other planes. They were calling in. *Lovely Lena. Ella Fitz. Lady Day.* He recognized the stubby, powerful P-47 that had been in the hangar when Crump landed his one-punch knockout. That was *Lady Day*. The other names belonged to the P-39, P-40, and P-51.

Wilkerson said, '*Bessie Blue*, do you visual us? We are your escort. We're at six o'clock, high.'

'I visual you, *Rainy Mama*.'

'*Bessie Blue*, please indicate your destination and fuel situation.'

'We're headed for Hickam Field, Hawaii. Glad to have you along, escort! I don't imagine we'll meet any Zekes or Tonys, but you can never tell.'

'Repeat, what is your fuel situation?'

Lindsey waited with James Wilkerson for Crump's reply. Finally it came.

'There must be something wrong with my instruments, *Mama*. They indicate low tanks. That can't be right.'

'Listen, *Bessie*, you only have a little fuel,' Wilkerson told him. 'Do you have your classified orders with you?'

There was a long silence. Then, 'I don't have any classified orders here, *Rainy Mama*.'

Wilkerson said, 'That's correct, *Bessie Blue*. You are under my personal command. I want you to drop below the cloud layer. We have a surface rendezvous to keep.'

Crump's old-young voice said, 'Is it safe to use open radio transmissions, General?'

'Not to worry, Captain. These are scrambled channels. All our planes have been retrofitted.'

What happened when you played into another's fantasy? Lindsey had never tried it with Mother. He'd always tried to get her to connect with reality. It seemed wrong to reinforce her delusion. But maybe Wilkerson could make this work. Maybe . . . Lindsey sensed that Wilkerson was sweating as much as he was.

Wilkerson had geared back the Lightning, trying to hold its speed to that of the lumbering B-17. He banked the Lightning. Lindsey watched the B-17 dip. It disappeared into the clouds.

Over his earphones Lindsey heard

Crump's young-old-man's voice. 'What's that?' He sounded excited.

Wilkerson said, 'Hold on.' He banked and circled, then dropped the Lightning's nose. Whiteness swept up around the Plexiglass dome. To Lindsey it seemed that the plane had dipped into a giant wad of soft, opaque cotton. He became conscious once more of his perspiration. Then, suddenly, the fluffy cotton was overhead, beyond the Plexiglass. Beneath the Lightning Lindsey could see *Bessie Blue's* lights, and beneath and beyond *Bessie Blue*, a huge illuminated football field.

Abraham Lincoln.

It took a few seconds for Lindsey's eyes to adjust, then he became aware of the tiny lights hovering near the aircraft carrier. Those must be the helicopters Commander Jarrold had promised.

Still another new voice came over Lindsey's earphones. '*Abraham Lincoln* Flight Control. *Bessie Blue*, we have your special cargo ready for loading. You are cleared for landing. Approach at landing speed and welcome.'

Crump's voice replied, 'Roger, wilco.'

Roger, wilco. What was going on in the man's confused brain? If he had snapped back to 1945 and he was planning to be a hero, he might think that the *Abraham Lincoln* was carrying the first nuclear weapon. *Bessie Blue* would pick up the bomb and continue on. The war would end, and Lawton Crump would end it.

More voices crackled over Lindsey's earphones. He looked over his shoulder and saw a vee of lights drop through the cloud layer.

Lawton Crump's youthful voice sounded in Lindsey's headphones. 'Nice to see you boys. Nice to see the 99th again. I've missed all you fellows.' A moment later Crump said, 'Who's flying today? That you, Linson? Linson Blackney?'

Lindsey sent up a silent prayer that the Knights were as quick on their mental toes as they were at the controls of their aircraft.

One of them said, 'I'm here, Lawton.' Over his shoulder, Lindsey saw the Curtiss P-40 waggle its wings.

Crump said, 'Who else? Clemenceau Givings? You there, Clem?'

'Here, Lawton.' The sleek North

American P-51 waggled its wings.

Another two planes responded to Crump's fantasy.

At Wilkerson's touch the P-38 leveled off. The four Knights held formation. The P-38 surged forward until it was positioned parallel to the B-17.

Lindsey could see the external lights blazing on *Bessie Blue's* body. He could see inside the bomber's cabin, in which was the tiny form of James Wilkerson, Junior. He even thought he could see the miniature Fortress in the boy's hand. He could definitely see Lawton Crump in the pilot's seat beside Jamie.

Crump turned and looked straight at *Rainy Mama*. Fleetingly, Lindsey thought that they had made eye contact, Lawton Crump and himself. Then he realized that Crump had edited him out of his reality. The old man was watching James Wilkerson, Senior with something very much like hero worship. He raised his hand in a smart salute.

Wilkerson said, 'Captain Crump, there's a special weapon awaiting your pickup. It's a single bomb that could end this war and bring victory to our country. I want you to land so they can stow it on your aircraft.'

From this altitude the *Abraham Lincoln* no longer resembled a football field, but rather a large, illuminated parking lot. Maybe that was what it was. Lawton Crump's voice came over Lindsey's earphones. '*Bessie Blue* here. I'm lowering my wheels. I'm on my landing run.'

The B-17 dropped toward the *Abraham Lincoln*. Lindsey's body had turned to ice. He sent out psychic waves to help Crump land the old bomber safely.

Crump brought the B-17 in over the stern of the aircraft carrier. The flight deck was canted. Crump seemed to have slowed the Flying Fortress to a halt in mid-air. That was impossible. Without forward motion the wings would lose their lift and the bomber would stall, would fall into the sea.

Lindsey watched as the Flying Fortress swept along the carrier's deck. Crump had kept the bomber near the edge of the ship. If he centered the B-17 over the flight deck, its wingtip would clip the carrier's island and spin the aircraft into a mass of flaming wreckage.

A moment earlier *Bessie Blue* had seemed to hover above *Abraham Lincoln*'s wake. Now the bomber was racing along the deck.

The Fortress bounced visibly when its wheels hit the carrier's flight deck. It settled again and rolled forward. Smoke rushed from its engines as Lawton Crump reversed his props' pitch and gunned the Cyclones. *Bessie Blue* slowed. The bomber was approaching the forward end of the flight deck. If only it had been equipped with a tailhook — but that was a futile wish. How could the airplane be moving so slowly, yet approaching the end of the deck so quickly? What was going through Lawton Crump's mind? What was going through Jamie Wilkerson's mind?

Closer to the end of the deck.

And slower.

And closer.

It rolled slowly to the very edge of the flight deck, teetered, then tipped forward in slow motion, and almost frame by frame plunged nose first into the Pacific.

14

The angled flight deck of the *Abraham Lincoln* meant that *Bessie Blue* splashed into the Pacific beside the prow of the carrier, rather than beneath it. The carrier swept past the airplane.

Lindsey heard a moaning. He couldn't tell whether it was his own voice or Wilkerson's. As Wilkerson banked the *Rainy Mama* above *Bessie Blue*, Lindsey could see the bomber settle onto the choppy ocean surface. The plane had dropped off the flight deck at an acute angle, but once it hit the water it toppled back and lay on its belly. Lindsey heard his own voice. 'Wilkerson, how long can they float?'

'Ten minutes, maybe. Maybe only five. They couldn't have rigged to ditch; they didn't have time. There go the choppers.'

Navy rescue helicopters were racing toward *Bessie Blue*. They aimed spotlights at the bomber. To Lindsey the B-17 suddenly took on the aspect of something old and tired, something that belonged in the past. Something dying.

A big chopper was hovering over the B-17. Lindsey could see a speck descending from it. It had to be a man. The speck reached the airplane.

Wilkerson circled low over the bomber. Lindsey could actually see waves washing over the ditched airplane's wings. He could see it settling lower and lower in the water.

The speck from the helicopter was balancing on the bomber's wing, still attached to his lifeline. A wave rocked the airplane and the man was knocked down. He slid to the edge of the wing, caught hold and pulled himself back. He crawled to the fuselage and pulled himself up onto the edge of the cockpit. The cockpit window had been slid open. Something black, something far smaller than the black shape that was a wet-suited rescuer, emerged from the window.

The airplane was settling faster now. The upper surfaces of the wings were awash.

The rescuer leaned into the window. A moment passed. He pulled away. He still had the smaller shape in his arms.

The helicopter lifted, the double black speck dangling at the end of a lifeline.

Bessie Blue was gone.

The line shortened and the black specks disappeared into the helicopter.

The *Abraham Lincoln* had moved far past the sinking *Bessie Blue*. The helicopter followed the carrier. Major Wilkerson brought the Lightning up to a safer altitude and followed the chopper until Lindsey saw it land on the carrier. Crewmen swarmed toward the chopper.

The voice of Flight Control crackled. '*Rainy Mama*, you and your flight will return to your land base. I hope you all have enough fuel. I don't want any more attempted landings without tailhooks.'

Wilkerson surveyed the Knights. They could all make it back to Oakland.

★   ★   ★

There was a night game at the Coliseum. Lindsey could see the huge lights and the

328

colorful clothing of 50,000 spectators. He wondered if any of them could see the military planes in the sky, or if some bored fan or distracted outfielder might hear the engines, turn his eyes upward and see a formation of 50-year-old fighters circling in the night.

Their flight path brought them back toward North Field.

Lincoln Flight Control had told them that Jamie Wilkerson was safe. He was drenched and half-frozen and terrified, but he was being cared for on the carrier. Once he was checked out and fed he'd be ferried back by jet. High offered to send Marvia to the air station in a police unit. She accepted. She'd pick up her Mustang later on.

Lindsey thanked God for the Navy. It had saved Jamie Wilkerson's life.

It had not saved Lawton Crump's. Crump must have been a hell of a pilot in his day. And his day had lasted until his final act. He had gone down with his airplane. Lindsey would wonder for the rest of his own life what thoughts had swirled through Lawton Crump's mind as

Bessie Blue plunged to the bottom of the Pacific Ocean, carrying him along with her.

Maybe it wasn't the vigilance of the Navy. At least, not that alone. Lawton Crump's skill, too, had saved Jamie Wilkerson. But Crump had also killed his own brother — smashed his skull and spilled his brains. He had re-enacted the first murder in the world.

Wilkerson said, 'There's plenty of room. Here we go.' He swung the P-38 into a banking approach, lowered its wheels, opened the air brakes and touched down on the tarmac. Riding high on its tricycle landing gear, the Lightning flashed past hangars, parked aircraft, police cruisers, emergency vehicles. It slowed and halted 100 feet from the end of the runway. Major Wilkerson could never have landed this airplane on the *Abraham Lincoln*.

Wilkerson popped the canopy open. He climbed onto the Lightning's wing, hopped agilely to the ground and ran. Lindsey realized that his face was a giant ache and his body stiff and sore from its cramped position behind Wilkerson in the

Lightning. Moving gingerly, he followed Wilkerson.

The moon provided some illumination but the runway was lighted mainly by ground lights, supplemented by the headlights of police cruisers and emergency vehicles.

Lieutenant High and Sergeant Finnerty were waiting. High said, 'Lindsey, are you all right?'

'I'm okay.' He looked for Marvia, but the first female he recognized was Ina Chandler. She had tears in her eyes.

'I heard. I heard,' she said. 'Lawton is gone.'

Lindsey stood still.

Marvia Plum had run up to him. She held him and said, 'Jamie's safe. They radioed. I heard his voice.'

To no one in particular, Lindsey announced, 'Crump was the killer. He was our monkey-wrench man.'

Ina Chandler was still there. Red-eyed and wet-faced, she said, 'No, he wasn't.'

High whirled. 'He wasn't? Wait a minute! You go first, Mr. Lindsey. Give me a 30-second version. We'll take a full statement at Sixth Street.'

Drawing Marvia to him, Lindsey complied.

Before High could say anything, Ina said, 'No. No, he didn't. He couldn't have killed that man. I was with him when he found the body, don't you remember?'

'He was alone in a room at the Pare Oakland,' Lindsey said. 'He left the hotel and went to the airport twice. The first time was very early in the morning, maybe a little after midnight. He had his meeting with Jefferson King, not Leroy McKinney. That's something I'll explain when we get downtown, Lieutenant High. He returned to the hotel, waited a while, then met you, Mrs. Chandler, and came out here again. The second time, he found the body he'd left here the first time.'

Ina said, 'No.' She caught her breath, then she said, 'He couldn't have come out here in the middle of the night. He was with me.'

High said, 'I thought he was in his room, all alone.'

'He was in his room, but I was with

him. It was — it was a one-night thing. I knew he was married. But he was so lonely, I could sense it. His stories, all the things he'd done, all the places he'd been, but he was still alone somehow. When we finished our day's work we ate dinner and talked and talked. We went to his room and talked some more. He didn't want to be alone. Neither did I. We had a couple of nightcaps. And . . . ' She found a bandana in her jeans, wiped her eyes and honked into the bandana. 'It wasn't anything cheap or evil. It was — suddenly we just — just needed each other. We were both adults and we knew what we were doing. No one would ever have to know. But we could remember that night forever. For all our lives.'

High patted his pockets, came up with a notebook and pencil, and jotted busily. He said, 'You'll have to come downtown, too, and give us your statement. Mr. Lindsey, you made a nice case. I don't know that we could have proved it; I'd need to talk it over with the DA and see what they have to say. But if Mrs. Chandler alibis Crump, it all blows up.

Unless we can shake her story.' He turned to Ina. 'I've said too much already. We'll need your statement. We'll never get one from Mr. Crump, of course. More's the pity. And as for you, Mr. Lindsey, you've been keeping me informed, but we'll need to have another talk very soon, won't we?'

Lindsey nodded and turned away. Marvia was still in his arms. James Wilkerson, Senior stood beside them. He looked baffled and useless.

Marvia said, 'James, thank you for all you did.'

Wilkerson mumbled.

Nearby, within earshot of Lindsey, High said, 'Sergeant Finnerty, will you take Mrs. Chandler downtown, please? She's not under arrest — she hasn't been accused of anything — but before you take her statement you'd better Mirandize her just to be on the safe side. Is that all right with you, Mrs. Chandler? Do you understand what we're doing and why we're doing it?'

Ina nodded. 'He could be a little stiff, even a little harsh, but he was a sweet person. And there was pain in him.' She reached toward Lindsey's battered face. 'I'm sorry for what he did to you. But if he killed that other poor man, if he killed his own half-brother, why didn't he kill you? He could have. Why didn't he kill you?'

Sergeant Finnerty led her away.

High said, 'She has a point, Lindsey.'

Lindsey shook his head. The pain had receded whilst he had been distracted. Now it came back, washing over him a wave that buckled his knees. Now it was he who clung to Marvia until the wave receded. He said, 'I — let's sit down.'

They walked to Double Bee's hangar office. Lindsey leaned on Marvia all the way. She helped him to a chair. A moment later he had his hand wrapped around a steaming cup. He didn't drink its contents, didn't even taste them. He just held onto it.

High said, 'Can you handle this? Can you talk, or should we hold off 'til tomorrow?'

'Go on,' Lindsey said. 'Once I'm out, I'm really going to be out.'

'What do you think of Chandler's story?'

335

Lindsey shrugged. 'Could be. I mean, it fits together. Maybe we could try to check it with the other Double Bee people or the Pare Oakland. But unless somebody saw them, it's just a question of whether you want to believe her or not.'

High said, 'With Crump at the bottom of the ocean, there's no reason for her to lie for him. What difference does it make?'

Marvia said, 'You're not a woman, Lieutenant. It makes all the difference. Will he be remembered as a murderer, or as some kind of hero? It makes all the difference to her.'

'Accepted.' High was jotting notes now, the way Lindsey so often did. 'I've seen people come apart before. I'm sure you have too, Sergeant Plum. But this was like something out of *King Lear*.'

Lindsey said, 'I thought there was something odd at his house in Holy City. As if there were all these Lawton Crumps — the boy in Louisiana, the young man in the Air Corps, the older man. He never had any children to keep him connected to the present, to the changes in the world.'

He closed his eyes to rest them. The light was like needles. 'Not that I have any. But Crump never got over those peak experiences he had in the Tuskegee Airmen. When he killed Jefferson King, that knocked him loose from his bearings. He was really looking forward to flying bombers in the Pacific. The war ended too soon for him, and he never got over it. Here was this 70-year-old body with all of these minds in it. They were all Lawton Crump; he wasn't a multiple personality like the ones they keep making movies about. He was always Lawton Crump but he was many Lawton Crumps, Lawton Crump at different times in his life.'

High said, 'An interesting theory, Lindsey. I think you're nuts, but it's an interesting theory. I'll tell you one thing. If that alibi Mrs. Chandler gave him holds up — if Chandler doesn't wobble — we're back to square one on this thing. Maybe we go back to Richmond and try working through the Luther Jones connection. Nobody else knew about this alleged meeting that Crump was supposed to have with Leroy McKinney. And

I've got so much other work to do.' He
shook his head mournfully.

Lindsey said, 'Somebody else did know
about the meeting.'

High perked up. 'Who?'

'Nellie Crump.'

★ ★ ★

Lieutenant High pulled the police cruiser
across the driveway on Call of the Wild
Road. From the passenger seat, Lindsey
could see Nellie Crump sitting in the
shiny Oldsmobile. The engine was running. Despite the night's darkness, its
exhaust was visible in the headlights of
the cruiser.

Lindsey had drunk some coffee. He
could have handled a juicy steak and a
stiff drink as well, but that would have to
wait. He'd got cleaned up as much as he
could without a complete change of
clothes. He longed for a hot soak.

Somehow he felt he could function for
a while longer. He knew he would pay all
the higher a price, once he did crash.

Behind the wheel of the police cruiser,

High whistled softly. 'What do you think of that? It's a good thing we didn't wait for morning, isn't it?'

High and Lindsey walked to the Oldsmobile. Lindsey's body ached with every step. High tapped a coin against the driver's window. Nellie Crump turned her face toward the two men. She wore a dark cloth coat and a tiny hat and appeared to be composed. She reached for a switch, and tinted glass descended into dark green metal, hissing like a spaceship door.

When the window was open Lindsey could hear the Oldsmobile's radio. It was tuned to an all-news station.

'What do you want?' Nellie asked.

Lindsey said, 'Mrs. Crump, this is Lieutenant High, Oakland Homicide.'

'Mrs. Crump, we'll need to ask you some questions, if you don't mind.'

She frowned. 'I do mind. My husband needs me. At least, I'll have to identify the body. I'm going to him. Please get your car out of my way.'

High shook his head. 'I doubt that they'll ever recover his remains. I'm really very sorry. In any case, there's nothing you could do for him.'

'You let me decide that.' She glared at Lindsey. 'You are a viper. You come around here with your polite questions; you 'just want to help'. Now look what you've done!'

'But I haven't done anything, Mrs. Crump. I've — '

High stopped him with a hand on his arm. He said, 'If you'll just get out of the car, please. We contacted the San Jose PD and the San Mateo Sheriffs Department by radio. Everything is nice and orderly. We do need to speak with you, Mrs. Crump. Please.'

She looked from High to Lindsey, and back to High, then shut off the Oldsmobile's engine and its lights. She got out of the car and said, 'I expected Lawton to come home tonight, but I wasn't really worried. I know he stays late sometimes; I know he stays over in Oakland. I don't mind that.'

High said, 'No, ma'am.'

'But I was watching the late news and they had this story about this airplane. I thought it was a hijacking. Then they showed the tape. I saw it was a B-17. It was footage of the *Bessie Blue* from this movie they're making. Then I knew it had to be Lawton. What happened? What happened to him?'

Lindsey told her.

High said, 'I just wondered if you could help us out with this, ma'am. I'm sorry to disturb your mourning. It's a terrible situation. Maybe you could help, and then we'll be on our way.'

Lindsey had seen this act before. He'd even been on the receiving end of it. He waited to see how Nellie Crump would react.

She said, 'I don't follow you. Are you accusing him of that awful killing at the airport? What are you saying to me? What kind of help do you want from me?' She shivered. Lindsey realized that all three of them were sending plumes of breath into the cold night.

High said nothing.

Nellie said, 'If you're going to keep me here, at least let's go inside and be warm.' She led the way into the house. High and Lindsey followed docilely. She brought them to the yellow kitchen and switched

341

on the fluorescent ceiling light.

Lindsey sat in a wire-backed kitchen chair. High stood in the doorway. Nellie busied herself with the coffeemaker. Always the proper hostess.

High said, 'We do have to resolve the murder charge. We have to find the person who killed Leroy McKinney or Jefferson King.'

Nellie dropped a measuring spoon on the tile counter. Coffee grounds rained onto the bright floor. She dampened a sponge and dropped to her knees, then wiped up the scattered coffee grounds, brushed them into the sink, knelt and cleaned up a few grounds that she had missed. 'Why do you keep saying that name? I never heard of Jefferson King. I doubt that Lawton did either.'

Lindsey started to speak up but High gestured again. 'You didn't know that your husband found a body in the hangar at North Field? Didn't he tell you about that?'

'He didn't even know who that was.'

'The man was carrying ID.'

'Of course I remember that. Lawton

told me about it. Lawton always tells me everything. I want to see his body. I demand that the Navy recover his body. I want to see the responsible authorities in the Navy. You can't keep me here like this. Who do you think you are?'

High said, 'Please. Just a little longer. You have not been mistreated in any way. Mr. Lindsey is a witness to that. Please pay close attention, Lindsey. Mrs. Crump, you say that your husband *did* tell you about finding the body. Is that correct?'

'Of course he did. And it was in all the news, too. It was in the paper and on the TV. But that was Leroy McKinney.'

Lindsey said, 'You knew all about this last time I was here.'

High gestured angrily. Lindsey shut up.

High said, 'Your husband killed Jefferson King. Or Leroy McKinney. King was using McKinney's name.'

Nellie Crump said, 'Mr. Lindsey is right. I know who the McKinneys are. They're Lawton's family in Louisiana. But he couldn't have killed this man.'

'I disagree, ma'am. It works out very nicely. He sneaked out of the Pare

Oakland Hotel, drove to the airport for a meeting with King or McKinney, killed him, and returned to the hotel. Later he drove to the airport again with Mrs. Chandler and pretended to find the body. We're very certain of this. He doesn't stand a chance. Now there's no way we can bring charges against a — against a deceased person. So we'll probably close the case. But we need to get the facts together before we do that.'

Nellie slid onto one of the wire-backed chairs. She said, 'It wasn't Lawton's fault. He had to do it. That man was draining him. Draining us. You think we're well-off, don't you, with this house and two cars? But we're in debt, we're deeply in debt. That man was draining Lawton for years. We could always keep up, but then he made a big demand. And Pan American is bankrupt. Lawton worked for them faithfully. He gave them his lifetime. We've been together for 50 years. We made our way together in this world, Lawton and I. I wasn't — Lawton wasn't going to let him ruin it. He wasn't going to let that horrible man ruin us by taking

344

our money or ruin it for us by dirtying our good name.'

'Then he did kill McKinney?'

She reached for a roll of paper towels and tore one off and wiped her eyes with it. 'He did it. He told me. He made me promise not to tell anyone.'

High said, 'What about the gloves? We found bits of canvas and rubber gloves burned in a stove at the site of the killing.'

'He borrowed a pair of my gardening gloves. He was afraid of leaving fingerprints, so he took my gloves. Then he burned them after . . . after.'

High pulled a Miranda card from his pocket. He said, 'Everything you've told us up to now, Mrs. Crump, concerns other people. Before we ask you any more questions, you must know what your rights are. You have the right to remain silent. You are not required to say anything to us at any time or to answer any questions . . . ' He droned on until he came to the end of the Miranda warning. Then he said, 'Lindsey, you are witness to this.' Lindsey nodded. 'Mrs. Crump, do you know Ina Chandler?'

'I know who she is.'

'You wouldn't say she is an attractive woman?'

'I never met her.'

'Mrs. Crump, do you and your husband have what — how shall I put this? Pardon me. Do you and your husband have what used to be called an open relationship?'

'You mean are we fornicators? Speak plainly, you dirty little man.'

'Yes, ma'am. I don't mean to be indelicate, that's all. But that's exactly what I mean.'

'Then, absolutely not.' She stood up and turned her back on High and Lindsey. High reached for his hip. Nellie Crump looked at the coffee maker. She opened a cupboard, took out cups and saucers and began to pour. She put cream and sugar on the table and placed a cup in front of High and one in front of Lindsey. 'Lawton and I have been married since the Second World War and we have maintained a decent and moral relationship all these years. We are not fornicators.'

High said, 'You husband didn't kill Jefferson King or Leroy McKinney. He couldn't have. He spent the night with Ina Chandler in the Pare Oakland Hotel. They were in bed together when the killing took place. As far as I can determine, Mrs. Crump, you were the only other person who knew about the rendezvous.'

'What rendezvous? I don't believe you, that my husband would just — that Lawton and this woman — that — ' She sputtered into silence. After a long pause, she said: 'I met her once. I was at the hotel. She shook my hand.'

'Who did?' asked High.

'That Chandler woman.'

'You told me you'd never met Mrs. Chandler.'

'Well I did. Once. I should have made him come home every night. Or I should have stayed in that hotel with him. He was a weakling.'

'Your husband was a weakling?'

'Such a hero. Strutting around. Did you see that living room? Paintings of him, photos of him, all his war mementoes. He kept his old uniforms in the closet, and his newspaper clippings. Like nothing had happened since 1945. Like the world ended in 1945. I knew he was sleeping with her. The way she buttered him up, played up to him, fluttered around him.'

That wasn't Lindsey's impression of Ina Chandler, but maybe it was Nellie Crump's. Maybe it was all in the eye of the beholder.

High said, 'You knew he was supposed to meet Jefferson King? How did you know? And why didn't your husband keep the appointment with King? Did he know you were going in his place? Did the two of you arrange it together?'

'He didn't know about the meeting. He knew Leroy wanted a lot of money. But Leroy used to call here and talk to Lawton. Or to me. He was always careful about what he said to me, but I keep the checkbook; I knew what was going on. He'd call, and sometimes I'd answer, sometimes Lawton would answer. They'd talk, then Lawton would buy a money order for his mother. But they weren't really for his mother. I knew they weren't for his mother.'

High said, 'What about that night?'

'I made the meeting for Lawton. I let him sleep at the hotel. I knew he was sleeping with that harlot. I went to the airport in his place. Leroy didn't know who I was at first, but he recognized my voice. I told him I'd come in Lawton's place. I got there first. I had the wrench behind me. I'm a strong woman. He just looked surprised. I only had to hit him once.'

High said, 'You've heard all this, Lindsey?'

'Yes.'

'You'll have to come with me, Mrs. Crump,' High told her.

She said, 'I'd better disconnect the coffee maker first. It could be dangerous. It could start a fire.'

'Yes, ma'am. You'd better take your warm coat, too.'

'Yes, I think I'd better.'

15

For some reason it seemed right to visit Kasper's again. The proprietor, Harry himself, greeted Marvia and Jamie like old friends. Then he said, 'Nice to see you again, Mr. Lindsey. Nice to see you with Marvia and Jamie.'

Lindsey said, 'Call me Bart, please.'

Harry said, 'The usual?'

Marvia said, 'For everyone. And a chocolate drink.'

'Make it to go, though. Please.'

They put their food in the Mustang's luggage space and drove a few blocks to a tiny park hidden in a street just off Telegraph. Jamie took his hot dog and ate it sitting on the spring seat of a giant frog. Marvia took Lindsey's hand and they sat on a wooden bench, watching. For the moment, they were the only ones in the park.

Marvia said, 'Jamie's getting over Lawton's death. He loved him. He's too young to understand everything that happened. It was all a wonderful adventure for him, even the scary part when they went off the deck and *Bessie Blue* sank.' She looked at Jamie and waved. He rocked back and forth on the green frog, munching his hot dog, and pretended not to see his mother's wave.

Lindsey took a bite of his hot dog. He said, 'I didn't know your father was sick, Marvia. This is the first chance I've had to talk to you about him.'

'He isn't sick yet. His doctor's monitoring him. He'll get the best of care when he needs it.'

'But there's nothing they can do for that, is there?'

She shook her head.

'You have any idea how long?'

'No.' Her voice was almost inaudible. 'Probably a couple of years, the doctor says. My mother has to get the information from the doctor and tell me on the sly. Daddy won't talk about it. Says he's healthy as a horse. He is — or as strong as one, anyway.'

'We had a good time, Jamie and I.'

Lindsey walked to a trash receptacle and deposited the napkin his hot dog had been wrapped in. 'He said he wouldn't mind living with you and me.'

She looked at him. She didn't say anything. He looked at Jamie. There was the B-17 again in his hand. Today he'd showed it to Harry, and Harry had amazed him by launching into his own stories of aerial warfare. He'd been a flier 50 years ago, as well. An immigrant from Armenia, fighting for his new country, just as Lawton Crump had done.

Jamie finished his hot dog and ran back to Marvia, demanding his drink. She said, 'Where did you put your napkin?' Jamie produced it from a pocket. Marvia took it and wiped mustard from his chin. She stuffed the napkin back in his pocket, opened the bottle of chocolate drink and handed it to him. He started back to his frog.

Marvia looked at Lindsey. 'We can keep on for a while. My father's all right. Tyrone helps out, too. We're okay.'

Lindsey sat on the bench and took Marvia's hand. He felt like the Phantom of the Opera, like Lon Chaney and a score of other Eriks taking the hand of Mary Philbin and as many other frightened sopranos. He said, 'You're just putting it off, Marvia. You can keep it up for a while, but what happens when your dad can't handle Jamie anymore?'

She said angrily, 'I won't marry anyone just to get a father for my son. No way.'

'I'm sorry. That would be the wrong reason, wouldn't it?'

'I could always contact his father. Eat a little crow. James would roast me a little, Claudia would give him hell and love doing it, but they'd take him.'

'Marvia, I want to be your husband and I want to be Jamie's dad. That's why I want to marry you.'

She said, 'I'm on the late shift. I have to get Jamie to my parents' house.'

'All right, let's go. Wilkerson and his wife are gone. Ina Chandler and Double Bee are cleaning up and getting ready to head back to Hollywood. The Knights of the Air have taken their airplanes back to Texas, all except the B-17. They sent me a bill for that.' He had to laugh.

Even Marvia smiled. She said, 'I'm sorry, Bart. I didn't mean to be cruel to you. Please give me a little more time.'

★　★　★

Mrs. Blomquist glanced up from her work and said, 'Have a seat, Mr. Lindsey. Mr. Richelieu will see you as soon as he gets off the phone.' She turned back to her work, then did a double take. 'Mr. Lindsey! What happened to your face?'

Lindsey managed a smile even though it cost him a twinge. 'You wouldn't believe I ran into a doorknob, would you?'

Mrs. Blomquist laughed. Underneath her Gibson Girl hair-do and pale powder, she was starting to seem almost human.

A light winked off and she said, 'You can go in now.'

Richelieu waved Lindsey to a chair. 'I don't know what to do with you, Lindsey.' He looked sad rather than angry, like a teacher whose star pupil had been caught in a cribbing scandal. No, not angry. Just disappointed and terribly, deeply hurt.

Lindsey felt like apologizing but he said

nothing. He was acutely aware of the tape on his painfully set nose, and his fading black eyes. At least he hadn't lost any teeth. The rest would heal. Lawton Crump had done all that with a single punch. What a wallop he must have packed when he was 20 instead of 70.

Richelieu said, 'Aside from the media uproar, the first information I got on this matter came from Elmer Mueller.'

'I don't imagine Elmer was too kind, was he?'

'But you know, I got a very different report from Ms. Wilbur. Very different. I don't know what I'll do for information, now that she's retiring.'

'Ms. Wilbur sent you a report?'

Richelieu leaned back in his heavy leather chair. 'Surely you wouldn't expect me to rely on a fool like Mueller.'

'I'm glad to hear that.'

'I'll find somebody else; not to worry about that. In the meanwhile, I've had several conversations with Ms. Johanssen at National about you. And a fax from World HQ.' He said the last the way a humble parish priest would have said that he'd had a fax from the Pope. No, more than that. The way the mayor of a Japanese fishing village would say that he'd got a fax from the Emperor. The very phrase set the air to vibrating with powers and portents. *World HQ*.

'Now suppose you give me a very brief summation of the matter,' Richelieu said. The teacher again, hoping that his favorite might somehow provide mitigation for his unforgiveable misconduct.

Lindsey said, 'I've been talking with Lieutenant High and with the Alameda County Prosecutor's Office pretty regularly. Mrs. Chandler is sticking with her story about spending that last night with Lawton Crump. They've grilled her pretty hard, and she won't budge.'

'That gets Mr. Crump off the hook. Not that it matters. You don't have posthumous prosecution in California, do you? No, not even California would be that nutty. I want to know where this leaves International Surety. Legal's been getting into the act, too, and they'll want to have a long meeting with you, you know.'

'That's all right with me.'

'Is your friend Lieutenant High still out to hang this on Mrs. Crump?'

'I wouldn't quite put it that way, Mr. Richelieu, but yes, that's the essence of it. The forensics lab has done a lot of work. They never did get anywhere with the murder weapon, but they were able to match the burned rubber and fabric in the hangar stove with the rubber and fabric of Mrs. Crump's gardening gloves. They're an unusual brand; most gardeners don't like them because they make their hands too hot.'

'Can't hang her on that, can they?'

'They took some scrapings off the chassis of the Oldsmobile and matched it with the oil and dirt from the North Field parking area. That particular combination was just about unique. And everybody agrees that Lawton never used the Oldsmobile. Never. Only Nellie drove it, and she'd been denying that she ever parked at North Field, so High has her on that. And all the financial records support the connection with Luther Jones, via Leroy McKinney. That is, Jefferson King.'

'So Crump was subsidizing his half-brother all those years, bleeding away month after month until the Pan Am bankruptcy threw a financial scare into him. What a pity. Uncle Sam has stepped in. Those pensioners will be all right. I wonder how many people are suffering.'

'The Richmond police have been working on their end of it. Crump wasn't just supporting Jefferson King all those years. He was bankrolling him. He was never bleeding. Nellie thought he was bleeding, but Crump was a silent partner in the whole Hasan Rahsaan Rasheed operation. That was how he managed his lifestyle on his salary from Pan Am. You know, he earned a decent living, but that house, those furnishings, two new cars — he didn't manage that on a mechanic's paycheck. There was no way.'

Richelieu steepled his fingers. 'Now there was a man I could really admire.' His grin turned his silvery waves into a halo.

'Crump never did get over World War Two ending before he could become a bomber pilot. And then he never got to be an airline pilot, just a mechanic.'

'Well, we could kick this around all day, couldn't we? What I need to determine is what it means to International Surety. The Legal kids tell me that Lawton Crump stealing that plane and kidnapping the youngster constitutes moral turpitude; and since Crump was an agent of Double Bee, we're off the hook.'

Lindsey shook his head. 'I wouldn't be so sure. If Crump was legally insane when he stole the *Bessie Blue*, there's no moral turpitude. And we'll have to pay.'

The jovial, almost paternal Richelieu disappeared. In his place, an ice-blooded fury glared out from behind gold-rimmed glasses. He leaned across his desk and almost launched himself at Lindsey. 'Whose side are you on? It's your job to save this company money, not throw it away.'

'I think I can even work out a way to get something for Latasha Greene and her baby. Reverend Johnson and I have had a few more chats, and he's offered some great suggestions.'

'Mr. Lindsey, I am prepared to accept your resignation from International Surety as of close of business today.'

'Mr. Richelieu, I am not prepared to tender my resignation. And after all the wonderful things I've said about this company to those reporters from *Time* and *Newsweek* and CNN, I don't think you'd want to tell them why you fired me.'

'Out,' Richelieu snapped. 'Goodbye. I'll talk with Ms. Johanssen and you'll have your next assignment.'

Lindsey rose and headed for the door without shaking hands with Richelieu. As he reached for the door, he was stopped by Richelieu's voice. 'I promise you, it will be one that you love.'

Lindsey said, 'Thank you, sir.'

He walked past Mrs. Blomquist. Her powdered face betrayed no expression that Lindsey could clearly identify, but as he strode toward the elevator he couldn't help wondering if he'd seen a wink that lasted no longer than a fraction of a second.

★   ★   ★

Lindsey winced and groaned.

Marvia said, 'I'm sorry. I just wanted to touch you.' She pulled a tissue from its box and wiped her eyes. 'I don't know why I'm crying. I think it's because Jamie's all right. Or what I would have done if he hadn't been all right.'

Lindsey put his hand on her cheek. He didn't say anything.

She said, 'Or maybe it's because you do look funny, Bart. At first you looked — I was frightened. I see some gruesome sights in my work, but when it's somebody you — somebody I love . . . ' She looked at him and started to laugh. 'But now you just look so ugly and so funny — I can't help it.'

He said, 'Come on, let's go get some dinner. It's our last night in Denver. Let's enjoy it. I guess I can stand the stares. Let 'em wonder what happened to me.'

They wound up at Morton's, where parking cost more than Lindsey would have paid for most meals. He turned over the rented Thunderbird to the valet with a flourish. The valet only stared at Lindsey's discolored and bandaged face briefly; he spent more time admiring his companion.

Marvia liked to dress down, Lindsey knew, and she carried that look well. But when she wanted to turn heads — he pitied Ms. Claudia Ferré. Lindsey pictured Marvia in her flame-colored blouse. Poor Major Wilkerson would never be the same.

Tonight Marvia wore something that was green in one light and blue in another, and a strand of beads that drew eyes away from Lindsey's ravaged face. Over a shared chateaubriand he proposed to her again. They'd been drinking champagne, blessed by a waiter with tolerant ideas of what went with what.

Marvia said, 'I can't say no anymore, after what happened at North Field. It wasn't what you said to James and Claudia at the Pare. That was sweet, but that wasn't what won me. It was when you said you were Jamie's father. When you said you'd exchange your life for your boy's. For Jamie's.'

'I might not have said it if I'd thought about it. I didn't have time to think. It just came out. After — after, I thought, how could I say that? Wilkerson was his father. I know you wanted a black father for him. I thought, what kind of role model would I make, anyway?'

'That's why I love you. We tell the truth when we don't stop and calculate. When what we have inside just comes out. That was then I knew. If you felt that way about Jamie . . . I knew how you felt about me, but I had to know how you felt about Jamie. It won't be easy to be his father, but in your heart that's what you are.'

He said, 'Let's get out of here and get back to the Brown Palace and celebrate. You'll just have to be careful of my nose.'

'I have to take care of you. Eat your dinner. Your body needs the protein. And married people don't have to hurry back to bed. They have all the time in the world.'

GRAVE WATERS

Ana R. Morlan and
Mary W. Burgess

Two cunning, cold-blooded killers board the cruise ship *Nerissa* disguised as an elderly couple, with a deadly armoury at their disposal courtesy of the Russian Mafia. Meanwhile, members of a mysterious cult called the Foundation have infiltrated the passenger list, with their own sinister agenda to take over the ship. When they strike, they disrupt the on-board wedding ceremony of police officer David Spaulding. Can the ship's captain, aided by David and his new friend, author and anthropologist Richard Black Wolf, regain control of the *Nerissa* before it's too late?

THE OTHER MRS. WATSON

Michael Mallory

Who was the elusive second wife of John Watson, trusted friend and chronicler of the great Sherlock Holmes? The secret is now revealed in *The Other Mrs. Watson*, eight stories featuring Amelia Watson, devoted and opinionated wife of the good doctor, and intrepid (if a bit reluctant) amateur sleuth. Jack the Ripper is back, and up to his old tricks . . . Ghosts and demons materialise to trouble the living . . . An old acquaintance of Holmes's reappears, with cut-throats on her tail . . . And murder seems to lurk around every corner!

MISSION: THIRD FORCE

Michael Kurland

In the late 1960s, the Cold War threatens the survival of mankind. To help keep the uneasy peace, a new group of mercenaries is born: known as Weapons Analysis and Research, Incorporated. Whilst WAR, Inc. does not supply fighting troops, it provides training, equipment, systems, advice and technical expertise . . . Now former major Peter Carthage leads his men into the hostile jungles of Bonterre to prevent the overthrow of its government by guerrillas — and the mysterious Third Force known only as 'X' . . .

WEDDINGS ARE MURDER

Geraldine Ryan

When DI Casey Clunes visits Oakham Manor with a view to holding her wedding there, the last thing she expects to discover is a body. Planning her big day quickly takes second place to solving a murder . . . A woman disappears from her family home in mysterious circumstances — but are the grieving family victims, or villains? And what is so important about the contents of some old love letters, that their now-famous author will go to any lengths to stop them being made public?

STORM OVER UTOPIA

A. A. Glynn

After the Second World War, Britain looks forward to a brave new future. The University of Central UK creates an experimental model of society: a push-button environment of ease, with an artificial brain at its heart. Located on a remote Scottish isle, it starts off with great hopes. Then snags arise. The great electronic brain begins to malfunction in an alarming manner, and the ideal society is thrown into turmoil . . .